THE ONLY STORY

CAMILLE DUPLESSIS

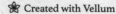 Created with Vellum

This story hinges on self-forgiveness and self-
acceptance, as well as the forgiveness and acceptance
of our friends. It exposes what's under David's careful
façade while extending the story that started in the
first book. Events build directly on *Like Silk Breathing*,
so it's best to read them in order. I know standalones
are very popular, and I just want to manage expectations at the start so we're all on the same page. (Love a
good dad joke!) Soon, you'll also be able to discover
more about Paul and Alastair in my short story, "The
Kraken and the Canary," which is a prequel to the
present trilogy.

I should probably say that I never intended David
to be a villain, even if he caused a minor crisis for
Theo the last time we saw him. He's a consummate
overthinker, was definitely repressed as a kid and
young adult, and maybe he's a little overdramatic...
but he's not heinous. I wasn't interested in creating
"villainous" queer characters; I'm so tired of queerness
being vilified in reality – with deathly consequences –
that I chose not to. I'm more intrigued by letting these
made-up people wrestle with various inner demons
and the complexities of their relationships.

Lastly and as a fun aside, some readers may be aware that the Sir Garnet Wolseley public house in Norwich was known variously as the "Baron of Beef" and the "Punch and Chop House" — I've stuck with the Sir Garnet here in 1901 because I found some records referring to it as such in 1898. (It may be a creative liberty if the name changed again in that short period, so get in touch if it did. I'm curious.) I used to spend a lot of time there, and couldn't resist a little nod to it.

For N. As per usual.

You really liked David in the first book, too, so there's that.

1

JANUARY, 1901

Cromer

Even though not a moment prior, David had silently vowed just to listen to Theo, he blurted, "Are you intoxicated?"

Part of himself despised that he asked, while the other could not help it. What was more, he knew Theo wasn't. He wasn't given to extremes, and certainly not extremes related to intoxication. As soon as he thought so, though, he frowned. It was the Theo he believed he knew who wasn't prone to extremes.

Whatever was underfoot, it was clear he had not actually known Mr. Theodore Harper as well as he'd assumed. He shivered in his coat and wondered again why they had to discuss this outside. Not that he wished to be indoors in The Shuck where anyone could eavesdrop. He studied Theo, watched the sunlight filter through the clouds and refract gently on his dark hair where it inched out from under his hat.

"No, I've taken nothing, and I've had nothing to drink," said Theo, rubbing his thumb gently against David's arm. David glanced at where Theo's arm was intertwined with his. "Though I do imagine what I'll tell you may cause you to doubt that. It can't be helped."

They walked slowly, ambling as though they were on a pleasurable stroll, but David knew better. He might not know exactly what had happened between Tom and Theo, but one didn't leave a note in the middle of the night and go to someone else for no reason at all. David often had strong feelings in his gut that he tried to restrain, not that it would have taken one to know something was happening.

He would rather wear a dirtied coat and smashed hat than admit he inferred more than he reasoned. The tendency drove him to slight agitation, so he generally ignored it. He liked things orderly, he liked things mundane, and he liked them to have boring conclusions. Unfortunately, he didn't get the sense that life was going to give him orderly, mundane, or boring right now. "What is it you have to say?"

Theo hesitated. "You know your family lore about being descended from witch-hunters?"

What an exceedingly odd entree into any conversation at all, but especially one about ending of a relationship. He shrugged. "Of course. Fireside stories for children, aren't they?" He tried to be flippant.

"What if they weren't?"

David opened his mouth before closing it again. There had been a time when he believed they were not simply stories and he'd secretly never stopped, so this was a dangerous thing for Theo to ask. Though the less human-looking creatures, like Old Shuck, certainly frightened him, he was not fearful of witches.

In fact, he liked to believe himself a witch whenever he was left alone to daydream as a very young child, and the dark seemed to meld itself to his imagination. Sometimes he saw glittering, thin threads, but when he'd blink or move, they'd be gone. He'd thought all of this was a usual part of perception – until he began to have tutors and asked them if other lads could see what he did. This question instigated some strange looks and calm, but firm, assertions that no, other lads could not.

Anyway, it was the Mills' ancestral belief that witches needed to be caught and stopped. Even if he was a witch, it wasn't meant to be.

Once this creed had been properly explained in a way he could digest, he was horrified. At first, his young mind hadn't understood the binary of witches and witch-hunters. To David, they sounded like they had similar skillsets, and he couldn't see why anybody would *hunt* anyone else. But, as Father had explained when he'd deigned to tell stories at all, one was marked as good, and the other was decidedly not. Besides, said Father, there could be no such thing as witches. And what he said, he expected David to believe.

"Don't be absurd. You know they're just stories." Yet, as he said it, he *knew* they weren't. He shook his head as though he could physically dislodge the knowledge, much like a horse might flick a fly with its tail.

Rationality said he must have imagined how comfortable he felt in his childhood bedroom at night, thinking up fantastical scenarios, arranging his toys in strange conferences. But he'd often felt he was communing with things beyond the natural. Mother called them imaginary playmates, but he always wanted to say they didn't seem so fanciful. At one point, he'd had one called Nick who originally stepped out of the wall of their kitchen wearing an old, Elizabethan-style hat.

Apart from Nick, there'd been an older lady who

smelled of sugary biscuits. She liked the rocking chair in the corner of his bedroom. There was usually a sleek ginger cat who accompanied her.

Nick, who looked no older than eleven, never said much. David always heard his speech in his own mind, or at least, he took that to be Nick's brand of talking. Mostly, however, Nick just smiled and nodded and seemed particularly taken with a stuffed toy duck. At the age of seven, David didn't have many friends, so he just believed they were generally quiet sorts of people who admired toy ducks and pretended to take tea with you. The older he got, the less often he saw Nick, yet Nick himself never grew older when he did see him. Neither did the woman in the corner. The agelessness, too, David took for granted.

Eventually, he stopped seeing them at all, but he felt it must be because he was busier, more sensible, and didn't have a need for playmates. Two of those things were definitely true.

"David?" said Theo gently.

Wanly, David smiled a little at him. For a moment, he wanted to ignore everything that had happened in the last few weeks, all the little rows and belligerent tension and the strange sway Tom Apollyon had over Theo. He wanted to coax Theo back to the house overlooking Chapelfield Gardens. They could go back to Norwich and carry on like they always had. Even if he'd been more optimistic in general, this could never happen.

Too much had been strained between them, and he'd more or less planned on leaving Theo before they'd even come to Cromer. But trying to keep everything as it was, especially when Theo addressed him with such tenderness, felt enticing. He recalled something and opened his mouth, then sighed before he could speak.

Theo studied his expression and asked, "What is it?"

"You said inside that I'd taken something of yours. You were right. I should give it back. And apologize." He thought back to the juvenile way he'd taken what seemed to be an item of sentimental value, an old fur, and hidden it away. Not very well and not with much craftiness at all, but he had done it. If Theo was going to walk out of his life, then he should at least give the thing back. He had no use for it, not even as a memento and certainly not if Theo himself valued it.

There'd been no deeper intent to the decision; he'd simply wanted to do something petty. *Then again*, he thought, *maybe it wasn't so important*. He'd seen nothing that linked Theo to the object, no fine, glimmering threads or chains. But that was neither here nor there, for the sight only ever happened sporadically after his childhood years.

With a shade of amusement, Theo said, "Oh, you *should* give it back."

Peevish, for he'd been about to tell him what it was and where to find it, David said, "Well, what did I take?"

"An old fur pelt, one that you often genteelly maligned."

Blinking, David replied, "And... you divined this... how?"

"That's what I need to tell you." Theo smirked slightly, and the David of a month ago would've felt his knees go a bit weak at the expression.

The David of this moment knew he was about to be discarded. Kindly discarded, for Theo was a gentle sort of person, but discarded all the same.

"But I need you to suspend your disbelief, which I know in your case is prodigious," said Theo.

It's actually not. But he admitted that of all the disguises he'd constructed for himself and of all the secrets he'd ever kept about his internal thoughts, the way he appeared married to logic was the most grandiose. It was the most false, too. But it also was what people saw most, he felt. True, he did not believe in God. That didn't mean he didn't believe in anything at all. As David was musing, Theo continued to speak. "Can you *promise* you'll just... have faith that I'm not lying to you?"

This was new, this note of desperation, and David disliked it. Specifically, he disliked being the one who had summoned it and he was saddened that he had. Well, he *had* behaved like a pompous fool. He'd taken something and hidden it simply because he felt agitated and slighted, and he wanted attention even though he would probably rather die than actually admit the desire for what it was. That kind of behavior didn't encourage trust or warmth.

Although he quelled the wisp of shame that began to curl through him like woodsmoke through a winter morning, he supposed it was a good guide for what he had to do next. "Yes." He had to ignore his own feelings and pay attention. That he could do.

"I *need* that skin, so I've always taken it with us when we travel. Always. You may not have seen it because I did not want you to, but it's always somewhere near me."

Right, so he must have been prone to more fretfulness than he let on, and his tranquil, careful, charm was a well-cultivated skill. The fur could be some kind of secular talisman; it was similar to how some men might carry a little rock that held significance only to the owner. "I see." Then he thought of Tom's Julian of Norwich medal, which was the same sort of thing for him and had arguably started all of this. No, he couldn't be annoyed with Tom. *He didn't do this. You did.*

"You don't," murmured Theo. "I... fuck, this is more taxing than I thought it would be."

"You've spoken to me almost every day of your life for quite some time. What's so difficult about it?"

"I was hoping that would make it better, but..." eyeing him, Theo shook his head. "You are... a very... logical sort."

He watched the nerves surface on Theo's expression and had to ask the most obvious thing that came to mind, though it hurt him. "Have you and Tom..."

"No, but we did break into the house."

"You have a key! Why would you have to break in?"

"Well, I didn't; he did. Christ, that's the easy part to talk about. Let's begin with that. I thought my fur might be in the house once I realized only you could have taken it, so that's why I rushed here."

"For a bit of fur," said David, struggling to understand how it was so significant that Theo would abscond to Cromer without any forward planning. "And... he broke into my house?"

"He picked a lock. Nothing was damaged."

Only moderately mollified, David said, "All right... sorry, I do keep interrupting. But you are being quite circular, in my defense."

He watched as the muscles in Theo's neck moved while he swallowed. "You told me, once, that when you were a boy, you wanted to believe witches were real. That magic was real."

David was about to interject with, *Not that, again.* He also wished he had told Theo even more than he had about wanting the witches and the magic and the fairy stories to be real. Spoken things that self-discipline wouldn't allow him to say because it was far more than self-discipline that stopped him; it was fear of rejection and derision.

But as Theo carried on, those words died. "The light in your eyes when you said it... it was one of the early things that made me want to share my life with you. I loved your whimsy. Under a very... polished exterior." Theo stopped them walking and glanced at the sea, then back at David. "What if they were real? What if all of it was true, one way or another?"

"I don't know," was what slipped out, before David could stop it.

He was still struggling to say what he actually felt and believed. He believed that it was probably all true, but this made him feel like the earth was dropping out from under him, and therefore, he never brought it up. Unless he was alluding to old family stories that his father had always turned into didactic parables meant to tell him who to be.

It had never eradicated David's belief in the fanciful, but it had pushed it down somewhere much too small and caused it to fester. The resulting discomfort of trying to ignore things he valued, things called boyish at best and sinful at worst, made him trepidatious and prim.

Apologetically, David continued. "If you want to end our arrangement, you don't need to concoct a grand story. I'm more than able to..." he took a deep breath. "You don't need to make anything up. I... look, I let you go." He mumbled, "Fuck knows Tom Apollyon did something for me, so I won't say I can't see the appeal. He's only gotten better with age, too, but don't tell him I said that."

"I might." Theo smirked, but it was a kind one, a sweet one. "He needs to hear better things about himself, what with all the terrible ones he says in his own head. You and he are alike that way, I think."

The wisp of shame returned, bringing with it a longing for something David couldn't name because of how deeply it went. He didn't think it was for Tom, precisely, or even Theo, though it might be for something like what they'd evidently found together. Companionship, understanding.

"I'm pushing you in if you don't shut up." David nodded to the cold water.

"Wouldn't matter."

"It would be very cold," said David flatly.

Theo sighed, his shoulders rising, then falling. "Thank you. For letting me go. But I still think it's important that you hear what I keep trying to say."

"All right."

"I shall just... say it."

"I'll believe you will, once you have," said David, softening it with a smile.

"I needed the skin back because... I'm... a selkie. I would be useless without it. Well, I'd be ill without it, and I assume I'd essentially be yours forever. Or not forever, but until you died."

First, it took David a moment to recall what a selkie was. Then, he felt two conflicting responses: dismay because something had been kept from him and an immediate relief that he now knew what it was. Unfortunately, it all came out more like anger than dismay or relief. He found anger was closer to the surface than ever, these days, even if it was motivated by gentler things. "What the hell are you talking about, Theo?"

Theo finally relinquished David's arm. The fear

and sincerity roiling from him felt real as the sea moving beyond where they stood. David couldn't see why a man would make up something like this, and what was more, he did not need to be persuaded. "I mean what I say."

"I believe you."

Apparently, Theo had been bracing himself for more of a melee to persuade David. His mouth gaped. He closed it, then opened it again. "You do?"

"Yes. Maybe *you* don't know me as well as you think you do."

Cautiously, Theo said, "Perhaps I don't."

David murmured, although he felt he knew the answer, "Why wouldn't you have told me?"

"I was scared."

"Of me?"

"No, not you. You have to understand, my father always told me to be very careful who I told. He was very clear while I was growing up that being truthful was a risk, and he made sure I understood what it felt like to be separated from the skin."

That made sense. As David kept his nerves at bay, something else conspired to sway him to accept what Theo said. He counted the days in his head, thinking back to before they'd departed for Norwich. "What does it feel like?"

"Pardon?"

"The... if you spend time away... from your... skin."

"Like a bad cold." Theo had been poorly of late, David knew. "It can vary. But it feels worse if it's taken out of malice or a desire to control, I'm told." Theo's brown eyes were full of warmth that David wasn't sure he deserved. "You didn't take it to keep it."

In truth, it had been a puerile little impulse. "No. Well, I didn't take it to... keep you. How could I?"

"You didn't know."

"So... when you started to feel ill..." Given the timing and how quickly Theo had located the thing, it hardly seemed plausible to argue against what he was saying.

The tiniest bit of festering belief was given a little more space, and David sighed, trying to decide if it felt better or worse.

Both. Better, because it was the first time in years he had allowed himself to believe what he believed. Worse, because the allowance itself felt frightening. A selkie was just one thing, one element of folklore and fables. There were more, and some of them were to do with him. These were bits of himself he'd carefully filed away, the same as a librarian would save obscure books meant to be preserved and catalogued. He never wished to destroy them, but neither would he look at them.

Theo said, "I didn't suspect at first, but when I started to feel worse the longer we were home..."

David wasn't entirely ready to think about witches, or witch-hunters, or any of the rest, but he could begin to reconcile himself with this, he supposed. He owed it to a man who, if all had gone according to plans that his father had ingrained in him, would have been relegated to a lesser tier in his life. Theo would have watched David start a family while being denied the comfort of his constant affections.

If given a moment to articulate it for himself, that was not how he wished to treat anyone. He might not entirely understand what Theo was telling him, but he would resist keeping him. That was enough to make his soul feel a little less heavy, and David did the only thing he felt was ethical. He apologized.

He took Theo's right hand, and after a quick

glance to make sure they were not being observed, he lightly kissed the back of it, then gently let it go. "I'm sorry." He was, in short, horrified at what he'd done. "I... am so glad I did not hurt you more than I did by accident."

"Don't be too sorry. I planned on leaving you when we first arrived here." David knew the wry words were simply deflection; the gratitude in Theo's countenance spoke more eloquently of his feelings than what he said.

"I suppose," David said, "you were going to swim off into the sea."

"Truthfully... no better exit for me than the North Sea."

2

AFTER BELTANE, 1901

Cromer

Theo was shocked at the chaos he had unleashed. He had not meant to, of course; he had meant to help. Still, he should have realized how many men did not do well with surprises, and now that he thought about it, he'd undoubtedly come back to The Shuck with a surprise.

Paul Apollyon's lover never left him. At least, not in the sense Tom had once assumed. He'd died and his son had come to claim to the body without informing Paul where it was to rest. That was the next-of-kin's prerogative, but Theo couldn't fathom being so cruel even if he could make sense of the motivations. While Paul and Alastair had never proclaimed their love publicly, it was still sinful in the eyes of many and illegal by the law's measure. All of that, Tom had been told already.

He also had a surname and birthdate he'd surreptitiously taken from one of Paul's many diaries. But what he hadn't known was where Alastair was. None of them knew, which had been the problem Theo thought he'd solved by retrieving the answer.

He hadn't solved the problem, it seemed, and the surprise was apparently too much to bear.

On one side of the bar was Paul, hands on his hips, and on the other was Tom, mirroring his stance and laughing with a little disbelief. In short, Theo had never seen uncle or nephew engaged in a proper argument and this one had been underfoot for at least twenty minutes. Tom wanted to know why Paul wouldn't just go to Scotland and see the grave; Paul wanted to know why Tom cared so much what he did.

They were both generally prone to scowling or taciturn silence when displeased. Paul in particular could go hours, even days, without uttering full sentences. Tom once assured Theo that it was not always an indication of a foul temper, it just intensified when he was in one. So this scene of overt displeasure was fascinating as much as it was shocking, though he would not say so to either of them. He sensed they wouldn't see the humor and knew the subject that caused the disquiet was, quite exactly, serious as the grave.

"I would thank you not to go prying into my affairs, Silence," Paul said, not much louder than normal, which was to say, fairly quiet. For him, it was akin to a shout, and he didn't use "Tom," which was pointed.

Likewise, Tom was not terribly loud, himself. But vociferousness colored his voice. "No one pried. It was all a matter of public record."

"Well, it is if you know where to look," offered Theo. "I don't know how many people are interested in church registers or birth records these days." He was adept at scouring documents, having kept so many books in the past. Most recently, he'd kept David's business matters and appointments until they parted ways. But not everyone cared for the process and he had more patience for it.

"And I'll thank *you* not to meddle where you're not meant to, selkie," said Paul, keeping his eyes on Tom while he spoke to Theo.

"Ah, I see we're just going to toss that about whenever we wish now that I'm not in peril," said Theo.

"You were never in actual peril," Paul returned swiftly, with reference to David unknowingly capturing his skin.

Theo shook his head and smothered a chuckle. He knew it could have been much worse, as did all three of them, and hearing Paul say it in such a finite way tickled him. "I could have been." But he put up both his hands in a placating gesture, then let them fall. He'd only just returned bearing the knowledge he thought Paul would have wanted, and out of respect, he had not gone directly to the grave itself. He felt Paul should have the honor if he wished it.

Perhaps he did want it and shock was getting the better of the elder Apollyon, although it was difficult to tell.

If it were me, thought Theo, *I would want to know where Tom was buried.*

"Who'd believe me even if they heard me?" Paul's retort was almost amused, which was a good sign. Granted, it was a decent point to be made about most average individuals. They might; they might not. Probably wouldn't. This century, everyone was convincing themselves right and left that the old ways with all their lore and creatures had never been real. Theo had seemed to find the nearest and best enclave of preternaturally-inclined people who did.

But overall, Paul's rhetorical question was a valid one: in this day and age, evidence was considered more persuasive than folklore and Theo was not about to transform in front of anyone who demanded proof of his being.

"I told him to look," said Tom, after a breath of quiet passed between the three of them. "I told him to look for Alastair. It was my idea."

That was true: one evening they'd had free, Tom explained what he'd known about his uncle and the man who was essentially his husband in all but law. How, among other things, he'd become part of the fabric of The Shuck. So much so that the pub now owed its name to him. Originally, it had been known as The Queen Anne. But some years after Alastair had been in residence there, there had been a memorable incident with a drunk patron and a greatcoat in an upper-floor window looking like the ominous creature – from what Theo understood, there were claims Old Shuck was in the building.

It was, of course, not the folkloric black dog of usually ominous doom and gloom, but rather a greatcoat slung over a chair. Alastair had found it hilarious and jokingly said the pub should be renamed. Back then, Paul must have had more of a sense of humor. He'd agreed. And so, The Shuck became herself sometime in Tom's childhood.

Paul snorted gently. "Of course it was yours. You want me to have a happily ever after. But I've already had it, and this is what happens *after* that."

"I don't have to tell you anything," said Theo, glancing from Tom to Paul, whose shoulders sagged as he sighed. "If you don't wish it."

"I don't know," he said at length. "I've gone long enough without..."

"Visiting him," Tom said.

"Yes. I don't know if I should, or if I need to." Despite Paul's words, the longing on his face was plain. Not for the first time, Theo marveled at how similar his and Tom's expressions could be. "I don't know if it will make me feel better, or worse."

As though he was softened by the way Paul seemed to deflate, Tom came around the bar and joined his uncle. "Let us know if you change your mind, because now that we do know, it's not as though the location will be any different tomorrow or a year from now... or five years from now." He clasped one of Paul's hands in his own. Theo imagined that whatever Tom could sense emanating from Paul, it was deep and painful, the kind of bereft feeling nobody felt ready to carry. Yet only the lucky would get to bear it, if sorrow was the price of such deep affections.

Watching, Theo noted how Paul relaxed when Tom said, "I should have asked you first, Paul. If you even wanted to know where he was."

"Oh, yes, you should have," said Paul. He chuckled once and relinquished Tom's hand. "But what's done is done, and... who knows, perhaps it will be good to know after all these years." He gazed at the room as though seeing it as it had been while Alastair was alive. Or perhaps he was silently speaking to it in a way only he could manage.

Even having only frequented The Shuck since last December, Theo felt it was almost more like a person than a location. It seemed to have moods that changed, and a certain demeanor. Though Benson had been at it since January, it had only been within the last month or so that he'd truly transmuted some of the melancholy Theo had come to associate with the old girl.

Whatever David had managed by way of a bewitchment when he was young and feeling scorned, it was subtle, yet enough to keep things from flourishing. Theo knew witchcraft wasn't his own strength, so he didn't entirely understand anything Benson spoke about, but he gathered the process for reversing an accidental bewitchment was going fairly well. Witchery, he said, could take time. However, they did need David to finish the process.

Theo glanced at some of Benson's sigils on the crossbeams above his head. The Shuck felt happier, less tense, and even seemed to allow for more light within her rooms. It was impossible to confirm if this was just their changed perceptions, or something more concrete. They were all more content now than they had been, so it was possible the building just seemed different.

Or maybe Benson was right.

All of these things could be true. Theo was capable of holding many truths in tandem and didn't always insist upon choosing one.

"Perhaps," said Tom. He smiled ruefully and said, "Now that we have ruined your morning, we'll leave you and I'll return this evening to take over."

"You didn't ruin it; I'm just not as good at being shocked as I once was."

"Can a seer be shocked?" Tom asked.

This kind teasing was a language of affection between them, a slightly saturnine way of expressing their love and understanding of each other. It had developed as they decided to be more open about their thoughts and abilities, which was endearing to Theo, if somewhat mystifying to patrons or strangers.

"I offer my congratulations that you managed to shock one," said Paul. Then he added, "Maeve said she would be in tonight, so we shall have to remove the curtains when she does, or at least keep an eye to where she chooses to sit. I'm fond of the new ones and I don't want her setting them on fire."

"Fine," said Tom, and he hooked his arm into Theo's. They'd unhook them as soon as they went outside, but Theo wouldn't take these small shows of devotion for granted. "Think about it — think about planning a journey north," he told his uncle as they headed for the door.

"I will," was the soft reply, so quiet they almost obscured it with the sound of the hinges as they left.

The day that greeted them beyond the door was mild and Theo took a deep, grounding breath. "What do you think he'll do?"

"I know what I would do," said Tom, the worry in his hazel eyes reminiscent of that in Paul's slightly greener ones. "As to what he will do... I won't pretend I can say. That kind of a loss... I can't imagine how I would get past it."

Nodding and reclaiming his own arm, Theo went alongside him in silence, and they walked to the house, a cottage, really, that they now shared. He owned it, but they'd each cleaned it up, decorated, decided on the purchase together. Life had decidedly changed since Tom returned his skin – since they'd met under cover of darkness in David's empty house. It was full of ease, now, of a sort Theo hadn't ever experienced.

He had never lacked for money even long ago when it was him and his father. After his mother left them, they'd had to be mindful of what they spent, but he hadn't faced any particular material hardship. Then, one way or another, he'd moved through the world in such a way that meant he could make his own money, and because he was about a century old, he'd managed to save and invest more than many men who appeared his age.

But what he'd lacked was belonging, a sense of family and place, and he found he had it now. With Tom, and even with Paul and Benson.

He once thought he'd found it with David, but it wasn't as lasting as he'd hoped. *He could still be part of it.* As they reached home, he reflected on what he'd gained, and it made him wonder how David might fit in his life now. He had the nagging feeling that it might be the thing that helped The Shuck, and he couldn't elaborate upon why. That aside, he rather missed him as a friend.

Unlocking the door, he said, "Would you mind if..." then reconsidered what he was about to ask. Tom and David were not fond of each other, though it might have been much more accurate to state they shared a complex past. While Benson was unearthing the best way to reverse what David had cast upon The Shuck, nobody quite knew how to tell David he had the ability to do so in the first place.

The best way to involve him was, from Theo's perspective, to try being friendly first. They weren't lovers any longer, but he knew Mr. David Mills at least as well as he knew himself. Which was to say, at least he could read and predict his ways. He frowned. *That might not be entirely correct.* He'd expected David to balk when he'd told him he was a selkie, and David had not.

Perhaps Theo could still say what might win him over, though, and he suspected that would be friendship.

"Would I mind..." Tom glanced at him quizzically after he'd stepped indoors and sat down on a little bench to remove his boots.

Rather than try to be tactful, he just came out with it. "I think we should invite David round." He waited for the inevitable scoff, the huff of chagrin, both of which he understood given all David had said to Tom in the past, and what he had done.

But if there was anything the last few months had demonstrated for Theo, it was precisely that he should treat the past carefully. One needed to decide what sort of power it could hold over them. Whether that was Tom trying to wean himself off his entrenched need for drink, Paul slowly removing some of the old and disused things from his flat, or Theo deciding that his father hadn't been right about *everyone* and that some people could be trusted with secrets.

"I think that would be a good idea."

"You see, if Benson and even your uncle are trying to understand how..." Theo took a breath. "You... do."

"Yes."

"Even though he might make remarks about all of this?"

Theo waved his hand at their surroundings, which were tidy, warm, and breathed serenity, but were undeniably simple. Even as he said it, though, he did not actually know if David would say anything critical at all.

"I'll survive." Tom rose and took both of Theo's hands. "I was thinking, too, that it seems pointless to try fixing a problem he started when he has no sense of how he *is* the problem." His eyes searched Theo's face. "The trick will be convincing him that all will be well."

"Benson said it could be harmful to lift something someone has cast without their knowing. Or their help," said Theo. "To be honest, I don't understand why or how. But I gather it would go easier for all of us if David were around and aware."

"The first snide thing he says and I'll push him outside, I promise."

"We should see if he behaves, first," Theo said, but he smiled.

"You're remarkably calm about this."

"Well, so are you." Initially, Tom had been confounded by his grace toward a man who'd unknowingly captured the thing that could capture him. Theo had tried to explain – as time went by and Tom stopped grumbling if he so much as mentioned either David or Norwich – that he was simply too old to get angry about an accident. Ultimately, it had been an accident, and it would have been a far different matter had malice been involved.

"I'm trying to remember how he was before his father fucked us both over. That helps me be kinder. He was stodgy before, but not cold. Not cruel. To my mind, Mr. Mills the elder is the one who bewitched The Shuck... not to say I want to absolve David of any and all responsibility, but... I don't think it's entirely his fault."

Nodding, Theo said, choosing not to remark upon how begrudging Tom sounded, for this was a good change regardless of the tone and he wished to encourage it, "I think that's very wise of you."

"I *might* even be induced to see him as a friend, again."

"Oh?" Endeared, Theo concealed a smile.

"Might, I said. And he's been on my mind, today. Not specifically inviting him anywhere, but..." Tom let go of one of Theo's hands and reached for a letter resting on a nearby sideboard. Theo recognized David's penmanship immediately. "This came for you;

Paul said it arrived yesterday morning. Yet... as you may know... I was rather distracted upon my return home last night. Couldn't give it to you promptly."

Coyly, Theo said, "No, well, you gave me something else." A little abstracted, he paused, thinking about what they'd done and against which pieces of furniture in this very room. The table might be a little crooked permanently, now. But he found he did not mind.

Tom said, "I forgot to avoid marking up your neck. Noticed when you were dressing this morning." He did not sound apologetic at all, but rather, wistful and pensive.

"Collars obscure a great deal, Mr. Apollyon. I won't have you avoiding my neck unless you wish to start marking up my thighs, instead." He took David's letter, sighing, keeping himself nestled along Tom's body. "I wonder what he's said, then."

3

FOUR DAYS LATER

Upper St. Giles Street, Norwich

Balefully, David remembered what Theo had said to him once after he'd torn into this very office in a state of tension and Theo had been simply minding his own affairs and trying to work. It was something to the effect of paying someone to run his business while he went and wrote monographs. Theo knew he loved history, something he hadn't been allowed to make his profession.

At the time, he'd been too irked and anxious to enact such a plan, but even then he'd admitted there was something appealing about it. He just didn't know how precisely to make it happen. The Mills weren't people with terribly old money; they were in effect glorified merchants whose means were only about three generations old. Compared to anyone who considered themselves old money, that was nothing, and less-involved approaches to his business still felt unattainable to David because of this divide. On the other hand, Norwich did seem welcoming to enterprising sorts.

Perhaps it was time to consider hiring a manager.

He'd lost his sense of how to run things, and while profits were good, his heart was not in it at all. Earlier this week, he'd crumbled and written Theo to see if he would consider returning to work for the interim.

In short, David was overwhelmed, a feeling that had begun in January after they'd parted ways and only increased as spring approached and progressed. Despite all they'd been through, he still trusted Theo more than anyone he knew. If a certain mystical truth had been withheld from him, and it had, he could admit he was the person to blame for it. Theo also already understood everything about the operations.

The question was whether or not he was occupied by some other endeavor. And whether he would even want to work for David again. This time, naturally, *work* wouldn't be a euphemism for their long-term romantic arrangement.

He mussed his hair and stared blankly at the far wall with its old, fine crack in the white plaster. *How the hell did I get here?*

He thought back to what he'd thought life would look like at thirty when he was a boy, and it was far different from this murky standstill he found himself occupying. It felt like being stuck in a marsh or quicksand, and he'd been so preoccupied of late by questions that had nothing to do with daily life.

They were about magic and creatures, not economics and business. The more he delved and read, the less he understood, and the more he thought about all of it, the more he noticed things that could not be there. More threads, a few sparkling little auras around people.

None of it had anything to do with anything he'd been brought up to esteem or want or value.

It was true that much of that original picture of

success and progress was drawn by his mother and especially his father, as it had involved a wife and at least one child. He now knew it wasn't his own measure of success.

It had taken him quite some time to admit it, and Theo departing his role as lover and confidant made him certain. David knew such a traditional family wasn't for him and he couldn't pretend it was. He also felt, in a deeply unsettling manner, that this life of routine wasn't meant to be his.

The only thing that remained similar between his thoughts then and now was the line of business, for everyone had to do something and he'd never objected to cloth. It was not as though he went out and tended the sheep whose wool ultimately made the stuff or picked any plants needed for various fibers.

Although if he did, maybe he would not feel so unmoored. He'd be too tired and at least get to spend time around living creatures.

Worst of all, he was forced to admit in his newfound solitude that he was quite lonely *and* quite put out about that loneliness. He couldn't stand being near his old friends, these days, and had become something of a recluse, save for business appointments.

Grumbling, restless, he stood and decided he needed to go for a wander.

From here, he could walk to the market quite easily or even stop at home, though he knew his cook was not expecting him at midday. She would be flustered if he chose to go there. *Even that line of thinking makes you different from your so-called friends.* Very few of them would care about inconveniencing a servant.

In the end, he was much more at home with those who were, not to put too fine a point on it, a bit strange. Or elderly. Both, perhaps. He liked speaking to old men at the market, listening to all their odd stories and learning about the place where he'd grown up. They were likely to tell him all the things his family avoided discussing. Which of the lanes were where women of ill repute plied their trade, or which of the plague pits near the Cathedral were largest, or how exactly Kett had been tried for his part in the rebellion.

Yes, he was more at ease with people like that, or with people like Theo. *Or Tom.* He felt, by now, that perhaps they might be able to mend what had happened.

As he put on his coat and hat, he glanced at the top of his empty desk, devoid of any correspondence, and wished Theo would reply sooner rather than later. He was probably enjoying himself immensely and had little time to make prompt responses. The thought made David slightly bitter even though he knew they wouldn't have been together much longer, anyway.

And as Theo was a seal creature known for its elusive nature, David wondered if he would have left at some point regardless. All the obscure texts he'd recently trawled about the subject claimed they were quite fickle, and they were predominately women. Then again, it was not as though he had treated Theo so well that he would never want to leave, regardless of who or what he was.

He supposed he might like to see Theo be a seal, although whether he ever would was an entirely different question. It felt private, akin to asking a man to touch himself in front of him.

He locked the door behind him and set out for the street, lost in thought.

As he revisited old mythologies and tomes before

he tried to sleep, the more he felt confident that perhaps, he might begin to explore things. Nobody was around to tell him he had to be godly, or serious.

It all spoke to the internal sense of *knowing* that he possessed and often suppressed.

Why, what if Nick had never been imaginary? Perhaps someone who might see ghosts had to keep cultivating the skill, or maybe one grew out of it the same way a favorite food might change. *Seeing the threads never really left,* he thought. It was more muted until recently, almost as though giving it more thought brought it more life. *Perhaps ghosts are the same?*

There could be whole scientific reasons for the preternatural, just like there were such rules for the natural world. He was sure of it.

He grunted upon receiving a slight impact to his side.

A slender young man had walked into him, or he walked into the slender young man while he was thinking.

Incensed and trying not to be, he straightened his clothes and peered at the dashing person in question, who bestowed a rakish smile and no ready apology. "Things are rather uneven there, aren't they, sir?"

Rather than dignify it with a reply, for he had nothing polite to say to such an inane rhetorical question, David merely sniffed, shook his head, and kept walking. It might be fair that the young man hadn't apologized, because David hadn't been paying much attention to his surroundings.

And he didn't quite appreciate how he thrilled a little as he heard the stranger's husky voice, or the way their gazes caught for just a second and the stranger smirked.

It was not until he neared Gentleman's Walk that he realized his wallet was gone.

He liked that even less than emotional upheaval.

Rather than make for anywhere that served tea, which had been his original plan, he went immediately to the Sir Garnet Wolseley public house instead. Had he been less flustered by both voice and eyes, he might've remembered neither a shop nor a pub would furnish him something to drink without money. The landlord, however, took pity upon him as soon as David uttered the word pickpocket.

Peevish, knowing he was only afforded such grace because of how he spoke and appeared, he settled with his pint at a table upstairs and sipped, then gulped. He knew he'd be expected to return with proper payment once his affairs were in order. Being fortunate enough never to have experienced something like this, he hadn't any thoughts on how to recover his effects.

"I followed you here."

He looked up to see the very source of his problem, but felt so sullen that he did not even stand to confront the stranger. Instead, he took another drink of his ale. "Well, if you stole from me, you needed what you took, I am sure." Really, he knew no such thing, he didn't know the first thing about thieves, but he'd like to assume most of them — or perhaps just this one — was in need.

The stranger frowned, his vulpine face graceful in its small movements. He was perhaps a few inches shorter than David, with dark hair under a gray flat cap that had seen better days. It was still on his head even inside. His eyes seemed to be dark brown like his hair, but that could have been the light inside the pub. "Maybe I did."

Then he sat, and David could not find the words to tell him to go away. "Then why did you follow me here?" David watched as his own wallet appeared on the old tabletop between them. "That's all I had on my person. If you've come back for more."

"My name is Lennie," said the stranger by way of reply, though David had not asked for a name and wouldn't have expected a given one. Then again, had he been told anything more proper or more thorough, he might have expected it to be fabricated, too.

"Is it really? Why are you telling me?" Surely, he could bring Lennie before the law even if he had such minimal information. "And that wasn't even an answer to what I actually asked."

Lennie shrugged. "It is. It's my name. And you have trustworthy eyes."

At a loss, David said, "I have what?"

"And I followed you because I liked the way you walked."

That made him splutter. "I beg your—"

"Don't, or I'll just take it back," said Lennie cheerfully, nodding a bit to the wallet. "Not that there was as much as I expected."

Still attempting to understand if all this was kittenish or insulting, a trick to extort more from him, David huffed. "What the hell did you expect, then?"

With a chuckle, all Lennie said was, "More."

For no reason other than he simply didn't think Lennie was going to trick him any further, David let down his guard. Tiresomely, he also liked how Lennie said *more*. Sighing, he took out some banknotes and set them just near him. "For your trouble."

Evidently, his gesture surprised Lennie. His dark brows arched as he quickly and fluidly pocketed the money. Though David could not pretend to know why, he appeared relieved for a spell, as though he really did need the money for something important.

"My trouble? Think I could have caused you more trouble than you caused me."

"Be that as it may," said David. He reflected upon why Lennie felt so compelling and came up with no concrete reason for it. Maybe he was just that bored. Or lonely. "You did bring it back."

"Only after taking it."

Even amidst his confusion and pique, for he couldn't account for his lack of proper anger over the way he'd just been pickpocketed, then un-pickpocketed, David was mesmerized the more he heard Lennie speak. He had a local accent, complete with the vowels and almost-mumble that Father hated, and possessed a timber of voice that carried well in the pub's ambient noises.

Lennie said, "True." He smirked a little. "Well, now that I've returned it, I think I made the right choice. You seem quite sad, and really, I wouldn't want to add any more misfortune."

As he tried to think of what to say to that and his eyes strayed, David noticed threads, fine as a spider's web coated in morning dew, between Lennie's fingertips and his own. He blinked and they left his sight. Unlike him, Lennie had graceful hands and he wore no rings. "I am not..." David exhaled and didn't end the sentence on *sad*. It was the smallest way of telling the truth. He was sad, though perhaps not in an all-consuming manner. "I'm well."

"You can be well *and* sad." Lennie tilted his head. "I'm glad I followed you."

Because David was engulfed by his own feelings of gladness after hearing it, he took a long drink. He wasn't prepared to feel so pleased and found he was almost giddy, not just glad. "Well..."

"Never mind," Lennie said. "My mother always said I was too forthright."

"My father said the same of me," David said, before he could think better of it.

The smile he received was reward enough. "Then, from one forthright child to another... keep your shit up here." Lennie reached over and patted the edge of David's jacket, close to the left side of his chest. There was indeed a pocket within and perhaps he should have made better use of it. "It's more difficult for likes of me to steal from you that way."

Stunned, David stared at him, certain his expression was more of a glower, though he did not mean it to be.

But Lennie just laughed. "Perhaps I'll see you here one day. I come often enough."

After he had left, sauntering down a nearby flight of stairs as David gawped after him, he had only one thought. *He doesn't know my name.* Well, he could always just... make this his regular. He smiled to himself. He'd never had a regular: Father demonized drink, public houses, and anything to do with them, including the Apollyons.

Father had demonized damn near everything and none of it had killed David yet.

———

They weren't certain Mr. Garnet had ever been shown much by way of jovial teasing or flirtatious conversation. Lennie could not recall ever meeting someone who was so painfully dignified, though they supposed they didn't converse with many of their marks.

Most did appear quite proper, so they couldn't know for certain if they'd never actually met someone that prim. Pickpocketing was usually a quick transaction, and they were very good at their work. They were fast and light on their feet, even lighter of fingers, and they had a preternatural advantage that was a boon on most days.

Like their mother, Lennie'd had premonitions since childhood. With some determination and focus, they eventually managed to hone the ability: they could sometimes see the outcomes of their stealing if they concentrated. But it wasn't all Lennie saw, and they'd dreamt so many things that happened in life that they'd lost count of the occurrences. Insignificant ones, largely, with a few scattered momentous instances, like the time they'd known to delay crossing a road because if they'd done it any earlier, they'd have been hit by a cart that an incredibly apologetic farmer was running after.

Like Mr. Garnet with those blue eyes. They suspected he was going to be somehow important. They'd dreamt about him repeatedly. He didn't know it, but Lennie had seen him before. Just in dreams, which weren't realities for most people.

And Mr. Garnet wasn't his name.

Lennie chuckled quietly at how taken aback he'd been at their presence, so much so that he hadn't even bothered to introduce himself or bluster about getting the police. There was a sense of gentleness underneath those perfectly cut clothes and within that cultivated speech. It was almost timidity more than gentleness, and Lennie was charmed by it.

They were taken by the idea of conducting a little experiment while they spoke. They wanted to see if he'd volunteer the information, introduce himself properly.

He had not.

So for now, he was Mr. Garnet in honor of the pub. He'd stay named such until they met again, and they would.

Had Lennie realized who he was before taking his wallet, they might have refrained. All they'd felt before brushing against Mr. Garnet was a pull, a tug, and they hadn't bothered to interrogate it. Then he'd looked at Lennie and Lennie recognized his face from dreams, premonitions that they'd had several times of late. They always involved Mr. Garnet and took place in an old taproom whose crossbeams had funny little runes across them. Not much happened, really. Mr. Garnet and Lennie just spoke to a man of middling age with greenish eyes who had premonitions of his own.

The most irksome thing was, they couldn't hear anything, or if they could, they never recalled what was said.

All Lennie had decided was, if it kept coming back, it must be significant. It didn't feel like a normal variety of recurring dream, the kind anybody could have, and they had long since learned the differences. Dreams that were meant to happen felt vivid, almost lurid, and they were bright as lightning across a dark sky.

Glancing over their shoulder as they made their way along Gentleman's Walk, they almost hoped Mr. Garnet would follow them the way they'd followed Mr. Garnet. He'd just helped more than he had realized: with the banknotes he'd given them, they could pay Ralph, and paying Ralph would create a new world of more freedom.

Their stepfather, long given to making their life fairly miserable, had sent a letter demanding Lennie

repay him for room and board or he'd *expose them.*
That had been a fortnight ago, and it had taken the
first full week of the two for Lennie to calm down
about the communication.

Apparently, it didn't matter that Lennie had not
lived with Ralph, or Robbie, their stepbrother, for two
years this week.

Ralph, who was literate even if he wasn't elegant
when he wrote, explained it was a retroactive payment
for all he'd done: housing Lennie, and Mum, and
feeding Lennie, and Mum. The note itself sounded a
little deranged, which was in part why they meant to
obey it. It felt like a madman's ramblings more than a
letter, and Lennie didn't trust him even when he
sounded more cogent.

He also had a lifetime of disparagement and scorn
to evidence that if he wished, he would antagonize
Lennie for being not as he thought they should be, for
being wrong, for being mad, for being a waste.

Even though they didn't want to pay and had been
avoiding Ralph – mostly successfully, with the exception of letters like these – after that first week of fury,
they felt the best course of action was just to pay him
so he'd continue to leave them alone. He had done
this every month or two in the years since they'd made
their own way: he'd written and demanded money.
The reasons were usually less mad than the one he
gave now, but no less infuriating.

Had to visit the tailor.

Need new shoes.

You wouldn't want me to starve.

A doctor was summoned to the house; I'm ill.

This most recent instance, he'd asked for a larger
sum than usual and given the pettiest excuse. After
they paid him this time, perhaps they could consider

leaving the city and starting a new chapter elsewhere. They had no record with the police, never having been caught at their craft. Besides, they fancied a change and knew they could put their mind to other occupations.

It hadn't taken them long to come up with almost all of the money Ralph commanded, although it had strained their meager finances. Then came Mr. Garnet. Who'd given them the rest of it even after they'd tried to take it illicitly. Lennie grinned, knowing that to passersby, it looked like they were grinning at the air before them. They didn't care.

Even if he hadn't had such beautiful eyes, I'd give him a kiss for that, alone.

4

Cromer

There was nothing for it. David had made the mistake of mentioning *a man* in front of two men who knew him very well, in some way or another. Almost a week after being pickpocketed, he was still thinking about the person who'd tried it. Theo intimated that there could be romantic implications to this, not that he possessed any more information than David mentioning he'd met someone called Lennie.

Who'd tried to pickpocket him.

Well, who had succeeded in doing so, then reversed his actions.

"This thief doesn't even know your name?" Tom said. He looked like he was stifling a chuckle at David's expense.

They were *supposed* to be discussing Theo coming to Norwich to resume work for David until David could find a permanent manager. That was what he'd been invited here to do, as per Theo's reply to his letter. Instead, they were still talking about the mysterious, kindhearted Lennie, leaving David helpless in the wake of speculative gossip about someone he had just met under frankly criminal circumstances.

Not that I'm unused to meeting lovers under criminal circumstances. Though, there had not been that many besides the two men before him. A few more, here and there.

He was not quite comfortable enough with his own desires for the conversation to feel lighthearted or hopeful, or even very arousing. He could entertain the concepts of selkies, ghosts, and witches. Even shucks or grims or mermaids or whatever else. But he couldn't entertain the idea of such a chance meeting leading him to a new lover in the manner these two did. He eyed them, unamused. *You are meant for each other.* It was a forlorn thought. But he could see the give and take between them. Theo softened Tom and Tom moored Theo.

He'd also seen similar relationships once or twice while at university and it had driven him to envy. Now, he felt naught but dull longing, much the same as he felt when he contemplated Paul Apollyon and his lover of many years. They'd flouted the expectations society had of men. With the barest of internal winces, he reminded himself that even so, that had still ended in loss. He had not decided if such a risk was worth it.

"Must not have looked very hard at the contents of his wallet," said Theo, from where he stood next to David.

"I don't know if he... no, wait, he must have. He said he expected there to be more. More money," said David with a frown. "Perhaps he didn't look very hard."

Trying to keep calm, for he was not very good at being teased, however kindly meant, or at discussing his own internal thoughts, David sipped his ale and took stock of what he'd come to accomplish.

Luckily, Theo had already said he would step in. And David truly did consider himself lucky that he was getting that, given what he'd made Theo endure.

The letter he'd received yesterday morning said Theo would be happy to, and though he did oversee some of The Shuck's affairs, those were well enough in hand that he could probably do David the favor for at least several weeks.

While David had expected some resistance on Tom's part, there was none. Instead of combatting another man's jealousy or spite for the sake of his business, he found himself sitting in the taproom he'd once derided and making jovial conversation.

"What an impertinent thing to say to someone when you've just stolen from him," said Tom.

"It just means you are dressed very well, which you always are," Theo said.

"I wasn't wearing anything of consequence." Proudly, David managed not to splutter.

"But you forget you are attractive," Tom said. "To some people." He winked and David *did* splutter.

The changes Theo wrought in Tom since December were remarkable, or perhaps Tom himself managed them. He talked more freely now, brought up lighter topics, and let his dry humor come to the fore instead of his recalcitrance. David eyed him, once so sullen as to be taciturn and so wind chafed as to look a handful of years older than he really was.

But there he stood, rosy with warmth and more animation, still with a glass of something strong nearby, yet consuming it in a moderate way. Despite needing to grow more used to it, David found he greatly enjoyed the effect Tom and Theo's cohabitation had seemed to produce. It was much more the way Tom had been when they were younger, before Father had set them on an inevitable path against each other. Thinking of his father's actions caused a flare of anger that started in his stomach and felt almost like a punch.

Well, he couldn't shirk responsibility entirely. Father might have forced him to end things, but he hadn't forced him to behave priggishly. Some of it had to be related to his own choices and temperament, and David was prepared to acknowledge it.

"Tell me again about his hands," said Theo, arching an eyebrow.

Flushing, David took a drink of his ale. He might have alluded to adept hands earlier in their discussion, once things had turned from the Mills family business to a thief on Upper St. Giles. "I'd thank you not to raise the topic while we're in public."

"So... it's like that, is it?"

"Theo!"

"No one is listening to us."

"And they're all drinking," said Tom.

"Be that as it may, it's not... seemly." David looked around the modest throng in The Shuck, unused to seeing this many people within it, but pleased for the Apollyons' sake they were here. He did not recognize any of the faces, which were all generally of the older and more florid variety.

He'd expected to see the old eccentric whom Theo had pointed out and mentioned was in residence. Theo felt they should meet properly. Something about a regional historical undertaking. Figuring he was due a hobby, David was intrigued by the idea.

"You aren't convincing me his hands were of no

matter, then," Theo said. "If it were seemly, you wouldn't care about telling me. Right now."

Tom, who was repairing one of the decanters that had a metal hinge and looked more medieval than modern, snorted. "I'd have kept your purse or your wallet or whatever I'd taken from you."

David did not say the reason given for the safe return was that he'd looked sad, for even though he was surprisingly happy to be here in The Shuck talking to them like he was among friends, he just wasn't used to sharing such emotional information. "Of course you would have. You're incorrigible, my man. And..." he sighed and looked at Theo. "They were lovely."

When Tom looked up from his work and smirked, David compulsively lit a cigarette to have something to do. He sounded bewildered and he knew it, and he wished to play it off as though he were not. Taking a breath and exhaling smoke, he considered the rest of what he wanted to say.

"Sounds like they were splendid," Theo said, raising his eyebrows. "I have never seen you this addled — polished Mr. Mills — not once."

"And how addled is that?"

"Besotted," said Tom, his voice smooth over the collective chatter.

Even though there was nothing in his expression but warmth and a wry kind of smugness, David mumbled, "Fuck you."

"No, thank you. I find myself quite satisfied."

Seeming to take pity upon David, but still chortling, Theo said, "David, you have to understand, seeing you like this is... a surprise. But love is a very human thing, is it not?"

"Love?" David said, and it emerged on a squeak.

"Fine... to lust, then, is human. Maybe. Though, I

don't believe all of us experience lust. I think some people don't experience any attraction at all."

"Can we change the subject?"

"Selkie!" None of the three of them said it. But the old man with the regional history project had appeared, presumably from the rooms he rented upstairs, yet also seemingly out of nothing in the space between patrons. David was grateful for the intrusion, but he glanced at Theo to gauge how he might feel about the word being veritably shouted over a bar toward him. True, nobody seemed to react and they probably wouldn't, for this local eccentric was well marked as such and smelled keenly of gin.

"Benson," said Theo. He was, thought David, remarkably tolerant. "One day, you will have everyone believing that is my given name."

"Don't think so," Benson said. His rather dirty beard glittered with what David thought were beads, but on a closer look were seed pearls and tiny charms. It was as close as he wanted Benson to step; he did not prefer gin and quickly found that the scent of it warmed by a person *and* mixed with the odor of his unwashed body was rather nauseating.

"What can I get for you, then?" Tom asked.

"Nothing I have not already poured myself. *Something* told me to come down." Benson tapped his florid nose.

With the merest flicker of a glance at David, Tom said, "I see."

David did not, for this seemed like any halfway decent evening at a public house, and if one lived here, it seemed unlikely to prompt any special consideration. He put out his cigarette even though it wasn't near to being finished. He thought this might be his perfect time to exit and see himself home.

He'd slept last night in his family's house without telling anyone he planned to arrive, so the place was devoid of life and slightly dusty. There were the mouser and the caretaker, both of whom were somewhat shocked to see him. The stalwart man said they could quickly hire a woman to clean, but David insisted there would be no need while the cat wove happily between his and the caretaker's ankles. He just liked Cromer and wished to stay a couple of nights, that was all.

He supposed he could have easily taken the train back, but he'd hoped being near the sea for a short while would have a lulling effect on his mind, which seemed to go quite quickly toward everything he did not want to think about, these days, or prove itself a traitor to his old thoughts. Though those old thoughts had been direly in need of an overhaul, he would have appreciated it if they could change in an orderly fashion. So far, that had not been the case.

But he was not too bothered to be within the house, even if most of its furniture was obscured by covers and there was no food in the kitchen. He could not even spot signs of any forced entry on Tom's part, though judging by the rumpled bed — his bed, ironically — he wondered if either he or Theo might've rested there the night they took back Theo's skin. He did not want to consider if they'd done anything else. Theo said they hadn't, so that was what he chose to trust.

"I shall take my leave, then?"

They hadn't really decided on the details of Theo's return, but he could always come round The Shuck in the morning before he caught the train.

"Oh," said Theo, "actually, I had wondered if I might introduce you both, remember?" Benson then eyed David with some expectation, and David stilled himself and turned toward him. "This is Benson. Benson, this is Mr. David Mills." Apparently, Benson went by one name and that was enough.

David did not question it. And because of how the man looked, he expected a handshake at best; they weren't done much in polite circles, but someone like this might try. Or perhaps he'd utter some sagacious but senseless quip. He was obviously somewhat drunk, or appeared so.

But then, Tom had often been somewhat drunk without anyone knowing, so David did not know why he thought he could divine another's drunkenness with accuracy. Anyway, some of the old men in the reading rooms he frequented when he had a day to himself often smelled just as pungently of various liquors, the only difference being that they did not look as unmoored as Benson and clearly had more means to take care of themselves.

"A pleasure," said David. He squinted at the tiny pearls in Benson's beard, for they seemed to be refracting the gas and candlelight more intensely than they had a moment ago. It could have been the ale impacting his perceptions, to be sure, for Paul was known to produce slightly intense brews. According to his father, anyway.

David shook his head slightly and met Benson's eyes instead of allowing the pearls to catch his attention. Without any pleasantries, Benson said, with the same quotidian tone as someone who asked for directions, "So, *you're* the witch."

5

Someone in the corner dropped their glass, or threw their glass, in the pause between Benson's words and David's next breath, but he was so stunned that the shatter sounded far away even though he could see the sheepish, thin man who'd caused the mild commotion. Tom cursed so quietly that David could not catch what he said. Then he moved to help clean it up, walking to the source of the noise with a dustpan and broom before anyone might cut themselves.

That left Theo to look between Benson and David with an air of equanimity. But David wasn't fooled; Theo's expression was colored with an undertone of wariness.

"I'm sorry?"

"You, you're the witch."

"Benson," Theo said, evidently trying to defuse the situation, "this is who I thought could help with your history proj —"

"Don't insult us, selkie, either of us. He might be fond of his books, but he's not going to help me with any history. He's going to help me with the bewitchment he's put on this place."

"Clearly he's had too much to drink," David said, grasping at regularity and ignoring the way the hair on the back of his neck was standing up while Benson scrutinized him. The reaction itself didn't feel natural, and he remembered the spiteful things he'd told Tom about The Shuck, how he'd said that it should be cursed.

If Benson was mentioning *selkie,* too... frowning, David chewed at his lower lip and sensed there was so much more here than he knew. It brought to mind the way he'd felt when he found out Theo and Tom had met, which was to say, like he was on the edge of an abyss.

"I've nearly always had too much to drink," said Benson, and the illusion of him being an elderly man with a tenuous grasp on social niceties and the present shifted. An intentness was in his eyes, the color of which David could not tell in the smoky light. "And now that I see you for what you are — have done for months — I have to question my ability to spot anything. I hadn't known, but I should have understood well before."

Theo had opened and closed his mouth several times during the course of Benson's speech. Perhaps understandably, he found nowhere to interject. David could not help but glance at him for some guidance, some indication of how to respond to any of this, none of which was the usual order of any conversation he'd ever had with a new acquaintance. Annoyingly, he liked the irregularity of it.

Waiting until Benson was through, Theo said, "We ought to decamp elsewhere if you *insist* upon doing this."

"Doing what?" David said.

"Don't worry," said Benson. "You didn't mean to do it. All shall be well, shan't it?"

"What will?" David wasn't even insulted, but he was perplexed.

"All of it."

"Benson, don't make me bring Paul down here," Theo said.

For a moment, David wondered if Paul had come to an intimate understanding with the personified pile of rags before him. He peered at Benson, trying to decide if Theo made the threat because Paul could leverage a romantic connection to get Benson to stop speaking.

Then he recalled the last few exchanges he'd had with Paul, and he did not think this Benson would suit the elder Apollyon at all. He had not known him for more than a few minutes, but he was the sort of man most adults would avoid on the street. Small children, meanwhile, might either taunt him, or cry at the sight of him.

"As though he frightens me."

"No, I don't think you are scared of him... but he is good ballast for your frankly *alarming* conversational style." Theo spoke as though he had experience with Benson's erratic choices of discussion.

Benson sipped from a battered pewter flask he'd had at his hip. He looked slyly at David. "I said to Silence, once, that you'd look at me like shit on the bottom of your best shoe."

"Am I?" David did not think he looked so openly disgusted. For one thing, he was not. For another, he was thinking about too many things to look at anyone with much intent. "Looking at you so poorly?"

"No." Complacently, Benson continued, "On balance, I suppose things are going better than I expected them to."

Had David been a child, Benson's unpredictability would have been frightening — yet paired with Benson's words, it would have intrigued him, too. He had so often longed to be special, to be part of something beyond what others thought possible and saw before their eyes. Part of it must have been because he grew up an only son and only child who'd received little warmth.

Some only children, he knew, were well-loved and cosseted, but that had never been his experience. Mother was more loving and lenient than Father, but she was rather timid and did not go against him to demonstrate more affection than he deemed seemly. By the time David was twelve or so, Father had started to treat him with even more strictness. His imagination, any fancies or lurid pretending, none of that was valued or encouraged.

Seemingly everyone who had an opinion of him, Tom and Theo included, believed he was prim and stodgy. Or that he had become a prim and stodgy man even if he had not been such an unpleasant child. But the truth of it was, primness was a facade he built to keep Father out of his affairs and stop him from interfering overmuch with his life. It had robbed him of genuine connections with others, he was sure, but it had also protected him.

Inwardly, he thirsted after the incredible. At times, he was bitter he'd kept himself away from it. Now, much of the time, he found himself furious with his father for having created the circumstances that made him behave so self-protectively.

"That's something, isn't it," said Theo. He eyed the corner where Tom still tended to all the broken glass.

Benson nudged David with his left knuckle. Blinking, David noted silver rings on his gnarled fingers, some of which were set with pearls to match those in his beard. When he glanced at Benson's beard, though, the pearls were gone. *No, they must be behind more hair.* Benson seemed to be in constant movement, so it was probable that his thick, dirty beard was just obscuring them now. Unless, of course, they were not physical at all, but instead preternatural.

"Look there."

David followed Benson's gesture, glancing above their heads at one of the nearest crossbeams. "At... some wood from a couple centuries ago?"

Theo coughed, but it was more of a chuckle and David was heartened.

"No," said Benson. "Look at what is *on* the wood."

It was stained from years of smoke, and David had never been any good at identifying types of wood because it wasn't fibers or cloth — and nothing about it looked remarkable. He huffed, about to tell Benson he was uninterested in this game, then he squinted. The crossbeam bore evidence of a fire. He felt Theo's eyes on him and wondered why, but he kept looking at what he thought were scorch marks. No, they were marks purposefully burned into the wood. Letters, drawings.

"Runes," said David, realizing what they really were. "Sigils?"

He glanced at Benson. His own knowledge of symbols like these was rather boringly intellectual, but he imagined Benson had a much more esoteric understanding of them. Well, perhaps they had been here for generations. Norfolk was home to plenty of folk beliefs. He had never bothered looking above his head in The Shuck long enough to notice, being too busy paying attention to Tom to direct his notice anywhere else.

How things changed. He was happy to be civil with Tom once again, and even being on bantering terms with Theo again was a good thing. But he would be lying if it did not feel somewhat strange, like he was returning to himself after a long illness.

He was relearning how to be jovial just as one might be cultivating the endurance to walk again after a long period of inactivity. It was easier the more removed he became from his Cambridge set, and the less he had to pretend to adhere to artificial codes of gentility.

"Yes, just so." Benson was almost patient while he addressed him. "And how do you feel?"

"How do I *feel?*" The question made no sense.

Tom returned, having replaced the dustbin and broom in the corner where they were kept. "I'm always happiest when that kind of accident is precisely an accident. No blood, no shouting." He looked from David to Benson, his face settling into an expression like he was braced for the worst. "Oh, hell, what *else* has happened? We're doing this, now?"

"He's asking me how I feel... under some runes burnt into an old bit of wood up there." David felt well enough but failed to see what it had to do with anything.

Sighing, Tom barely glanced at the ceiling. He said, his eyes beseeching, "Come round to ours after closing."

Suddenly envious, David thought of the house Theo had said he'd bought sometime this spring. He and Tom lived there together, simply bachelor renters to any outsiders, but far more if the eye knew what to see. "Why?" David had never visited, but it seemed like a refuge of sorts, the kind of place he would never have and might well upset with his presence.

"Don't look so cross. We need to talk to you."

David was willing to ignore the comment about looking cross until Theo rested a palm on his forearm. "Please?"

He took a stuttering breath and shook his head. "No... whatever it is, it can wait, and I'm not so sure I want to discuss it under any circumstances." The last time Theo had spoken to him alone, it had been to reveal he was one of the seal folk.

Now there was some old man going on about witches, saying *he* was a witch. If pressed, David could try to explain that yes, he knew, thank you very much, but he needed time to come to all these conclusions on his own.

He *wanted* to listen to stories, to entertain the thought he had always been right to believe in them. It just felt like too much to do when prompted by someone else. But because no one pressed him and he was not very good at explaining what he felt, there were only three pairs of eyes, two familiar and one alien, gazing at him with various amounts of concern, he panicked.

"I need to... go... outside."

Theo did not let his hand fall so much as jerk it away, and the gesture stung. David put on his trilby and couldn't continue looking any of them in the face, carefully navigating himself through the gaggle in the taproom.

He couldn't be certain of where it came from, but as he showed himself out, he thought he caught a strong whiff of burning wood.

—

"Should I... go out and try to convince him to

come?" Theo wrinkled his nose. "He... his arm got hot. Under my palm."

Theo's guileless concern did him credit, thought Tom, but it was exactly how Theo would react. "I don't know." He scowled at Benson, who was watching this unfold without any indication of distress or much urgency. "That wasn't very well done of you. I told you we'd handle it. You are too... much. I thought you would frighten him, and I think you did." He exhaled and took a quick breath in through his nose. "What's that smell?"

Tom was glad he could now ask without fear. Before meeting Theo, he'd assumed everything was a trick of his mind and never asked for either confirmation or denial without feeling nervous about the answer.

Benson, his lips drifting into a lazy smile, gently gestured up with his flask. "He felt cornered."

It had been weeks and weeks since Benson began his process of understanding the bewitchment The Shuck was under. He'd been at it since January, at least, and he must have been doing something invisible, for the premises did feel better. Things seemed to go smoother, more money seemed to come in. Tom was still not much closer to understanding much of it. Though, he also spent a lot of his time navigating sobriety. Or as near as he could get to it. "What does that mean?"

"Tom, look at the runes," sighed Theo, following Benson's gesture with his eyes.

They were darker, more charred, and although it wasn't easy to confirm in the already smoky air, Tom thought they were giving off a little smoke of their own, more the way incense would once it was lit. In a much different tone, more resigned, he asked, "So...

what does *that* mean?" Worried for David, he added, "Have they hurt him?"

"No," said Benson. "But without a doubt, it means he absolutely did bewitch this place."

"We already knew it was so," said Tom, pouring both himself and Theo a dram. Theo accepted his with a soft murmur of thanks. "But you mean... he... did that. Made them smolder."

"Sort of," Benson said. "They reacted to his emotions because that's what I put those there to gauge. If I'm to help him — and righting The Shuck *will* help him, in the end — I need to know what triggers his reactions. *Especially* if he chooses to withhold his thoughts from us, or if he continues to rationalize."

"You goaded him," said Theo.

"A bit." Without remorse, Benson shrugged. "It was helpful to me, at any rate. And all the sigils over the doors and windows are there to protect the place. They're the protective ones. Remember, we all decided to lift the bewitchment without causing him harm.

"Of course we did," Tom said.

"I could do it without him, but to do so would mean some kind of illness or injury. For him." Benson did not appear unsettled at the thought of hurting or inconveniencing a toff, but Tom appreciated that he was too ethical to set those events in motion for the sake of an expedient result.

"So, he won't burn the place down." Tickled in spite of the serious circumstances, Tom chuckled.

"Can he?" Theo's voice rose. "Set The Shuck on fire?"

"No, that little smolder up there is no evidence of that," said Benson. "I doubt he can manipulate fire. I think *we're* more alike than he shall ever want to hear." Benson did not elaborate. "And anyway, we have

Maeve to do that. She's a fire witch, herself, though she rarely uses it for anything of consequence and often gets too drunk to control it."

Unimpressed by Benson's pragmatism, for Maeve had lost them several sets of curtains and caused Paul to impose an edict on where exactly she could sit, Tom murmured, "We just need to talk to him. He's scared."

Everything about David, from his expression to his speech to the colors that permeated his being, all attested to fear. He'd thought hard about how he wanted to treat David after the initial fury over how David had jeopardized Theo, and his conclusions had varied depending on how long it had been since his last drink, how much sleep he'd gotten, and how charitable toward humanity he felt.

Sometimes they changed based on who dredged up the subject of David with him: Paul got more of his sourness, whereas he felt he owed Theo a little more grace. But when he was alone, he could admit to himself that it would not be easy for someone like David to contend with information that would change how he saw himself. It was obvious to those who knew him that appearances mattered very much to him, and Tom had only lately started to wonder if David's clinging to a good public image was defensive, not necessarily what he valued as a person.

After all, if he was above reproach, it was much harder for his father and others like the odious man to ostracize him. He sighed and glanced at Theo, who mirrored the same understanding he felt. It was not easy to question and reassess all one thought one knew, and David knew rigidity as he did breathing.

6

An hour past closing time for The Shuck and any other public house that abided by the law, David was drunk.

He had first returned home in the hope he could calm down with some quiet seclusion, but he found himself foundering and searched the compartment in the cupboard under the servants' stairs where he used to hide liquor from Father. Theo hadn't known of the hiding place, for David feared he'd be laughed at, and even good-natured laughter was liable to put him in a foul frame of mind.

That wasn't the case now; he thought he could stand to be laughed at by the right person even if it made him rather uncomfortable, but he wanted something to blunt his thoughts. If he was going to think of witchcraft and folklore and... *men*, one man in particular, he at least wanted to feel less guilty about it. Intoxication would help.

"Perfect," he'd said to the empty house, or the ghost of his father if he was present, as the panel slid aside and revealed an unopened bottle of something he and Tom had filched from The Shuck years ago.

It was unlabeled to begin with, but he reckoned

anything that hadn't been opened and exposed to any air would still be safe to drink years into the future. Anyway, he was willing to take the chance if it was not, so he'd sat right on the floor and opened the bottle without a second thought.

The David of last winter would have remembered there was no food in the house and there was little by way of comfort to be had, because nothing at all had been prepared for him. He had to go back to Norwich tomorrow morning. Drunkenness and any illness because of it weren't going to be pleasant under these circumstances. But this David lacked the foresight. Decades of preparedness and rigidity were eroding under the pressures of new self-knowledge and the questions it bred.

He was still on the floor near the servants' narrow stairwell and corridor after one-fourth of the bottle was gone. Rather than examine those questions, he wanted to feel good.

"I see why Tom did this for so long," he murmured. His head swam, no, floated, and he was warm despite the lack of any lit fires. Best of all, his thoughts had slowed and predominately turned toward Lennie. There might be a chance he could see him again if he just went back to the Sir Garnet. Sobriety would have called this nonsense, not much of a plan at all.

He liked how the alcohol lowered his usual objections and made the most tenuous of rendezvous seem plausible.

And after Lennie, he thought of Theo, who'd caught his attention and kept it even after any embers between them had flickered and died.

You should have broken things off with him before you came for Christmas last winter, he thought. That had been the plan and he just couldn't execute it, and his indecision had ultimately embroiled him in something that was still changing how he regarded the world. He did not know if he could let himself change, but he knew he didn't have a choice. It was either let go, or be dragged.

David laid down on his back, stretching in the corridor and pressing his palms to either wall. *He can show you he's a seal.* That would certainly supply the answer to at least one question, not about himself, but about the world he thought he knew. As quickly as he'd decided to recline on the floor, he hauled himself up, sitting for a moment. *But when you see that he is, what then?*

"Then you can stop pretending you might decide he isn't," he replied, standing on legs that felt weighted by lead feet. He already knew he wouldn't, so it was pretending indeed to entertain the thought. "You can stop pretending you might believe you never spoke to ghosts as a child." He took his bottle with him, sure to close the servants' door behind him as he walked outside. He even locked it, as he would have under normal conditions. "You'll stop telling yourself you just imagine all of those... threads."

—

The little house looked like any other local cottage, but David would have known whose it was even if he had not been supplied with the address earlier that day. It radiated an energy that looked almost teal against the night, and a fine thread of the same color seemed to trail loosely from his pointer finger to the location itself.

He grimaced. Whatever he'd stolen from Paul Apollyon so long ago, and he couldn't tell because it tasted like the fumes coming from tar, it was potent stuff. Without bothering to consider how terrifying it would be to hear pounding on one's door in the dead of night, he pounded on the door. He did not accompany it with words to declare who he was, which might have mitigated any alarm.

A few moments later, Tom opened the door, his face murderous.

Then he saw David. "Fuck, you gave us a fright." His countenance softened a little.

David couldn't find the words to say anything of consequence, or sense. He registered Tom wasn't wearing a shirt or any kind of coat, only a pair of trousers that was not done up. He was holding them at the waist. His feet were bare, his hair was wild.

But David wouldn't expect a man who'd never bothered with many social niceties to throw much on before opening his door in a circumstance like this. He found he enjoyed the view, much as he had before. The moon provided enough light for him to see that there was more muscle to Tom's form now, and more assorted, small scars, likely the result of nonthreatening accidents or even just the mundanities of his previous trades. Laborer, fisherman, whatever else. All very physical in nature.

The worst I have to contend with is a paper cut, he thought, feeling a little inadequate.

"Are you all right?"

David was staring at Tom's navel when Tom spoke. He wasn't really attempting to see lower than that where a soft, dark trail led, but he'd lost control of his gaze all the same. He looked him in the eyes at the question. "I don't know."

Tom glanced at David's left hand, which was still clutching the bottle. He paused, licking his lower lip just a little. "How much of that have you had, then?"

"A little."

Instead of only telling David to come inside, Tom took a step over his own threshold, and firmly but carefully guided him the short distance indoors with a hand on his waist. Once David was inside the cottage, Tom reached past him and shut the door. "Sit."

Without bristling, David did as he was told and dropped into one of the wingbacks by the stove, mystified by the drink, the feel of Tom's hand, and all the uncertainty in his mind. He took another swig. "Thought you of all people would just turn me out on my ear."

"No. Well, Theo's been a good influence on me. And frankly, you were never so bad even at your worst. That always seemed like bluster, and it broke my heart. Your father, on the other hand... I'd happily turn him out, and more." Tom knelt and brought the stove back to life. "You need tea and something to eat... you *don't* need to wander about until you trip and hurt yourself. Luckily for you, Mrs. Lloyd brought us some cake and there's still a little left. I'm a terrible baker, but she's fantastic."

"Why are you doing this?"

"Doing what?"

"Being kind." David watched while Tom rose and turned to him. He was able to study his features with the help of the moonlight dripping through the windows, paired with the stove's faint glow.

Tom moved well in the dark, familiar with his surroundings. Placing his palm on David's shoulder and squeezing it through his coat, he said, "Because we wouldn't have been set against each other if it were up to us."

"Do you think?"

"I know."

Theo entered in a shirt that had to belong to Tom,

for it was a little large on him. Although David had seen him completely naked before and on numerous occasions, something about witnessing the intimacy of this casual state caused David to blush. "I'd rather you were naked, honestly," he said cheerlessly, without elaborating upon why.

However, Theo seemed to understand the problem. He put his candlestick on the table that served as end table and dining table, and sat at it with a grin. He was illuminated by the candlelight, gone golden where Tom was more silver. "Does it bother you? I could try to find one of mine, if it's causing you any kind of pain." He was being playful, though not callously humorous. "His are much softer, though."

"Because they're older," said David mulishly. "And they've been washed more." He didn't point out that some fine cloth was perfectly, beguilingly soft at first touch. *I would know; I'm an expert.*

Tom set water to boiling and finally took a banyan from a hook near the door and covered himself. David was left sitting in the wingback and wondering if it had ever been in The Shuck, because it seemed vaguely familiar. He took another drink from his bottle.

Tom asked him, "What is it?"

"This?" David peered at it, then shrugged. "I don't know. It's something we took from your uncle and hid under the servants' stairs ages ago." In that moment, he couldn't guess why Tom gawped with horror. "What? It's not fucking... pig's blood, or vitriol, or ink..."

"Was it unopened?"

"Oh, that," said David. "Yes, it hadn't been touched." He knocked on the glass like it was wood. "Airtight."

Tom seemed to relax slightly at the knowledge. Part of David registered that this was actually pleasant, sitting in a warm room with two attractive men who did not seem to be aiming to cast him outside. He had been in close, drunk quarters with friends who were not so sweet as these two, though he was reluctant to admit that so many of those he called friends were anything but kind.

They all seemed to circle each other waiting for one moment of weakness that they could deride and mock.

Over time, it became easier to mock and deride before one could be mocked and derided oneself. Hazily, he remembered one such moment in The Alexandra when he'd been very quick to put Tom on the spot for his appearance, all for the benefit of a so-called friend who'd been visiting Norwich from Cambridge. He hadn't expected Edward to be anywhere near that particular pub, and wouldn't have expected him in Norwich at all. But in he strode to The Alex, and out strode any of David's decency toward a childhood friend and first lover.

Tom was an easy target in front of someone like Edward, who was everything David was supposed to be or emulate.

"Silence?" David started. Theo glanced at Tom, perhaps to see how he might react to being called such.

But Tom was looking at David with the air of one trying to solve a riddle. He didn't seem especially vexed about it, which encouraged David. "Yes?"

"Do you remember that time at The Alex... around Candlemas, oh, forever ago... and I called you a ragpicker?" It had been something like that, anyway, and though he couldn't recall exactly what he'd said, he could recall the wounded bafflement on Tom's face when he said it. Even at the time he'd wanted to take it back, but he couldn't. It was either eat or be eaten. "In front of Edward?"

Tom took his time to reply. "Yes. Not that I knew his name. It was someone you were trying to impress. Some new acquaintance."

"I'm sorry."

"That was years ago, David."

"Still, I am." He needed to apologize for a lot besides one moment, but somewhere in his more rational mind, he was pleased and amazed he'd even started the process of making amends.

"Thank you," said Tom, so low it was almost nonexistent.

It was the ever-peaceable Theo who spoke next when Tom did not say more. "David?"

"Hm?"

"Why have you come?"

"You told me to come. Well, he told me to. After closing."

"Yes, but... with us while we walked. Not... quite like this."

"Do you walk home?"

"What do you mean?" Theo asked, handing Tom the tin of tea leaves as Tom prepared the teapot.

"You could swim, couldn't you?"

"It would be a little out of my way to swim, but I suppose I could. Just because I can doesn't make it more efficient all of the time." Likely because he had overheard Tom saying David needed to eat, Theo readied him a slice of cake and handed it over carefully. "Go on, then. I don't think you should try to stand until you've had something to eat and drink that isn't... whatever that is."

"I like it. In here."

Then, before David could protest or stop him, Theo took the bottle from David's grasp while he was occupied by cake. He sniffed it and took a nip of his own. "It's whisky."

Grunting, Tom said, "If it's *truly* been closed all this time, nothing will have happened to it. It just won't taste very good."

"It *doesn't* taste very good!" David said, struck that he hadn't realized until now. It burned, but spirits always did, and it was rather caustic, but whisky always was. He didn't even like it under the best of conditions.

Tom laughed, and David didn't see the joke as he said, "He'll be fine."

"Will he?" David said.

"Yes, you will."

"I have been... thinking about a lot of things." Right now, he was thinking about how wonderful this domesticity was, and how well Theo seemed to bloom within it. It was impossible to put to words how awful he felt for having treated Theo like more of a convenience than a partner.

It was usual to marry for material or practical reasons, not love; David had grown up being told this. His inclinations themselves were rarely openly addressed once Father had banned Tom Apollyon from his life, but the topic of marriage was addressed frequently.

Really, he should never have entertained the thought that Theo would be his lover alongside any phantom, future wife. He should have been bold enough to seek another way of being. Theo deserved someone who would do so for him, and he had found that man. David said none of this as he thought it, but Theo seemed to gather he was thinking something too serious.

"Stop thinking for just a moment and eat some of the cake," said Theo. David frowned, sure he was being teased. "You're too drunk to think so much, whatever you're thinking about. And I know it isn't doing business with Jarrolds or Curls."

Tom sighed and sat in one of the spindly chairs next to Theo, who retook his chair, and David scowled but took a bite of cake. He also changed the subject.

Rather, he voiced a different subject from the one he was silently ruminating upon. "No, I'm not thinking of shops or stores. I believe you about being a selkie. I think... I know I do. Believe you. But..." Speaking thickly, he said, "But you have to understand, I was never given any room to enjoy the kinds of novels *he* did." He nodded to Tom, who arched an eyebrow.

"Can't think of many about selkies," he said. "None, that I know of. Maybe I found some in books about folklore, but..."

"You know what I mean," said David. "Anything fanciful or romantic or... any of it. It wasn't allowed."

"You're here because you want to talk about me?" said Theo, the confusion suffusing his speech more than his lovely face, which remained placid.

"I'm here because I want you to show me."

That did elicit more of a response. Theo said, "I don't think that's wise." Had David been sober, he would have agreed. He would have regarded it as invasive and insensitive. But as things were, he couldn't see what the trouble was. He ate more cake, wondering if perhaps he could employ Mrs. Lloyd to bake cakes for him all of the time. It was superb.

Tom waited for him to finish eating the full slice until he spoke, and didn't address the matter of his lover turning into a seal on command to satisfy

David's tangled whims. "David, you're coming to bed. You're going to sleep. Then, in the morning, you're going to feel terrible, but you'll be in a much better way to talk. I don't think you're going to remember much of this, anyway."

"What, with both of you?" David, whose self-loathing was never far from the surface but seemed closer to his thoughts when he was drunk, was perplexed. He thought of everything one might do in a bed that was not sleeping, and assumed nobody would really want to do it with *him.* Anyone who had must have been granting him a favor, or they were bored. "Why the hell would you want to do that?"

"I don't want to do anything."

This made more sense to him. "Of course not. I wouldn't want to do anything with me, either."

In an undertone, Theo said, "There's always the chair he's in."

"Too pissed," said Tom, passing a hand over his mouth as though to wipe away the small smile upon it. "He's too pissed. He'll fall right out of it, I'd bet, or end up sleeping doubled over, and then he'll *really* feel like shit in the morning."

"Good point," said Theo. "Do you know, I've never seen him this drunk..."

"Neither have I."

"He's right here," said David. Feeling as though he needed to get in a quip to prove he still could, he added, "And you'd know all about being too pissed, wouldn't you?"

Tom ignored that, and David was disappointed.

"Sofa?" Theo said quizzically.

"He's tall. I doubt he'd even fit."

David said, again, "He's *right* here."

"I'm surprised you aren't just demanding he be put

on the floor," said Theo, with an adoring look at Tom
that nearly broke David's heart, because he was certain he would never receive such a look himself.

"I'll sleep on the floor," David supplied, thinking
he was being somewhat helpful.

"No, David," said Theo with a chortle. "You won't
sleep on the floor."

"We're too old for that, now," said Tom.

"If you two are, I don't want to know what you
think of my age," mumbled Theo. David just peered at
him, wondering why he'd say such a thing at all. "I'm
older than both of you combined."

And although he was stunned by that answer,
David was still malleable. He was bundled off to sleep
between a selkie who was too kind, and a witch who
might've been kinder than the selkie. He'd have no
memory of the transition to the bed, and indeed, the
witch was right: he also wouldn't recall much of the
preceding conversation.

7

L ennie woke and peered into the pearlescent gray light of morning, wondering if someone had broken into their room or perhaps their landlady's house. She was a lovely soul who looked like easy prey, but in fact she was the last person Lennie would want to rob. Mrs. Peters was reputed to be a deadly shot and given the rumors, Lennie wouldn't be surprised if she had a veritable arsenal in her bedroom under all the lace and paisley upholstery.

Actually, they might consider sending someone who irked them Mrs. Peters' way. That could be a fun and enlightening little situation, for they were sure Mrs. Peters would emerge the victor.

As they listened to their own breath, they relaxed when it became clear they'd woken themself. The more breaths they counted and the longer they studied the ceiling above their head, the more Lennie felt...

Drunk?

Whoever this belonged to, and they didn't care who, Lennie was furious.

They had things to do, including going to pay

Ralph. They'd been putting it off for days, now, although they knew they should have gone the moment Mr. Garnet had given them those banknotes. It was just that Ralph never did right by them. He was never even polite to them. Purposefully or unintentionally, they'd just avoided it.

The longer Lennie laid there, the more they determined they weren't entirely drunk, but they were quite ill in the way one could only be the morning after too much to drink. Lennie didn't consume much alcohol, having long discovered that in their line of work, it was much better not to be intoxicated. Drunk people made mistakes; drunk people got caught; drunk people ended up jailed. Mumbling indeterminate curses, knowing that even if they did manage to keep down a home remedy or induce vomiting, the revolting feeling wouldn't pass until its owner felt more the thing.

"Who the fuck is this?" Lennie promised themself they would find out, but nothing could be done to solve it until whoever it was stopped feeling like dog piss. They groaned and clung to the bedclothes.

If they focused on the feeling, it was unpleasant. But it might be possible to single out who was directing such poor choices in their direction, or better yet, force them out. They hadn't followed these strong, intrusive feelings since they were a child. Their stepbrother, Robbie, was prone to deep emotions and flights of temper, which unfortunately had spilled into Lennie's consciousness more than once. The first time it happened, they were almost ten years old and thought they'd lost their grip on what was real, but as it happened, Robbie was being maligned by his father for being scared of the dark at the advanced age of seven. Poor Robbie, it seemed, had crept to their parents' bed in tears only to be turned back in a harsh way. *"Men aren't afraid of the dark. Don't you want to be a man?"*

What Lennie had seen in their mind's eye, and they'd been dead asleep moments prior, was their parents' room through Robbie's eyes. What they'd felt were Robbie's dismay and sadness. They hadn't been sleepwalking and gotten there themself, so it wasn't happening to them, and they weren't dreaming.

After being rebuked, Robbie came back to his and Lennie's room and tearfully explained the whole thing, which corroborated what Lennie saw. As time went on, Lennie had learned through Robbie that they could direct what they saw through such a connection while it was active, just as they could defend against it.

Normally, as an adult, they just blocked it off. They erected walls and did not look. This was both to satisfy their sense of honor, and so they wouldn't be driven to distraction when the connection was there. Thankfully, it didn't happen too often. Tentatively, they closed their eyes, following rather than fighting the illness. They ended up in a bed that was not their own.

"Where am I?" Lennie frowned, eyes still shut: that was Mr. Garnet's voice.

He was capable of getting so pissed he was sick the next morning?

He'd looked like he could barely handle the pint they'd seen him with in the Sir Garnet. Lennie was slightly impressed.

"You're safe, first of all." The reply was reassuring, at least.

Mr. Garnet must have opened his eyes, for Lennie stared at a handsome, dark-haired man sitting in a plush chair near the bedside. They felt Mr. Garnet knew him, because the sense they had while they looked was one of warmth mingled with regret. This must be an intimate friend, they decided, and not without a twinge of jealousy. They weren't entitled to it and they weren't used to it. Being jealous was not their normal state, and it was audacious to be jealous over someone they'd only just met under the circumstance of pickpocketing.

But they had to admit the jealousy was there. Usually, they didn't get jealous over anybody they were attracted to, so the feeling was quite marked as belonging to them. It wasn't Mr. Garnet's at all.

"That's not where, that's... what." A wave of nausea followed the talking. Lennie saw the backs of Mr. Garnet's hands; they recognized the small rings he'd worn that day on Upper St. Giles. Family heirlooms, perhaps, for they weren't too ostentatious and looked rather old. *"Shit. Ah, whose bed am I in?"* At that, circumstances seemed far too familiar for them to keep following, so Lennie pulled themself out of the connection.

Mr. Garnet needed a talking-to, and what was more, they wanted to give it to him. No matter. They knew where he lived. They'd observed him walking home after realizing who he was; the route he took to his office was short and unchanging. They frowned, again, and it was more of a wince, this time. This fixation of theirs wasn't terribly useful. There were two men in their premonition, but Mr. Garnet always felt much more important than the slight man with greenish-hazel eyes.

Why else would they give back a wallet, feel this connection, be transfixed by those ridiculous eyes? It was a proper tendre, was what it was. The word wasn't one they felt comfortable saying aloud, but they'd once heard a heroine in a play say it.

Mum said the sight was unpredictable, even if you think you know it.

Irritated and impatient that there were still things they had to discover in time just like anyone else, Lennie grumbled. They might not know his name; they might not be able to tell the whole future. But they certainly knew where he lived in a charming house by Chapelfield Gardens, and that knowledge was almost more useful. Until they could deliver the dressing down, they'd build a little berm that separated them from Mr. Garnet.

No proper walls until they knew he'd arrived home, otherwise they might lose track of him. This was a much more interesting endeavor than deciding what to do about Ralph.

—

"Where am I?"

Theo answered him from somewhere to his right. "You're safe, first of all."

David opened his eyes and gazed at him. He was reclining in a tufted chair near the bedside. "That's not where, that's... what." He turned his head, which was on a pillow, and immediately felt the need to vomit. Though he did not, the dizziness did not abate. He glanced at his hands, which were clutching a sheet. "Shit. Ah, whose bed am I in?"

"Ours. Seemed better than trying to get you to sleep on the sofa... you're too tall. And you were too drunk to leave in the wingback; you kept slumping over."

"Not *ours*," said David. Now that he was not too drunk to be left anywhere on his own, he was made of pure embarrassment.

"Don't be pedantic," said Theo. He smiled a bit in the grey light, looking tired, which David guessed he would be. Some drunken lout had come and disturbed the entire night.

Fretting, he said, "How'd we all fit in here? Did we?"

"You'd be surprised. You're tall, not especially wide."

Somewhere, his father was fuming and screaming. He'd spent the night in bed with two men. Never mind that he had not spent the night in bed with two men *doing things*. Father would have found the mere physical contact, the comfort, wrong in and of itself. If David was not already comprised of embarrassment, he'd be thrilled.

While it had taken him some time to admit that he was a romantic creature, and he still wasn't adept at being romantic due to years of disavowing it, he'd realized he liked comfort and camaraderie much earlier. Both of those could be found in subtle ways, and they came under less scrutiny than trysts or romances. Of course, after Father found him in the arms of Tom Apollyon, even more of how David behaved came under examination.

Little of what he did was private after that, not unless he was at university and nowhere near his family. Frowning, David said, grasping at one of the very few things he fuzzily remembered, "You didn't turn into a seal just because I asked you to, did you?" He had to know. It felt manipulative, and it was absolutely poor form of him to demand anything of anyone while drunk.

He had an idea of what had actually transpired, which was to say nothing. But he wanted confirmation. Past eating the entire slice of cake with the candied orange peel on top, then being chivvied somewhere soft — here, he now knew — he did not recall much else. Presumably, he'd just fallen asleep.

Alongside Theo or Tom, or between them.

I hope not between them.

Theo shook his head. "No. If I ever do it for you, I don't want you to be so pissed while I do it. You might just think you imagined it, for one thing, or you might not even remember."

"Has..." Feeling like he was prying, David stopped speaking.

"Hm?"

"Has he ever seen it? Tom, I mean."

"No."

This was extraordinary to David, and yet seemed so completely aligned with Tom's character that couldn't be surprised about it. "He just believes you."

"Yes."

"Do you think it's... worse, somehow... that I want to see?" He hadn't made up his own mind.

Considering, tonguing the edge of his lip as he thought, Theo said, "What, as in... is it a moral failing? No. I think it's probably quite natural, isn't it? Someone tells you something outside your realm of experience, so you want to see it." He shrugged. "I can't blame you." But that was the trouble; whatever Theo was, he was not precisely natural. Or maybe he was, and science just had not caught up to the idea.

David scowled as philosophy jostled his already addled brain. After a silent pause between them, he said, "I like how you are around each other." Without waxing too poetic about it, he and Tom had been more like fuel and fire, whereas while they were dealing with his drunken, adamant stupor last night, Theo and Tom brought to mind sky and sea. One pairing seemed far less abrasive, even if wind could make the sea dangerous. Or maybe he was still drunk to be thinking in such metaphors.

"I like it too," said Theo.

"I feel like I'm seeing you for the first time," David said, and he smiled to soften the weight of the sentiment. It did make him sad, but he was encouraged that he was actually happier for Theo than he was sad for himself. "I feel like I'm understanding you, I mean to say." Rather than steer the conversation in a maudlin direction, he asked, "What time is it?"

"Eight."

"Fuck, I didn't sleep long at all."

"Drink will do that to a man," said Theo. "It'll put you to sleep, but I've found it doesn't keep anybody there for long." He spoke knowingly, and David realized he must have helped Tom through this state more than once. From their few recent and brief meetings, he knew Tom's imbibing was much slowed. But that had to have come about slowly itself or it might've killed him. "I stayed here because I had an inkling you'd be awake sooner rather than later. Tom's with Paul and a new grocer, and that's really not my end of things."

Trying to decide what to do, David mused, "I need to go home. Norwich home, not here, home."

"If you try to go now, I doubt you'd make it to the station without casting up your accounts. You look a little green."

"So I'm just to lay here in my ex-lover's... lover's... bed?"

"That's about it, yes." Theo rose and quit the room, and David heard him shuffling about. "Though," Theo called, surely trying to have a bit of fun at David's expense, "I own the place, so the bed's also mine by law."

Giving a long sigh, furious with himself for being weak enough to get that drunk and come to these two, of all people, David stared at the backs of the tawny linen curtains, then at the edges of light that shone around them. He very slowly brought himself into a sitting position, and was not comforted to see he'd been stripped down to his own shirt.

When Theo returned with a cup of tea, David said, "You would have every right to tell me to go."

Eyeing him from across the little room, Theo said, "I know." He carefully stepped forward and held the cup until David grasped it himself. It wasn't a dainty china teacup and had no saucer, which was an advantage while David's hand trembled slightly from tiredness. "You're here because I want you to be." He couldn't have held both a saucer and a cup.

He looked at the tea and had to smile. It was the right shade. Months and months of companionship seemed to have instilled that knowledge within Theo forever. "Why?"

"In short?" Theo sat down at the foot of the bed. "I'd like to consider myself your friend, still."

David wanted to say this went beyond friendship, but he wasn't sure if it did. His own class might have the wrong idea of friendship as something more transactional, or at the least, rigid. Very few of his friends would have done this for someone who wasn't a lover. He knew they might not even treat a lover this way. "Does Tom?"

"He's very protective of you, even if he doesn't admit it," Theo said.

It neither confirmed nor denied, but that was fair. Whatever he and Tom were to be, he suspected it would take a bit of time to determine. "Fine."

"There's nothing at all the problem with us being here like this. He trusts me. He trusts you."

A small flare of envy surfaced again in David's heart, and he quelled it. He couldn't tell what instigated it, exactly. Rather than lash out when he was being shown consideration that he felt he did not deserve, he chose to be gracious. "That's something."

Theo shrugged and said, as though it was nothing at all, "Some people have more than one partner, anyway, not that I'm saying we all need to dive headfirst into such an arrangement. Drink some of that tea."

With a huff, David did. Not only was it the right color, it was the right sweetness. "Leaving that kind of unorthodoxy aside, I didn't come last night just to see you be a seal."

"No, well, you've made up your mind about it already, even if you want to see it," said Theo. "I can tell. Was it Benson? I regret to say, he's usually right about the things he goes on about."

Sipping, then sighing, before he spoke, David said, "Oh, he's right."

Whatever Theo had been expecting him to say, it was not that. A line formed between his brows. "You agree."

"I've been thinking about it since you spoke to me in January."

In an instant, Theo gleaned the cause of last night's drunkenness; David saw the knowledge light up his eyes. He knew so many of the Mills' beliefs and habits that he could instantly see the trouble. David found the mere understanding brought so much relief that his own eyes almost welled up.

"You must have been ripping yourself to pieces since then," said Theo. "I wish you'd sought me out."

"I was ashamed at how I'd treated you. Not just...

what I did with your skin. But there was so much I took for granted when you were with me," said David simply, believing it was past the time to keep this to himself. "You had to have felt it. I didn't think you'd want to talk to me about things that were so personal."

"You're not irredeemable," Theo said. "I've only ever watched a man who struggles with who he is and making that conform to what he was told to be." His eyes met David's and he spoke with confidence. "And an *unkind* man would have left his father to rot at the first sign of senility. But I also think you would have been justified to just consign him to the care of others... to pay staff to look after him here in Cromer, perhaps, while you went off and lived your life. He treated you horribly. Yet you never retaliated."

Transfixed, for he hadn't realized these were things he needed to hear, David found he couldn't interrupt or demure. He waited for Theo to finish. "What good would that have done? It wouldn't have helped me, wouldn't have made me feel any better. Certainly wouldn't have undone the past. Wouldn't have undone any *bewitchments*."

To that, Theo just smiled. "Do you see my point?"

"I suppose."

"You could have come to me. I'd no idea you were thinking about my revelation in relation to yourself."

David drank more of the tea while it was still warm. "It started when I reread all the fairy tales my father said weren't suitable for me."

His head was pounding as he tried to remember what he'd read first. He had no children's books about selkies, but he had found things on mermaids, and inevitably, when he'd finished those, there was a whole slew of stories about witches. That, then, made him think about Father's love for their witch-hunting relation who'd claimed to be an intimate friend of Matthew Hopkins. Though, not the sort of intimate friend David would seek out, of course.

It all felt immense, but not like he was rediscovering something. From the outside, he imagined even someone so astute as Theo might presume to say David was remembering bits of himself he'd disavowed, but it was far more complex. When he let himself consider that he might not be what he he seemed, he allowed himself to have something that he'd been denied his whole life: the ability to explore. To decide for himself.

He'd have thought the liberation would be easy.

In point of fact, he was finding it to be terrifying. When he thought about it, he supposed it was because this was the largest rebellion he'd ever engaged in. Larger, even, than loving Tom, which was originally supposed to remain indefinitely covert, and loving Theo, which he'd planned on keeping similarly clandestine.

Overhauling his sense of self was not a process he could keep internal or quiet, and it would affect everything.

"David..." Reassuringly, Theo put his hand on David's ankle, resting it over the quilt. "You need to let your father die. Really die."

There was undoubtedly more work to be done than that, but David agreed. He tried for a smile. "Every time I do something I want to do, or think how I want to, it seems he's there in my head. Maybe not in the exact moment, so that's something, but hours later... when I'm trying to sleep."

Theo squeezed a bit. "How could he not be? He was there for all your early moments. For better or worse... Fathers often have that kind of sway, don't they?" He grinned. "But that's why you need friends. It's why you need to talk. Replace his voice with ours, until you can find our own."

Friends. He rolled the word around in his mind.

"Is Benson a friend?"

"Despite how he seems... yes," said Theo. "I think he could be. And I am, and even our cantankerous Tom seems willing to be. I can't speak for him, but he did let you inside."

Curtly, although he was secretly warmed by the gesture, David said, "Can't recall." He finished his tea and set the cup on a nightstand.

"He's the one who said you needed food. And it wasn't poisoned cake we gave you, either. That happened to be one of Mrs. Lloyd's; she's very concerned about Tom getting too thin."

What sort of world had he landed in, where heartbreak was rewarded with cake? "Very well. I shall try this business of having friends who aren't simply trying to compete with me, or who say awful things to me for a laugh." While it felt alien and new, David also knew already that it was preferable to his old one of rules, rightness, and severe consequences.

Near Chapelfield Gardens, Norwich

David was perhaps behind his peers in a pertinent way; he had no family. But on the other hand, he had not lost the Mills' business any profits, he had not succumbed to his modest vices, and he generally functioned well enough. Until these last several months, he had not given much thought to what could be or what he wanted.

The only thing he'd firmly decided was that he was alone and disliked it. It was a day later, and he was still thinking about his conversation with Theo, who would come the week after next to begin the sort of work he already knew so well. The office on Upper St. Giles would no longer be so empty and David looked forward to that immensely.

He *should* be thinking about an appointment he had tomorrow morning with a jolly Mr. Davies who wished to order a prodigious amount of cloth for his own shop, and here he was sitting in his parlor musing on Benson — whose second name he still did not know, unless that was his surname — and colored threads. But not the sort that made cloth. When he was not thinking about that, he had been thinking about new and old friends, or old friends made new again.

He sipped strong coffee, gazing out of the window at the public garden lit by sunset. This time of year, it could be lovely, but he saw very little. He was still in the throes of a prolonged hangover, which accounted for some of his abstraction. Drinking when one was thirty was apparently much different from drinking in one's younger years. He'd never felt so poorly for so long after one night of drunkenness.

You didn't have to drink something so old, either, did you?

Right as he had almost decided to pour himself another cup of the coffee, a loud crack came from downstairs. "Fuck."

He hoped Musgrave, his man of all work who was part footman and part gardener, had not lost control of himself and broken a window again. It sounded a little like that, though perhaps more like wood than glass breaking. He supposed Musgrave could have broken a window frame, or a door, or some innocent piece of furniture. The poor fellow was addled from his years in military service and sometimes took flight from his rational mind. Mother had been fond of him and he had always been kind to David.

Honestly, most of his staff in Norwich and Cromer, not that there were many of them, had stayed on after Father died. They did not all have the most jovial of relationships with the new Mr. Mills, but that was mostly because Father had never encouraged David to be cordial with servants. Now that he was dead, no one knew how to comport themselves. Ironically,

Musgrave got on best with him, but that was likely because Musgrave wasn't entirely well.

Counting his blessings, David knew he hadn't heard a gunshot. Nobody was supposed to allow Musgrave near any kind of weapon, whether that weapon was makeshift or purpose built. Not even a fire poker. Still, it could happen. Anything could be weaponized, and while Musgrave did not wish to hurt others or himself, he was prone to seeing disturbing things that were not there. Figments from the battlefield, no doubt. It often led him to take questionable actions.

Sighing, David stood and made his way toward the noise as the sun dipped below the horizon and the room was cast in the shade of cheerful flames.

But after he made it through the hallway, someone careened into him on the stairs.

It was darker away from any windows and everything was cast in shadow. He would never expect to be careened into in his own home, anyway. Musgrave was not fast enough, and anybody else in residence was too sedate or old to go tearing around in such a way that would lead to a collision.

Even though some children might, servants did not careen about a house.

His cup went flying upon impact and broke against the wall behind him. It was empty, thankfully.

Whoever this intruder was, they grunted in consternation or surprise. David quickly took them by the forearms. He wasn't terribly athletic, but he was strong, and something was nudging the back of his mind to take hold of them. "Stop struggling, or I shall let anyone who has heard you have you arrested."

This person didn't need to know that due to the nature of his staff, there was a good chance they hadn't heard much of anything. There was also only Musgrave, Ellie, and the cook, not droves of people. Musgrave could only hear out of one ear, Mrs. Greaves was almost entirely deaf, and Ellie was usually off in a world of her own and noticed very little that went on around her.

Waiting a moment to see if anyone came bustling up, David tugged the intruder back into the parlor to get a better look at them. They weren't small, but being smaller than him, they were easy to maneuver even if they clearly did not want to be moved.

Still, they weren't struggling as much as he expected a thief to struggle, and that was odd. He saw why they didn't as soon as the light was better.

"Lennie."

Taken aback, he relinquished his hold almost instantaneously as the word left him; Lennie rounded on him almost immediately. "You need to stop drinking. And agonizing."

That was, doubtless, the strangest greeting David had ever received from anyone. All he could manage was, "What?" Even more strangely, he was not angry. He knew he should be livid.

"Whatever you're ruminating over, it probably isn't as bad as it seems," Lennie said. He straightened his cap. "Look around. How could it be so bad? You have everything you want, here, don't you? Whatever *is* troubling you, I doubt it'll harm you."

David was rapidly losing any sense of ground he had, so he asked the obvious question. "You broke into my house?"

Lennie shrugged. "I did."

Yet, it did not seem to be for the purpose of robbery. David narrowed his eyes, mostly to fight against his redoubling headache. "Why?"

"To tell you to stop fucking drinking."

David wanted to be unnerved, but all he could manage was a compelling curiosity. Something deep and persistent nagged at him, and it had to do with how Lennie knew he'd been drinking. The very idea should have been preposterous, but it was not, not after he'd spent the night in a selkie and witch's bed. "I fail to see why that would require you to break in. Just hand me one of those mad pamphlets about the evils of drink the next time you try to pick my pocket."

"And you don't seem angry that I broke in, at all," said Lennie. "Or even that confused."

The truth was, David was overjoyed and didn't know why, or how, or even where the feeling came from.

And he did not *agonize*. Rather than let that sour him, he stared at Lennie. Really, apart from being crashed into, he was happy to see him. He liked how the dying sunlight played on his graceful face, how its planes were lit with the same fire-like glow as the parlor.

It would not do to tell him so soon. It would not do to tell him something so painfully untoward at all.

"To be frank, I've rather used up my confusion on the matters that are causing me *agony*." David smirked, hardly aware that he was flirting.

Lennie's eyes widened, and if David was not mistaken, there was the flicker of a smirk on his face, too. "Well, at least today you don't look so sad."

"What's it to you if I'm sad, or confused, or angry that a miscreant has entered my home without permission?"

Lennie sighed and said, "I'll pay for the lock."

That must have been the crack. "I'm not concerned about whatever you broke to get inside. Or the cup that you also broke." He wasn't. He should be, but he wasn't. David was finding that there were a lot of instances of *should* that he should be living up to, and he simply couldn't be bothered about any of it.

"Look, just... please stop. Drinking. And... try to find someone to talk to about... whatever has you..."

David tried to meet Lennie's eyes, but Lennie kept looking anywhere but at his face. "Would you believe it if I said I don't know how to talk about it? I mean to say, I am trying, but that's a very recent thing."

A small bevy of emotions came across Lennie's countenance and David knew before he was told that Lennie understood. Neither of them spoke for a second, and David's attention was drawn to the way Lennie's hands moved nervously. His fingers were quick and adroit, appropriate for a pickpocket, flicking like a cat's tail against his lapels. Then a metallic glimmer caught David's eye. It wasn't the metal of a ring, modest or otherwise.

It was another fine cobweb wound around Lennie's left wrist, like the ones he'd seen in the Sir Garnet between their fingers. He looked down at his own chest, and the cobweb led directly to him.

—

Mr. Garnet was unnerved, but he didn't seem angry. Lennie thought it was admirable to be so comparatively calm when a stranger had broken into one's house, but the calmness also irked them. They would know how to respond if Mr. Garnet was angry: a row was much easier to navigate than whatever tangled emotions he exhibited. Warmth wound though his expressions, but so did fear.

While Lennie could understand both because they felt for this prim and yet unshakable man, they wanted simplicity.

Then what was your plan? Why do this?

There could be nothing simple about threatening someone in their own home, after all. It wasn't as though anyone caught in that position would do nothing about it. Mr. Garnet was not monstrously sized, but Lennie imagined he could injure someone if he put his mind to it, and at the very least someone could call for the police.

Now that they stood in a parlor with the man who'd forced them to be ill for a good day, though it did ebb as time passed, they could see how ludicrous this idea had actually been. There was no such thing as friendly threatening or forceful niceties.

Although Lennie took great pains to be sober while they worked and never had made a mistake, impulsivity had always been one of their less desirable traits. Their mother had remarked they were fearless, always had been, but Lennie couldn't tell if they were fearless or reckless. When they wanted someone, they did not tend to think the consequences of their actions through. But they were astute enough not to follow every attraction to another person. Not everyone would accept them, for one thing, which was an issue of safety as much as emotional importance.

And luckily, most people vexed them, so it wasn't often the case that they found themself lusting or hoping after just anybody. Mr. Garnet presented both the most persistent candidate, perhaps ever, and he was the most recent in a long while. Paired with dreams about that old taproom and the intrusive hangover that Lennie had glimpsed, he was compelling.

Not that they wanted to be here. Like this. They said as much. "I didn't want to break in. I don't want to be here as an intruder." They added, "And yes. I be-

lieve you... some things aren't easy to talk about."
Lennie had a short but powerful list of those topics,
not that they were about to enumerate them. Pausing
for a breath, they noticed Mr. Garnet was looking at
their hand. "What is it?"

"Nothing."

"Then don't stare. Didn't someone ever tell you it
wasn't polite?"

"Oh," said Mr. Garnet, as though enjoying a private joke. "Someone told me damn near everything
was. Asks the man who broke a lock to get into my
house." He grinned, actually grinned, and Lennie's
breath caught. "Should think that's a bit impolite. Not
to mention, you don't know my name, do you?"

They feigned nonchalance and turned their back
to look at a gilded clock above the fireplace. "Don't
need to know who you are, do I? You're just someone
with money." And they hadn't looked too closely at the
contents of his wallet, anyway. Normally, they were
after coins and notes, not anything more personal. If
they took very personal items, or anything with a
name or an address, there was a slightly higher
chance they could be traced. Better not to risk it, in
their opinion.

"David Mills." The tiniest tremble was in his voice
as he said it, and Lennie suspected they'd touched on
traits David did not like to acknowledge or discuss.
Money, status. They couldn't think why, for it was obvious he was privileged. "I'm David. And I want to
know why it matters so much to you that I was
drinking."

Their mother's voice, sweet but urging caution, reminded them not to say too much on the subject of
foresight and premonitions, empathy and visions.

They knew, now, that Mum said those things only *after* she'd learned discretion was important. She hadn't always been so guarded. It was something she'd had to learn and by the time she had, Lennie could benefit even if she couldn't.

Ralph taught her. Inevitably, a wave of guilt followed the thought. They couldn't think their way out of feeling culpable, because they'd sparked Ralph's idea to leverage Mum's sight for money, for his own gain. To their mind, there was no other explanation and they should feel like shit for enabling a lazy boor to take advantage of the person they'd loved most.

They shook their head. They didn't want to tell this toff anything they didn't have to, regardless of what was ahead for both of them. "You wouldn't believe me. Just forget it." Lennie turned to take their leave, knowing that some future event brought them and Mr. Mills together in some smoky taproom. But they could wait for it like any other person. "I'll send you money for the lock first thing tomorrow."

Mr. Mills inserted himself between Lennie and the door. "No."

"Wonderful, you don't want payment?" They scoffed and looked up at him. "Then I'll just be on my way."

"You did give me all of my money back."

"Except for what you gave me."

"True."

"I have never come across a man who was this polite to an intruder." Lennie frowned when David still did not move. This was more than politeness, though, and he had to have known it. A moment passed, and they savored the warmth that circulated between their bodies.

"Someone instructed me very well on civility. And I'm about to be even more polite."

"Yes, you're going to get out of my way."

"No, I'm going to ask you to stay and eat. You did say you didn't want to be here as an intruder, so perhaps... let us try having you as a guest."

9

Aghast, Lennie said, "Well, I am hungry." It was all they could think to say because they were, and David — Mr. Mills — was so earnest when he said it that they felt obligated to be amenable. It was an absurd request, the sort of thing someone would offer a friend rather than a housebreaker. Then again, that Lennie had broken into his home at all was absurd. Probably the most absurd thing they'd done in their nearly thirty years.

"Are you? Perfect."

Nothing about any of this was usual. All of it was absurd, including how Mr. Mills smiled and the way that smile filled them with anticipation. If the dreams and shared hangover were any indication, there was a certain association there, but they wished there wasn't. It was possible such a connection had come to the fore because they focused on him. Or perhaps it was the other way around? It already existed, and so it was easy to make him a mark. It had to have existed well before now, because they'd had those dreams for months.

But he was affluent, and that meant he might catch the attention of others who wished to take advantage of him. Who could say he wouldn't have ended up a target at the hands of a more ordinary thief?

Then their thoughts fell to Ralph. Luckily, their life didn't look at all the same as it had when their mother had died and left them to his whims. Lennie was, crucially, no longer dependent on him for room and board. But that didn't stop him from demanding money, and they despised how he had something he could leverage against them.

They shook their head, trying to clear it. "Mr. Mills, I..."

"The least you can do is call me David when you've destroyed one of my locks."

"David..." When David leaned forward as though beckoned by his given name, Lennie's heart softened toward him. They didn't say more than that, reluctant to proceed, and instead watched his blue eyes catch the light and go almost green, like sea glass. How did one go about telling the truth in this situation? It seemed impossible to tell a well-off, relatively genteel man any of it.

Their caution, in part, was learned. At first, Mum wanted to see the best in everybody and did not take pains to hide her intuition or premonitions from those whom she loved. Her trusting nature never had terrible consequences until she met and married Ralph.

By the time Mum started to tell Lennie to be careful who they were honest with, it was really too late for her to enact her own advice. *Might've been better if he and Mum never met.* Following the thought, Lennie was consumed by shame.

Softly, David cleared his throat. "Yes?"

"Never mind."

"No matter, we can talk over food." David gestured them out of the room and they hesitantly preceded him, lingering near the stairs they'd come up before crashing into him. Then David passed them as he went down, calling to someone, "Ellie? I've a guest. Have Mrs. Greaves lay two plates."

The difference between the man Lennie had collided with and this one was subtle, but it was like watching someone become younger, a little more spry. "I can't believe you want a thief to have dinner with you."

David glanced over his shoulder. "To be fair, I have questions. I might just be bribing you. And you haven't stolen anything if you just gave it back. Not a very good thief, hm?"

———

David didn't expect anyone to shout back at him. Anyone below stairs wouldn't, but he did expect Ellie's cheerful reply. The last he had seen or heard, she was airing some of his mother's old embroidery in the dining room while Mrs. Greaves was busy in the kitchen.

He also didn't expect to see a strapping blond man with the build of a pugilist in his foyer.

"Fuck," said Lennie.

He looked back at him. "Indeed." There was no reason for this man to be inside, and for all his muscle, he still had the air of someone who hadn't been treated properly since infancy. That was a dangerous look, David knew, and he'd encountered it in some of his university friends. It didn't always signify a literal lack of resources, of food or money, but it did often mean a lack of emotional fulfilment or care.

"Ralph's been worried about you," said the blond, all but ignoring David for all the attention he did not give him. "He says you need to come home for a visit. Been an age, hasn't it?"

"I'm too busy enjoying myself."

"Bring the toff, too," the blond man said. "I'm sure we can find some use for him, can't we?"

Lennie shook his head, inching closer to David and closer to the ominous stranger. David, for his part, tried to block him by taking a step back. With a noise of frustration, Lennie edged around him. "No, he's useless. And I'm not going with you, Robbie. So you may as well take a candlestick or a clock or something, and go."

David frowned, neither feeling useless nor like he wanted any of his things to go missing. Also, whoever Ralph was, Lennie clearly did not wish to see him, for his face had darkened at the name. David could only glimpse Lennie's profile, but there was a strained taut-ness in Lennie's fine, almost sculpted features.

"I would rather nobody took anything," David of-fered, possibly absurdly. He hadn't seen a gun, yet, but it was probable that Robbie possessed one. After all, he wore a coat that could have concealed both a large feral cat and a weapon of his choice. *Then again, he might just use his fists.* Like the rest of him, they were large, and he was in his prime, probably in his late twenties.

"You'll find I take what I want," said Robbie. At the moment, he seemed more amused than anything to find Lennie and David in a home that was growing darker as the sun fully set, but David gleaned his com-parative goodwill could change in an instant. "Was this a mark?" Robbie directed the words at Lennie.

A mark?

When Lennie did not reply, Robbie appeared to take that as tacit confirmation. He chuckled. "You've gone soft, haven't you?"

"God, Robbie, you've always been so dull," said

Lennie, and the taunt sounded more like one between brothers. Robbie and Lennie certainly did seem to know each other, at the very least, and there was an undercurrent of knowledge shared between them. Still, David shifted nervously from foot to foot, never having been accosted like this and unsure how to react.

He thought of Tom, who'd likely jump the fellow, and Theo, who would have charmed him into submission by now. *He* was just inert. He felt a fierce need to protect Lennie, which he'd examine later, if there was a later. He also hoped Mrs. Greaves and Ellie had gotten out of the house. Musgrave was nowhere to be seen, but had he been present, things might have escalated too much. He was far too jumpy to experience something like this without an incident and there was no telling which direction the incident would go.

"Dull? Don't put on airs. You're no better than me. Never were."

"I'm still older."

"Not any wiser, though."

"Well. Who's still under his father's thumb?" Lennie was disdainful and David wanted to ask if it was wise to taunt this newcomer, but held his tongue. "You always said you wouldn't be, but I can see he's still got you running his errands."

Then he thought, *Father?*

"I'm here for myself." Robbie sniffed. "He wants to see you. He says you owe him something. Then you can toddle to whatever shitty hiding place you've found."

Robbie came close, very close, and although David had tried to keep himself between Lennie and Robbie, he hadn't quite succeeded. Lennie was almost directly beside him, now, having inched forward during the conversation.

"No. I'll pay him, not that he needs it. But I'm not spending any time in the same room with him."

"How would your mother feel about that? She used to *love* him."

"Seeing as she's dead, I don't think she'd feel anything about it. She did love you more than him, in the end, if you want to know." A bit of pain colored Lennie's words, then they said, "Go away. You haven't even broken in to steal anything, have you?"

Robbie shook his head. This close, David smelled tobacco on his breath. The lighter strands in his hair caught the very last of the sun's light, and the entire foyer was now the bruised purple of dusk. "Followed you here. Happened to see you in the gardens and thought I was lucky. You're like a little fox, aren't you?"

Blinking, Lennie seemed to take a moment to adjust to the assertion that he'd been followed. David felt for him; although he'd been surveilled quite strictly as a child and younger man, he'd never liked it, either. A gun clicked quietly, and David glanced down at Robbie's right hand. "Ah, *there* it is."

Robbie eyed him. "I've no problem with you. Step aside."

"No, I don't think I will." It was probably the wrong thing to say, and he hadn't thought about saying it, but he was compelled to stay where he was. He registered that Lennie shifted, but because David was staring at Robbie, he couldn't see Lennie's expression.

"David, he'll let you go. You probably *should* just go." Nobody said his name like Lennie did. Wonder and exasperation commingled in the word, and David didn't know what he'd done to merit either.

"Leaving aside the way I may never feel safe in my

own home again even after he's gone... I'm not going," said David.

"Where'd you find a toff with mettle, Lennie?" Robbie asked. "How long have you been fucking him, then?"

David couldn't help gasping slightly. It had been too bred into him to be shocked whenever anyone was so crass about the matter for him not to flinch. Swearing or coarse language was one thing, but using it to evoke carnal acts still made him cringe just a little. Robbie didn't miss it, and he was fiendishly amused. "You're more disturbed by *that* than the way I could shoot you?" The metal of the gun nudged into David's midriff. "Go on. Scoot."

He didn't move. It wasn't fear that stuck him in place; his palms felt charged with anger and the fury seemed to keep him there.

Lennie said, "Robbie, just fuck off."

His voice seemed to unlock David just enough to talk. "I agree... you *should* fuck off." He didn't know what possessed him — and he imagined this was what being possessed felt like — when he lashed out and pushed Robbie hard on the chest. It was a ridiculous thing to do. His mind, at least, understood the risk. The gun could go off and hit anyone or anything, or Robbie himself could lash out just the same as he had.

None of those things happened.

There *was* a moment when Robbie's face still held laughter, but a quick, gentle pop and flicker of light, a spark, emitted from his chest where David's palm had landed. It didn't seem based in reality, for it took David a moment to realize he'd somehow initiated the spark by his own volition. Nothing about it hurt and the sensation was reminiscent of static in the air, yet the effect that followed was far more impactful.

Robbie met his eyes with incredulity and seemed poised to strike him, until he staggered back and appeared to faint. The gun clattered against tile when the back of Robbie's hand hit the floor, too. Luckily, it did not discharge.

Unluckily, Robbie probably did not hit his head hard enough to cause any lasting damage.

All David could do was stare at his prone body. Lennie recovered first and knelt to check the pulse in Robbie's neck, then brought their palm just under his nostrils to test his breath. "He's alive." He reached around and felt for, presumably, any wounds on Robbie's head. "No blood. I don't know. He took most of the fall on his back, I think."

David couldn't even muster a breath. "I don't know where my housekeeper is, or... my cook, or... Musgrave."

"Probably snuck out, if he just followed me in. I'm quiet, but he's not. They likely noticed him. I'm sure they're fine." Lennie was speaking as gently as David had ever heard him talk. "I would leave, too, if some enormous lout came in and I didn't fucking know him."

"You're not running away, now," said David. He turned and watched Lennie in the minimal light. "Why not? I didn't have a gun. I didn't even hit him, not really. But I did something. Did you see it? Hear it?" He wasn't yelling, but he was almost whining, desperate to either dispel or confirm what he'd just experienced. "And you know him, too. Aren't you angry at me?"

It was clear that they were somehow connected. David would guess siblings, but neither of them looked physically related. Siblings by marriage, maybe, for Robbie had mentioned Lennie's mother and Lennie had mentioned Robbie's father, whom David assumed was the mysterious, ominous, Ralph.

"Yes," said Lennie. "I know him."

"Who the hell is he?"

"My stepbrother. But I'm not angry." He took David's hand, the same one that had caused this chaos, and that calmed David more than anything else would have in that moment. "His father is a... terrible person. He... might not be."

"You're not scared?"

"Of you? No."

Trembling with nerves, David said, "Good. I don't think *you* need to be." He knew that, even if he knew little else, he wouldn't hurt Lennie. "But I don't even know... how..." his voice trailed away. "Why aren't you?"

"I don't think you'd hurt me, and anyway, that was something to do with magic. I have some myself," Lennie said succinctly, no fanfare, no apology.

He wouldn't argue, because it seemed that way to him, too. "I've never done that in my life."

"I was told it can kind of... leak out of you, if you're not careful. My mum made sure to help me learn about mine as soon as she realized I had any." Lennie was caressing his hand idly, so David concentrated on how his thumb felt against flesh. "I would bet nobody bothered to teach you a thing."

Oh, he'd learned a thing or two. "Just that witches were bad, witch-hunters were good, and God liked the latter."

With a faint smile at his sardonic words, Lennie inclined his head, took a small breath, and said, "Look, I don't want to frighten you, but we should go. I don't think we can go where I'm staying... I assume Robbie will wake up and it sounded like he knows how to make his way there. He's breathing, after all."

"I..."

"Can you think of anywhere?" Lennie squeezed his hand softly. "Just for a day or two... maybe a few days, until I gather my thoughts. I'll need to come back." He looked at Robbie's body spread at their feet. "He's right. Ralph thinks I owe him, which is the same as needing to pay him."

"Yes." The word came out with surety. He should have protested, he should have said any number of more logical things. They could have stayed in the house and alerted the police; he could have contacted one of his far more influential, or just adept with firearms, so-called friends.

"Good."

He could be asking more of Lennie, demanding to know what the hell was going on, why he owed someone who plainly frightened him money. What he owed money *for*. No upstanding person owed money under these shadowy circumstances, and David knew Lennie was a pickpocket. He'd also said Robbie's father was terrible.

That meant his own stepfather was terrible. David could glean that any money owed was less a good-faith matter and had more to do with something insidious like blackmail. Although he had no confirmation of it, he suspected Lennie was an invert. That could be easily leveraged against a man. Yet it was madness to consider just *going* only to come back after some stranger had *gathered his thoughts*.

He had a business, he had a life, he had things he needed to do and matters to think through. Suddenly, none of them seemed as imperative as Lennie. He thought of the kindnesses Theo and Tom had so recently shown him and wondered what it might be like to show some of his own.

It might be that he didn't have all the facts as he stood in his dark foyer with his heart pounding and mind reeling.

But perhaps the most pertinent fact? Lennie was in trouble. Yes, he knew a place, and the Apollyons might kill him.

10

I t grew late, but The Shuck wasn't closed when they arrived.

While on the train, David had hurriedly and disjointedly explained what it was, simply a public house, and that it had not always been called such. Lennie had an immediately distrustful look upon hearing the name. But David assured him it had been renamed by an outsider close to the innkeeper, which *he'd* only learned within the last few weeks. To him, it had almost always been The Shuck and was only something else when he was a child.

David was still too shocked to address anything else. So, they'd nattered about where Lennie was hopefully going to be allowed to stay for a short while. Funny what one might not know about one's environment. But until recently, David had not been the most pleasant of companions to anybody who might have been able to explain that a man from Scotland once had the idea to rename The Queen Anne. First as a joke, then it just stuck because the regulars, who were often intoxicated, thought it was hilarious.

The only disadvantage to it being open, whatever the pub was called, was that Benson might be underfoot. As far as disadvantages went, it was not enough of one to dissuade David from being there.

Still, as his eyes swept the gaggle of patrons in the pub, he hoped to see Tom or Paul or even Mrs. Lloyd, whom he didn't think was always present during the evenings.

Lennie lingered near his elbow. He said, "I like it here."

"Good." David did not need to be on his toes to see anyone, but he went up on them all the same, a reflexive habit, and found Paul in the corner speaking animatedly to a woman in a faded red dress. He had to reconcile his older perception of the man with the man before him; Paul was not what he would call animated by any stretch of the word.

Wading between tables and those who lingered near them, he approached Mr. Apollyon with deference. They had spoken on a couple of occasions since winter, but Paul had no reason to know that Tom, Theo, and David were now on good terms. Therefore, he had no reason to take any special pains to accommodate David. "Mr. Apollyon?"

Paul did not shift his attention until his companion looked at the man at her side and the two of them began a conversation about pilchard. Only then did he say to David, "Yes?"

"I... my friend has need of somewhere to stay." He'd thought this through and come to the conclusion that Lennie would be more protected here than in his private home. There were more people. There was more activity.

He hadn't expressed any of that on the journey here, which would account for Lennie's perturbed expression as he spoke. But resolutely, without looking at Lennie or uttering any apology to him, David looked at Paul and hoped Paul would understand the importance of the situation without context. Paul regarded him without blinking, then glanced at Lennie. David expected him to bring up something about the Mills family home, or all the less-than complimentary things David had uttered about The Shuck.

"We've room," was all Paul said, and he said it to Lennie rather than David. Then, already moving to the foyer where the small desk existed to house the ledgers, Paul spoke over his shoulder. "Is it for both of you, or one of you?"

"Just him," said David.

"Both of us," said Lennie.

They looked at each other. David spoke first, praying his cheeks were not pink. He enjoyed the intrusive picture of Lennie in his house after dark for just a moment. "I have... a house." Lennie's expression all but asked why they were both not residing in it, then. David had to admit it was a decent question.

"Fine," said Paul, flicking through the pages before him as though this sort of urgent need for a room was routine and not at all suspicious. "One of you."

"If you have a house, why would I be here?"

"If," said David carefully, "your... Robbie... or anyone. Comes looking. I'm sure they'll go there first." He had visions of devious folks rifling through his effects at home, perhaps pilfering though his post or correspondence, and tracing at least some of his property or his work endeavors. He had two houses, not a gaggle of properties, so it was not as though a handful of places existed to look for him or Lennie. Just two.

Thankfully, most of his important paperwork was locked away in his office and he carried the key to that safe with him. But he imagined it wouldn't be difficult for a certain unsavory set to determine who he was or where he holidayed. Where he worked. He was already prepared to miss all of his commitments tomorrow, including the appointment in the morning, and hoped no one would be accosted on his account.

"Why?" Lennie searched his face.

"Because there are just the two homes." He tried not to sound too entitled. He knew he was far more privileged than the majority of the country, and though the inequalities had not been obvious to him as a child, they were apparent now.

Why do you care about not seeming like the most pompous prick? He never really had in the past; Theo had gently teased him about it. He continued, "I have one here, and the one in Norwich. It won't be hard to deduce if I am not there, I could be in Cromer."

"Then why not stay here, too? Wouldn't it be safer?"

Hesitating, David slid the barest glance at Paul, who was busy writing in his ledger in a studied way. No innkeeper needed to write so much, David was positive. It felt more like a tactic to eavesdrop.

"It may... embroil others," said David. "If we're both here."

"We're used to being somewhat embroiled, Mr. Mills," said Paul.

Still, David did not think bringing any kind of ruffians to the Apollyons' step would be useful or kind. "Maybe not this way."

"You would be surprised," Paul returned. He did them the courtesy of finishing his writing, his dark greenish eyes flicking from Lennie to David, as unreadable as they had ever been. David abruptly wondered if Paul had ever killed anyone. Or perhaps he was some kind of fence for local smugglers. If so, he would take it directly to the grave with a mien like that. David hadn't considered the possibility until now, but Paul was reacting to all of this remarkably calmly.

Lennie said, "We might be safer together. Just until it... I..." he swallowed, and a range of conflicting and conflicted thoughts seemed to pass on his face. "I'm sorry."

"Why?" It burst forth before David could acknowledge there might be something to apologize for, and before he could question why he was so ready to defend Lennie even from himself.

Paul was rifling through a drawer; it appeared the key he would give Lennie wasn't behind him on the wall with the rest of the keys.

"I shouldn't have followed you. Even on Upper St. Giles."

This felt like a longer apology than not. David shrugged and shifted from foot to foot. He'd never been good at accepting or giving them. They had not exactly been incentivized in his family. "Perhaps not, but you can't help if some ruffian —"

"Followed me into your house, which I broke into."

Paul did not react much to hearing such an odd and criminal assertion, apart from pursing his lips. He might have been holding back a laugh.

David licked his own lips, slightly. "Well, moving past all of that, now, I think you'll be safe here."

"I could go somewhere else." Lennie tried to entreat Paul, now, who regarded him with faint amusement and more warmth than David had seen on his face in the course of their acquaintance. "I don't *need* to be exactly here. I don't even need to be here long."

"You shall do no such thing," said Paul.

Smug because Paul agreed with him, yet not being able to identify why he felt smug, David said, "There, you see? You are overreacting. We're not being trailed by bloody murderers. I just think it would be prudent for you not to be in my house."

Reluctantly, Lennie said, "I... they're not murderers. But Robbie and Ralph are not..."

"What?" David pressed.

"They're not... kind. They..." he took a shuddering breath. "God, never mind. I don't want to sound mad. I'll... I'll go upstairs, but I don't need to stay for long. Just enough to catch my breath."

Paul said, "You likely won't." He added for clarification, "Sound mad."

Selkies and talk of witchcraft *were* quite common within these confines, thought David. Anything Lennie might say would likely seem quotidian. He resolutely did not think about the fleeting spark that had traveled between him and Robbie.

But it seemed to be on Lennie's mind, too. "Then again, Robbie might proceed with caution because of you." He poked David square in the chest.

David found himself focusing on Lennie's mouth, the lines of his lips. "Me?" At first, he didn't quite understand what Lennie intimated. The short, quick jab was spreading from his chest to his heart. "Oh. Because of the... that." He huffed. "Seeing as I don't even know how to do it again, I don't think they'll have to worry."

"Still, *he* doesn't know that you can't do it on command." Lennie smirked, and David struggled to regulate the rate of his breathing. "That could work to our advantage."

"As riveting as this enigmatic conversation is, shall I show you up?"

Mouth slightly open, David looked sidelong at Paul, who spoke without impatience, but did look a little too knowing for David's tastes. "Right, yes, you should."

"Him, not you, Mr. Mills."

"You can come along," said Lennie, with the smallest air of a challenge, as though he believed David would abandon him. "Mr. Mills." Then his eyes lit with the faintest of fond glows.

David found himself glancing at Paul, who shrugged and raised both of his eyebrows. "If it's amenable to him, I haven't any rules about guests." Continuing in an undertone, he said, "Just do try to keep it down."

Then it was a keen battle between wishing to shake Paul Apollyon by the hand and knock him out cold.

David froze, then he said, before he could choose anything more polite to say, "Do you know from experience?"

"Both ways," said Paul. "From overhearing and generating." He winked, and David could have been felled by the touch of a feather. He knew Paul was capable of being quite a different character, but he'd never been around to hear such brazen declarations from him. "Come along, Mr. Mills' friend."

"Oh," said Lennie. "Lennie Campling. Is my name." He seemed to be adjusting to Paul's openness, himself, as he eyed him curiously, almost as though they had met somewhere and he was trying to recall where. David realized, then, that Paul had not been writing anything to do with the business at hand. How could he, without a name or duration for the stay?

He wanted to know if Paul would accept any payment.

"Mr. Paul Apollyon," Paul said, with a slow smile. "Pleased to make your acquaintance. I keep the keys behind the bar in the taproom. If I'm not about, my nephew Tom will be, and he'd be happy to help."

David could not help but snort lightly, for he'd never heard Tom described as such, but he knew the sentiment was true and Tom was in fact a helpful man.

Paul didn't miss the sound and slipped him a smirk of acknowledgement. Then he spoke to Lennie. "You may also take the key with you if you believe you shall be out for any large length of time. Though... if you're being shadowed, perhaps I would rather you didn't keep the key on your person."

That was a sobering thing to hear. David decided immediately that if he ever purposefully enacted his strange, phantom spark against another person, he would happily do so to keep Lennie from being detained or harmed.

A fleeting disquiet was in Lennie's voice. "I hadn't thought of keeping it here."

In a kind show of solidarity, Paul came around the desk to show Lennie — and David — upstairs, and grazed his hand against Lennie's shoulder. It felt remarkably forward. Not that anybody in David's own family was keen on exhibiting affection.

"I would try not to worry, Mr. Campling." Paul started up the stairs without waiting to be followed, his feet taking a route he'd taken thousands of times. "You are among friends, here."

11

T he room was better than any of the ones they'd rented or stayed in, and Lennie was almost embarrassed they liked it so much. David was used to better, undeniably. They knew that from seeing how he lived at home. *You shouldn't have let him come up.* But there was a pull that radiated from him and Lennie didn't know what to do about it.

It went beyond any vision or premonition. All they knew was they didn't want to be alone, and something about this fussy toff of a man had called to them. The sensation of need was quite new. What was almost comical, though, was Lennie knew David felt similarly and was just as unsettled by it as they were. They tried to disregard any feelings that they knew weren't their own, but it was hard to ignore his because they wanted to know more about him.

The night outside cooled the windowpane under their palm, and the more they thought, the more complicated everything seemed.

They just didn't want to contact Ralph; the man was odious, taking liberties and being supercilious about it. They also felt ashamed, for arguably they'd helped their stepfather build their own cage. Speaking to him felt like letting him win a competition they hadn't even consented to enter. Still, they could see no way around seeking him out, and they wanted neither David nor any decent strangers to get caught up in a row that had more or less started when they were a child.

"Do *you* think he'll figure things out quickly?" David's question grounded them as much as the cold glass at their fingertips. "Where you've gone, I mean."

"Who, Robbie? Or Ralph?"

"Either of them."

They kept their eyes on the dark sky as they considered how things might unfold. This was undeniably the pub they'd seen in their premonitions, right down to the smells. They didn't need to find the crossbeam with the runes to know; they already knew.

"I don't know. Perhaps I'm being overzealous and no one will care where I've gone." They didn't quite believe it, but it felt good to say. "You did try to lock up your house," Lennie said. "And I jammed the broken lock so that back door won't open." David locked the other doors. "That should help slow anyone down a little. I should think it would be Robbie who'd go back into the house to figure out things about you."

Chancing a look at David, they glanced over their shoulder to see him frowning so deeply it might have been causing him physical pain. He stood near the chair, but didn't sit. "Why does Ralph seem so stuck on you?"

Lennie was not ready to discuss it. "He's cruel. Always has been."

"And Robbie?"

"Not cruel, so much as forced into submission by his father." If things had been different, Lennie would have felt worse for him. They supposed that they did feel badly for him, no matter what, but it was easier to have pity when Robbie wasn't demanding they overlook their own discomfort with Ralph.

David's leonine features relaxed just a little. "How did he treat your mother?"

Lennie knew *he* meant Ralph. They paused, then said, "He treated her fairly well, or as well as he could, before they married. But it was only to get her to marry him."

Sighing, David nodded and seemed to understand. "Were you and Robbie ever friends?"

Tolerant of his curiosity as long as it stayed away from certain subjects, Lennie shrugged. "Sort of. It was harder to stay friendly when we grew older. His father set us against each other, you see. I think for his own amusement." They did not elaborate upon how Ralph capitalized on their talents, how he would berate Robbie for being ordinary and supposedly useless, leading Robbie to confusion and self-loathing that he luckily didn't take out on anyone but himself.

He wasn't the cleverest lad, but he was sensitive.

They had been almost-friends before Lennie opened their mouth and changed everything. *For me and Mum, especially.* They bit their lip gently, chewing idly at some dead skin, wondering what Robbie would do, now.

Dragging him outside had been almost fun in its way. They and David had managed to take him fairly expeditiously a road over, leaving him propped in a doorway like he'd had too much to drink and simply landed there. It looked similar enough to be convincing, but the minor miracle had been doing so without being observed.

Lennie frowned when they thought about Robbie watching them before he'd slipped into David's house.

They assumed he meant him, alone, when he'd mentioned it.

"I do hope Ellie and Mrs. Greaves and Musgrave are all right."

"You're much more thoughtful than you look." It was the kindest way Lennie had of expressing that most men who carried themselves like David and lived in a house like David's *and* had a second house in Cromer wouldn't be thinking of the help.

Wry, in a tone that melted Lennie and made them chuckle a little, David said, "Thank you, I think."

"It's a compliment. If you weren't worried about your help, I'd think less of you. My mother was a maid. Well, sometimes. She was a charwoman, a maid..."

"Wouldn't want you to think any less of me."

"No?" Lennie smiled at David.

"Not at all." He nodded to the chair nearest the window. "May I?"

"You don't have to ask."

Though David's reply was a huff of disagreement, he collapsed, mindful of the gun in his pocket. "I hate these things." He closed his eyes and Lennie watched him more readily than they previously had. Anyway, his eyes were so blue as to be distracting, the sort with very dark rings around brighter bursts of color. It was easier to watch him when they were shut.

"Do you have much experience with them?"

"Not with many small ones like this," said David. "But with rifles, yes."

That made sense. He spoke as though he was educated and with that came certain pastimes only afforded to a certain set of men. Rifles would figure into hunting. He'd said he was born in Norwich, but there wasn't a trace of the place in his voice, another sign of a specific sort of education and all its trappings. Lennie tried not to give a sigh or huff of their own. They were clever and knew how to read, write, and do sums. They were excellent at numbers. But they'd never been to university, which was surely something David considered a flaw.

A knock at the door made Lennie jump slightly, and disrupted their gazing at David. His eyes opened and met theirs for a moment. Briefly, he seemed to let Lennie see a genuine heat, then it was gone, a blue flame that mellowed into something less noticeable. "It's all right." That tone, almost more than the heat in his eyes, engulfed Lennie. It was soft, but protective, like a scarf made of some dear fabric.

Then David stood and opened the door. Whoever was on the other side of it, he knew them, because he said, "I thought it'd be you."

The man who entered the room bore everything needed to stoke a small fire. Though the day had been warm, the night had gone decidedly cool.

"Paul trusts you, you know, if he gave you one of the rooms with a fireplace. They don't all have them. But they're a risk with some people, aren't they?" Curiously, Lennie watched as he expertly started a fire while he spoke. He looked remarkably like the innkeeper even in profile, so they surmised this was the nephew, Tom. "He said you were in trouble. Sort of explained how."

Irksomely, there was also a shared dark blue haze that ebbed and flowed between him and David. It dissipated when Lennie blinked. That haze spoke of personal connections, possibly of physical intimacy, and Lennie became envious upon noticing its presence. They tried not to grimace, more at their own folly than anything.

"I never said I was," said David.

"What other reason is there to abscond to the rooms above a public house this time of night?" Crinkling a lean nose that looked like it had been broken once or twice when he was younger, Tom added, "Actually, don't answer that. Although, that *is* a brand of trouble all its own."

"Tom." It wasn't easy to tell what emotion David expressed by saying the name, but it might be exasperation. Fond exasperation, if Lennie had their guess. They stifled a mutter of annoyance. "Just... I *will* tell you. But... we've had a rather trying day. I'm going to miss several appointments tomorrow, one with someone from Curls, and my house was broken into..."

Yet again, David's fastidious side tickled Lennie. It might have been irksome in someone else, but it was endearing in him.

"All right. You do look shaken." Tom looked at Lennie and offered his hand. They knew, then, this was no dandy, no toff. No one of a high social standing would so readily offer their hand for a handshake. Or let their hair be this messy. Or have clothes that were clean and presentable, but several seasons old. And no hat. "Mr. Tom Apollyon."

Shaking it, feeling calluses but no squeezes or other attempts at seeming tough or dominant, which made them want to like him, they said, "Lennie."

A bare flicker of recognition shone in Tom's glance at David. Then a wealth of communication seemed to pass between them, for David said, "Yes, but stop looking at me that way."

Lennie did not have to be told that these two men had known each other for some time. Deciding to change the subject rather than make polite chatter, they asked, "If... is... there any way I might get some food?"

"It's past Mrs. Lloyd's usual hours," said Tom. "That's our housekeeper. And the cook has gone home for the night. But Mrs. Lloyd won't let you go hungry."

"She might let *me* go hungry," said David.

"No, she's not one to hold grudges. She might send up just a crust of bread for *you*, but she won't let you starve. Sit back down... you seem exhausted."

"I should go home."

Don't, Lennie wanted to say. They kept silent and instead removed their hat, setting it on a ledge opposite the fireplace.

"Why?" Tom paused on his way to the door. "You're going back to Norwich tonight after a burglary? Have I got it correct? Paul said something of the kind."

"No. Not there." David passed a hand through his own hair, having tossed his fedora, or maybe it was a brown trilby, to the foot of the bed. As Lennie realized where it was, they smiled a little at the thought that he'd probably never left any hat on a bed. "No, the house *you* broke into."

There was naturally a tale to be told there, but Lennie was too wearied to ask after it.

"At least have something to eat," said Tom. "And frankly, I... have questions. Don't just... go."

Sitting in the chair once more, David said, "I've answers. None of which make any sense and..." he hesitated and Lennie caught his glance. "I shall eat first, and then we can talk a little. I think... I may need that mad old man who called me a witch."

"A mad old man called you a witch?" Lennie asked. They sat on the ground near the fire, their back close to David's shins and shoes.

"All right," said Tom, as calm and without judgement as his uncle had been downstairs. "But he's
going to be leaving for his brother's in the morning.
Normally I accompany him, but I'm glad I'm staying.
Though, Paul can help with witchery. Maybe. If that's
what you're after. I also agree Benson is the man you
need."

With a blink, Lennie understood the conversation
was in earnest. Relieved beyond measure at the sincerity, they said quietly, "I can, too. Help. With
witchcraft."

—

Tom's hand dropped from the doorknob, the
movement accompanied by a little, indeterminant
noise of satisfied belief. He asked David, "Do you ever
think you meet some people because of... God?"

"I don't believe in God," said David. "Which you
know well enough."

"Choose whatever you'd like, then," said Tom.
"Fate. A saint. A pretty tree. Whatever you believe is
worth believing in. But *he's* the one who pickpocketed
you, is he not?"

The incorrigible man was saying it on purpose,
David thought. Lennie looked up at David from his
place on the floor. "You *told* people about someone
who pickpocketed you? People... who weren't the
police?"

"I..."

Tom was not helpful, for he only tried to make a
smile disappear from his somewhat chapped lips. Too
slowly.

"Why?" Lennie tilted his head, and although
David thought he might see censure or confusion or
disgust, his expression bore none of those things. It

was remarkably open, pristinely guileless, and his face was beautiful.

"Does it matter?" David asked.

"Answer my question, first."

At that, Tom tried to make a laugh into a sneeze.

"I was... rather... captivated."

"Smitten," said Tom. He glanced at David and shrugged. "Not that you said as much in as many words. You just went on about his hands."

"I know about witches because my mother was one," said Lennie, without putting more distance between his body and David's legs. That had to be a good sign. He faced the fire and stopped searching David's face for something. "Not the sort who gave out remedies or... birthed babies... or... nothing like that."

"That's a midwife." David couldn't see his way to saying something more sensible.

Any of his set would utilize doctors or chemists for babies and things like chest colds, but Ellie's sister was a midwife, so he'd heard rather more about them in passing than he'd ever expected to.

"Well, who's to say many of them aren't witches, too?" Lennie smiled, almost to himself, and watched the flames. David traced his profile with his eyes, savoring the lines outlined by firelight. "She could dream things before they happened. Saw them often while she was awake, too. All the time, honestly. I don't know how it didn't drive her to distraction, but it didn't. And she never treated it like a burden, or something wrong."

Immediately, David knew why Lennie hadn't been overly bothered about whatever he'd done to Robbie. If one grew up with the extraordinary being normal, being confronted with strangeness might not feel so terrifying. This was something David could understand in theory, at least, having only recently discovered his former lover was a selkie and admitted his imaginary friends might not have been imaginary at all.

Strange was starting to feel less startling. And the way Lennie mentioned his mother revealed deep love for her. There was more to it, too. He was curious to know more about Lennie's childhood, which even apart from their social standings, seemed so different from his own. "And... you?"

"Did I think it was wrong?" Skeptically, Lennie arched an eyebrow at him, and he felt his heart skip a beat or two. He didn't think that was possible, that it was just a thing mentioned in novels, but there he was, proven wrong.

"No. I wouldn't think you'd believe it was wrong. Could you do it?" *Do you, still?*

"Yes," said Lennie. "I can't remember not doing it. I still do."

"Paul can," offered Tom, with a little smile.

Lennie returned it. "I knew I liked him."

"He can? How long have you known?" David tried not to sound petulant, but he couldn't help feeling as though he had been left out of something. On the other hand, a lot about Paul's ambient strangeness would be accounted for if he had some kind of preternatural powers.

"Less than a year. He only told me after we first speculated that you'd taken Theo's... well." He shook his head, clearly thinking Theo's business wasn't his to divulge as much as Paul's might be. "Only since then."

"I am sorry," said David. "You shouldn't have to explain. As I said, long day. Afternoon. Evening."

A bit of wood crackled in the hearth and Tom nodded. "I'll bring you something to eat. And tear Benson away from packing his dirty carpetbag."

"I'd take a biscuit, anything," David said. "More of that cake I had."

Chuckling, Tom nodded and showed himself out, but not before saying, "Oh, her cake tastes even better when you're not drunk. We don't have any of the one with candied orange peel, like you had, but we do have one with strawberry jam."

—

Lennie was nearly ready to fall asleep by the time Tom returned with the mad old man called Benson and a small cake that David regretfully left to one side. It was soon clear why he wanted them to wait to nibble: Benson smelled so strongly of spirits, probably gin, that he tainted the air with it. Overall, it confused the appetite.

"What seems to be the trouble, Mr. Mills?" Benson appeared unbothered and he studied his filthy nails.

David, on the other hand, seemed both bothered and nervous. "I... knocked a man out with a... spark. From my hand. Fingers. Palm. I thought you might like to know. And... when you go to Norwich, do you think it would be possible to ask after a Mrs. Miriam J. Greaves?"

If any of this stymied Benson, who was dressed like a mendicant, Lennie could not see any evidence of his bewilderment. They were surprised that David simply came out with it, though. Perhaps shock had stripped him of some of his reticence.

"The man was my stepbrother," added Lennie. "And he'd broken into Mr. Mills' house. It wasn't really an act of aggression, just defense."

Something about Robbie's surprise entrance still nagged at them; they couldn't put their finger on why he had so abruptly taken an interest in their doings. He'd never followed them before, and the way he did so now was perplexing. It felt almost as though he was their keeper, or he'd been told to keep an eye on them.

Lennie shivered a little at the thought.

Leaving Ralph's dingy home had been a mark of their independence and freedom, so they hated the idea that he might have decided to encroach upon it. Perhaps they should move elsewhere entirely, if it did turn out that he was trying to. Then again, Ralph was getting on in years and his health was not good. They might be able to wait him out.

"Yes," said David. "I didn't mean to... do whatever I did to him."

Lennie said, "I've never seen anything like it, but that doesn't make it impossible."

Tom, who was lingering by the fire, raised his eyebrows at David's assertions and Lennie's additions, but kept his peace. Lennie looked at him, silently daring him to take issue with anything at all. But Tom shook his head a bit and watched the flames instead of rising to their wordless bait.

"I'll have my brother ask after this Miriam. He's far better with people than me," said Benson, still belying no astonishment at any of these revelations. When Lennie focused on him, he seemed to shimmer at the edges, much like David did, a little like someone outlined by a setting sun or heat rising from hot ground.

It wasn't consistent enough to be distracting, and it just told Lennie that he could or did practice witchcraft. They'd noticed it as soon as Benson entered the room, but it wasn't unpleasant. As they glanced at David, they realized David's own shimmers and flickers were more obvious now compared to when they'd stolen his wallet on Upper St. Giles.

It had been one of the first things Mum had taught them to see, to look for. Their sight wasn't as exact as a true science and there were probably exceptions to it, but Lennie knew enough to understand different abilities reflected in diverse ways for them. Paul, for example, did not have the same mirage-like quality as Benson or David. Neither did Tom, but both he and his uncle were flanked by gentle flares of shifting color.

Everyone else, those who might be considered ordinary, did not have any such notable signatures. They tended toward one or maybe two colors that did not flicker like sunlight on water. These colors would attach to things and places the person valued or frequented.

Lennie didn't know if all who shared their sight or abilities experienced things this way, but Mum did — at least to the extent that she saw colors and flickers and shimmers, as well as aspects of the future.

All of it was actually quite beautiful, and it was useful in determining certain aspects of various talents. *Or finding things people want to keep hidden,* they thought ruefully. Literal things, like their money or beloved heirlooms.

The human race was capable of attaching a rather startling amount of importance to material goods, and Lennie could follow spectral trails between most people and their precious things. They also left traces on their routes home, to places of work. All of that was what, after all, Ralph knew Lennie could trace.

And he relied on Lennie because they had introduced him to the very idea. Awash with guilt for their past actions, or the past actions of their childhood self, Lennie pushed the thought away lest one of these new acquaintances be able to read it.

"Good," said David. "Ah, thank you."

"My pleasure," said Benson, and it could have been sincere or purely satirical. Lennie couldn't tell, and suspected Benson wanted to keep things ambiguous for his own amusement. "Don't hurt anyone with your magical hand while I'm away."

"I... won't," said David, patently galled.

Benson let out what could only be called a cackle. "Wonderful. Don't think you will, but it was worth saying, wasn't it?"

Tom, who seemed used to playing Benson's keeper, turned to him. "All right, now you know, and now you know to keep a lookout for Mrs. Greaves. You have to be discreet, you realize?"

"Oh, yes, all of this smacks of a good little knotty problem, and I shouldn't like to add to it," murmured Benson. "Still, Mr. Mills, you chose quite a safe place to bolt, if I don't say so myself."

Whatever he meant by it, Lennie guessed it had to do with preternatural things, with charms and wards and a host of things they'd never learned to do themself but at this present juncture wished they could construct. If they had, perhaps they wouldn't be in this *little knotty problem.*

"And I wager we have more to discuss when you return," said David wearily.

Ushering Benson out the door, Tom said, "Right, if you don't go, you'll be talking to them all night and you'll miss your train in the morning."

"Very well," he said to Tom. Then he winked at David. "Good evening, Mr. Hand of Glory."

Spluttering, David barely had time to call after him, "I'm not dead, and I'm certainly not mummified, and I'm not a thief, and..."

But Tom had herded Benson out and the door

closed with a soft creak, so Lennie patted David gently on his shoulder in sympathy and went directly for the cake. They liked Benson already, but could admit he was quite a strong presence. And poor David, they imagined, was grappling with his entire perception of the world being shifted to something new.

12

For the second time in less than a fortnight, David woke in a bed that was not his. But he recognized The Shuck's dusty, tannic smells, so he kept his eyes closed, lingering in a haze between alertness and slumber. The bed itself was soft, but not overly so. He was in his clothes, or at least his shirt and trousers. While he savored the haze and became more aware of the slow breathing to his right, he was happy that Lennie had convinced him to stay.

After Benson left, they hadn't discussed much more beyond the marvelous cake Tom had brought up, a pristine little round thing topped with strawberry jam and served with cream. Exhaustion seemed to lead him and Lennie to a mutual accord: there was a moratorium on witchcraft talk. He couldn't imagine any productive decisions or revelations occurring after the day they'd had, and Lennie looked amenable to acting as though he hadn't broached the topic.

The more David thought about it while he ate Mrs. Lloyd's cake, the more he wondered if he had been meant to meet the Apollyons. He didn't want to tell Tom that his rhetorical question had stuck. He started to do a mental tally of everything that had ever attracted him to Tom. While physical attraction had always been present, underlying that had been something more sublime. Like recognizing like. Which at the time, he'd attributed to their shared status as so-called inverts and definitely rather odd boys.

Knowing there were witches and selkies, now, and having experienced something quite inexplicable literally by his own hand, he wondered if, without knowing it was a shared preternatural inclination, he'd recognized something essential in Tom.

Of course, he'd said nothing about any of this and concentrated on the sticky burst of strawberry jam on his tongue followed by mellow cream, and he let himself be privately mesmerized by the play of candle and firelight on Lennie's tanned skin. While he kept trying to leave due to a strident sense of propriety, he found he couldn't, although they were just eating cake and doing little of consequence. After an hour or so of idle talk, Lennie had turned to him and said, "You're staying the night here."

"I shouldn't," was what he said in response.

"Yes, you should."

The confidence made him smile slightly. "That's bold."

And it was. He'd been flirted with long before Lennie had started doing it in a beautifully, smoothly pointed way, so he was able to recognize it. Unlike what he suspected others thought of him, he could easily read such things. He'd just found it gauche to act upon the cues, or so he told himself.

In truth, it was more that he was terrified word of the liberties might get back to his family. While he might have ventured to take such freedoms before Tom, after Tom, it was more difficult because Father then insisted upon taking a tighter grasp on his social life. This had the effect of convincing him he shouldn't bother indulging himself at all, for even if he could sneak away to spend the night with someone, it felt as though Father would inevitably know.

While it was one thing to subject himself to the man because he had no choice in his family, it was another one to possibly expose someone else to his particular brand of coldness that was so intensely cold it always burned. Even Theo had not experienced much of it, for Father became quite ill while he and David were still together.

Theo's recent words floated back to him. *You need to let your father die. Really die.* Maybe he should. Maybe he shouldn't be the one keeping him alive in memory. There was nothing good that could come of it.

Rather than revisit his thoughts from last night, he decided to focus on this morning. He rolled to his side. That was enough to rouse Lennie, who was also mostly dressed. Both of their respective hats, coats and shoes were piled in the corner.

"What time is it?"

David's eyes were still not open, but he heard the sleepiness in Lennie's voice and it washed over his body like the tide. "I don't know. I've only just woken up," he replied. When he thought no one could see him actually enjoying himself, he liked floating on his back in the sea, he loved the pull of the waves and the caress of the air, and Lennie's barely awake voice reminded him of that sensation. He should be exiting the bed as quickly as humanly possible. All he'd been taught to believe about propriety demanded it. All he felt detained him. "I had strange dreams."

He vaguely remembered them the longer he was

awake; both involved Paul's Alastair, though David knew he probably wasn't correctly recalling Alastair's face. It made sense given where he was, where he'd slept, that his hindbrain would concoct those dreams. Each had been banal, anyway, he thought. In one, he'd just asked Alastair after the latest ale. Alastair had replied it wasn't Paul's concoction, but his own, and he was lucky he hadn't made anyone ill.

In another, he'd gone down to the cellar with Alastair, who said something about feeling at home in it. David had to resist making a quip about his relatives possibly residing in the old vaults of Edinburgh. Even in the dream, he'd recognized how slightly off-color it was.

Lennie asked, "Were they nightmares?"

"No."

"Then, can we go back to sleep?"

On a breath, David said, "I feel like someone owes the Apollyons a better explanation than whatever we kept going on about last night, and it ought to be me who supplies it."

"Well, they're not in peril, are they?" Lennie shifted so that he was draped against David's back. His voice felt like a purr. "The place hasn't burnt down around us. It's not burning now, either."

"No, but..." David wriggled a little as Lennie's voice produced sensations and reactions that might be welcome or unseemly. Or both.

"It's not very bright in here. It must be early. Besides, the older one seems like he can take care of himself."

Arching into Lennie very slightly, David said, "It's both of them you have to look out for. Tom's been through hell and back, and he's all the more unpredictable for it." Not that David knew that for certain, anymore, as Theo had seemed to temper the chaos.

At that, Lennie smiled. David didn't need to see it to know it. "You've slept with him, haven't you?"

"Years ago," said David, opening his eyes. Lennie didn't seem to be spoiling for an argument. There wasn't anything to argue about, anyway. "Was it so obvious?"

"To me," said Lennie, as he petted David's collarbone, his arm draped gently over David's shoulder. He was not a very large person and the weight was comforting. "Yes. Often, I see... well, I don't know what to call them. They're colors around people. I can definitely see yours. My mother could do it better than I could. She could see everybody's, see everything. But..." his breath was warm against the side of David's neck. "When he came into the room the first time, you two sort of... shared a color."

"And that means we've fucked?" He'd wished to ask, *What color am I?* But it didn't come out first. He didn't want to sound so sour or crass, and wasn't feeling as sour as he sounded. But it was early, his entire day and probably the next fortnight had been torn asunder, and more importantly, he did not want anything to happen to Lennie.

As far as business went, he was reasonably confident he could claim an illness without causing any offense whenever he did return. Even a new customer like Mr. Davies would understand the sudden onset of feeling unwell. He didn't know what to do about the rest — the potential thefts that might even be taking place this moment, for one thing.

Chuckling, Lennie said, "Usually, that's what it means. Now I know for sure. You're such a hedgehog, aren't you? All prickles, and rolling up when someone pokes you even a bit."

"Well," huffed David. "I quite like hedgehogs."

"Well, I quite like *you*."

He let out a slow, careful breath as several emotions vied for expression. "I like you, too. But I'm scared."

"Of me?"

"No, God, no."

Lennie's fingertips gripped his shoulder in evident relief and reassurance. "Good. I... mind you, I can be terrifying." David had to laugh at his words. "But I'd rather you weren't afraid of me."

"I expect we'll — all of us — talk about what scares me." It did all feel larger than he expected something like this would feel. On their own, he knew crimes like theft and housebreaking shouldn't feel like the cusp of the unknown in the same way contemplating witchcraft and creatures did. He'd been fortunate enough to avoid the real threats of crime until now, but he knew enough to understand they probably shouldn't feel like religious epiphanies.

Then again, if they were dire enough, perhaps they could.

He resisted falling into silent, pervasive panic.

Seeming to sense this, as well as the reasons behind the panic itself, Lennie curled more heavily around him. "I imagine it must be a lot to hear about... if you haven't grown up with witches or the like being treated the same as saints and almanacs. I forget it's not customary for everyone. But not everyone needs to know... and it's not as though we haven't good reason to keep quiet."

There was decided steel in Lennie's slightly hoarse voice, the hardness letting David know there was far more to that statement than he might ever understand. He inferred Lennie had learned that truth from personal experience, not that it was difficult to deduce. In agreement, David thought about the manic need throughout history to persecute witches. The very thing for which his father was proud of his supposed witch-hunter ancestor doing.

"Yes," he managed to say.

Regardless, even now, one might be thought mad or ill if they brought such things into conversation. That thought did not stem the panic; it stoked it. David wondered how many people locked up in hospitals or jails for madness were simply different, simply capable of things separate from or beyond reasonable explanations.

"David."

He swallowed. "Yes?"

"You're all right."

He forced himself to stay moored to the present, used Lennie's voice to steer himself and remain there, worked his jaw a little. "I want to be."

"You don't have to figure everything out all at once."

He so disliked letting problems remain tangled, but admitted this situation was more complex than the overwhelming majority of problems he'd encountered. What he wouldn't give to be dealing with a supply issue, or even a client who threw an inkwell at his head, which was a pitfall of their business that Father had never seen fit to warn him about. "It's not really in my nature to..."

"Be patient?" Lennie asked.

"No, I can be patient." He knew he could be and had been. Almost to the point of letting certain aspects of himself wither as he put aside elements of his

personality and own tastes to pass through the world
with minimal conflict. Often, he'd told himself, he
could come back to them, though even when he was at
his most hopeful, he knew it was a lie.

"What, then?"

"It's not in my nature to let things be... disorderly."
It was such an inaccurate word to articulate how rud-
derless he was feeling, but it would have to do at
present.

To his surprise, Lennie shifted away from him,
then tugged at his shoulder until they were both on
their backs. The bed was wide enough so that they
both fit, but not with much excess room. It was rather
ancient, the kind of thing that had never seen a
modern factory or assembly line. David found something almost erotic in the companionship, although
they had not touched one another in a marked way. It
thrilled and comforted him.

"I need you to know something."

"I'm slightly wary," said David. "The last time
someone said something like this to me, I found out
my former lover was a seal." Perplexed, Lennie's
mouth opened, then closed. "Never mind. I can tell
you about that later. What do you need me to know?"

"Part of my... what I can do. It's not just foresight. It
seems to latch onto certain people."

"Has it latched onto me?" He was teasing, slightly,
but Lennie's expression told him he was correct. "Oh.
Well, that's all right, isn't it?"

"Is it? I... it's how I knew you'd been pissed."

David watched his face, gauged how this made
him feel. A lesser man would have been, perhaps,
smug, but Lennie seemed to exhibit remorse. "What
do you mean?"

"The best I can explain it, I can experience things

through a person. Intense things, normally. Not... everything, and I work to keep up walls and not be nosy. They can just abate on their own if I don't try to..."

David brought a finger to Lennie's lips. "I can tell you're not going to use it against me, or for your own purposes. It's all right." He studied his eyes, relishing the closeness and distracted by their color. "Oh, your eyes are almost... golden."

"Well spotted."

"It's such a lovely color."

"Thank you."

"No, they're bronze."

"Are we going to talk about disorderly things, or will you be complimenting me all morning?"

David roused the courage to reach out and take Lennie's hand, lace their fingers together. "I know which I prefer."

"If you like my eyes..." said Lennie, in more of that delicious purr. "Wait until you see my —"

The door came open with a clatter.

Mrs. Lloyd, alongside Theo, almost tumbled forward. To her credit, Mrs. Lloyd did bear a tray of tea, toast, and jam, but Theo's skin was flushed pink, and he had the air of one who'd been eavesdropping. "Didn't I tell you it wouldn't be locked?" Mrs. Lloyd sniffed. "All this haste to get here and be safe, and your Mr. Mills can't be bothered to lock a door. Not that he's yours, now, is he?"

Resigned, for talk traveled quickly in the same building, David said, "What time is it, actually?" In all the chaos, he'd neglected to bring his watch along with him.

It must have been later than he'd thought despite the diffuse light, or there wouldn't be interlopers at his door. If he'd learned anything about Theo in the time they'd lived together, it was that he actually loved gleaning all he could about everyone around him. David now understood it was a means of defense, soft in its approach but no less thorough than obvious aggression.

If one knew things about everyone, one could act accordingly or even weaponize information, thus limiting the chances of being controlled. *Or having their skin taken.* Not that David had premeditated the act at all. And he suspected Theo's motivation would never be weaponizing information.

"Nine," said Theo, straightening his clothes and the small golden medal he wore at his throat. When Theo had first started to wear it, David would've given almost anything to return it to Tom. But it seemed very much part of him now. He smiled at Lennie without any malice or envy, not that David would've expected him to be openly envious. Theo was and always had been better at moderating his emotions.

Unlike me, thought David.

"Hello, I'm Mr. Theodore Harper. Theo."

"Have you been standing out there long, then?" Lennie sat up and regarded both of the intruders with wry, benevolent interest. Mrs. Lloyd had the grace to look dignified; Theo had the audacity to look like he hadn't been doing anything but eavesdropping.

"Might I?" Mrs. Lloyd asked David, lifting the tray slightly for emphasis. He nodded and she put it on a table under the window.

"No, not long," said Theo, "I was on my way up to Paul's flat to tend to some work, and Mrs. Lloyd was on her way up with tea to see if you were awake. She was about to knock properly. I have to confess I was the enabler, though; I'm nosy."

Sitting up, too, David murmured, "Thank God someone believes in the right order of things around here. Thank you, Mrs. Lloyd."

He didn't know if being on this bed with the most graceful man he'd ever seen would have led to anything. But the calmness around them had been interrupted by an inquisitive selkie and a housekeeper who baked the best cakes in Norfolk. If he wished to find out, he would have to initiate something later.

And he wasn't very good at initiating anything.

13

P aul's first response to Lennie's stories of various manipulations and abuses was calm and precise. "Your stepfather won't hurt you here."

They weren't used to anyone paying them such marked attention in a respectful way. It wasn't that it had never been supplied; Mum had. It was just lacking in their life now. Lennie cleared their throat and waited for Paul to reply to all they'd just explained. They recognized what they'd said was a little dramatic, and most of Ralph's qualities did make him sound a little like a penny dreadful villain. He wasn't quite that, but he was undeniably unpleasant.

They'd left out the part where they were to blame for Ralph's machinations. It wasn't something they could bear to describe.

Wanly, Lennie said, "He... it's not exactly that he *hurts* me, Mr. Apollyon." Ralph had never raised a hand against them, but he didn't need to. They glanced briefly at David, who sat rather stiffly to their right on a barstool.

Tom, standing against the front of the bar and next

to where his uncle sat, said, "He holds some sway over you?"

Lennie still had not made up their mind as to whether or not they liked him, and had to admit some of the ambivalence stemmed from jealousy. They wanted to ask David more about the relationship he'd had with him; it was clear that unrest and unresolved tension was present for both men. However, they did appreciate what seemed to be Tom's family trait of perceptive equanimity, and couldn't deny that he was astute. Watching as he took a short sip of something in a flask present on his person, they said simply, "Yes."

"Remember, we're friends, or we'd like to be," said Theo, who was easier to like than Tom, but roused the same jealousy over David.

"I'm not very good at having them," said Lennie with a chuckle.

"You're not going to find any judgement, either," said Tom.

Lennie sighed and tried not to be too frustrated. They understood that each of those present thought they were an unspeakable of a fairly common variety if one knew where and how to look. They weren't keen on discussing their more private details, yet could see no way around disclosing them. Ralph was no criminal genius and he was not particularly special: his capacities and beliefs were, so far as Lennie had seen in their experience, average.

If this conversation continued, they harbored a slight fear that the Apollyons, Mr. Harper, and David would all want to side with Ralph. They might have taken the chance of being seen and known to sleep with David, but they didn't think they could bear it if all four decided to regard them with disbelief, pity, or worse.

Nonetheless, they didn't think they could avoid the risk. There was no way they could blame only the preternatural for their stepfather's abuses; they'd just explained how Ralph had leveraged first their mother's preternatural abilities, then their own, for material gain. Ralph was not against the uncanny or the occult so long as it gave him something. Similarly, they could not pretend Ralph merely took issue with their love of men; they were in a room full of men who loved other men and seemed ready to offer them safe haven.

No, Ralph did not care that Lennie favored men. According to his view of the world and of Lennie, that was the correct order of desire. It was not their desire that was wrong, it was them as an individual who was wrong.

"What is it?" David asked, and it was so gentle that Lennie might've hidden their face in his lapel if they'd been in private. "Whatever it is, I promise you, we've all heard worse... and stranger."

"Ralph knows — thinks he knows — something that could see me locked away." Lennie studied a bottle of rum on a shelf past Tom's head. "It doesn't matter if he's wrong about me. Which he is. But many others, learned people, doctors, would side with him. He knows it."

"Is it..." David cleared his throat. Lennie did not have to be watching him to know he was likely exchanging a quizzical look with someone. The pause spoke volumes. "If you prefer men, yes, that's something you might be... treated for. Arrested for." All of them knew the realities, the truths that didn't need saying. "But... we can all... I can... we'll protect you. You never need to see him again. He can't use it against you if he can't find you."

"You could start again somewhere else, if you needed to," said Tom.

Lennie did not point out that David was now involved, that even if they managed to disappear, when David went back to his house, Ralph would already know whose it was. They wouldn't want to leave him behind to suffer any consequences. Since a vision had told them a mark was actually important, impactful, not as a source of income, but as something deeper, they felt very responsible for whatever might happen to David.

They kept looking at the rum bottle and not at anyone in the room, but they waved a hand dismissively and tried to act less terrified and conflicted. It was unlikely they'd succeed, because they knew their voice shook a bit. "No. It's not loving men that he could try to use against me." They tensed and decided to just press forward. After all, this was the room they'd had premonitions of, and David was in them. It had to count for something. "Ralph says I'm a woman."

Scoffing, David said, "You're not."

"You're right," said Lennie. "I'm not." They kept it at that, let the few words carry their own weight. They didn't need to explain how Ralph had known them as a child before they'd been able to articulate themself and be Lennie. He was convinced they were somehow addled, mad in the keenest sense. He also knew it was Lennie's deepest fear to be incarcerated or trapped.

Mum had championed them and questioned nothing, trusting Lennie to know their own mind; Lennie never asked her if it was because of a premonition or a vision. In the end, it didn't matter. But Ralph, who was already utilizing both of their abilities for his own greedy purposes by then, seized upon Lennie's truths as reins to be used for more control. He well knew that the likes of an invert could be locked away, fined, or blackmailed, and Lennie had no doubt he would have capitalized upon that, too, if he believed they were a man. He was cruel enough.

But he did not believe they were, and reminded them they were *a woman* at every opportunity. After Mum had passed and they'd put their mind to saving away enough money to live alone, they were able to let their own rooms and escape Ralph's daily abuses. Still, in his presence, they were always *she*. In quiet retaliation, Lennie never addressed him as Mr. Roylott, only as Ralph. He hated alliteration, hated his first name.

However, Lennie never did point out that Robbie – Robert – was also subjected to the same insult. Robbie did not feel so strongly about alliteration, though.

Paul replied first, breaking the pensive quiet. He spoke with an authority that from another person would have caused Lennie to balk. "You're not seeing him again."

With a smile, Lennie said, "I wish." At least they could look Paul in the eye, and when they did, there was no denunciation or apprehension.

He shook his head. "Maybe he'll come here if he figures out you've come to Cromer, but none of us will let anything bad happen to you."

"He's not violent toward me," Lennie said quietly, wishing to disabuse Paul of the notion that Ralph scared them for physical reasons, while also wishing they could be having any discussion but this one, "he's... oily. And demanding. And calculating." David shifted a little, which they only noticed from the corner of their eye. They were still too apprehensive to look at him properly. "I appreciate being brought here, but perhaps it wasn't the best place to come."

"Why not?" Tom said.

"Ralph isn't given to bouts of physical anger," said Lennie, choosing their words carefully and selecting the best rationale that didn't make them feel weak. "But he once worked as a caretaker for a barrister's office... though he never dealt directly with him, he did become friends with the barrister's secretary. He fancies himself clever because he picked up some idea of little loopholes and jargon. I wonder if he may act out."

In actuality, nothing he knew was enough to convince a court or an authority to do anything, and what was more, he did not appear at all moneyed, so few in power would be motivated to help him. And if his latest letter was any indication of his mental state, he was not terribly well within his mind. Whether he could manage to behave as he had when he was more hale and hearty was debatable.

Lennie just did not want to say that they feared how his words impacted them, how the smallest remarks from him could cut like a knife. They'd worked to get out from under his roof, and wanted to avoid experiencing it as much as they could. This felt like a feebler reason behind leaving Norwich than being physically hurt by someone.

If Ralph was doing them such harm, then they could look these men squarely in the face and explain why their first instinct when they'd seen Robbie in David's house was to run. Men were often expected to fight, they knew that, too. Nonetheless, if Ralph had a pattern of being violent, few would expect Lennie to subject themself to it. Most would be more understanding of their urge to bolt.

But Ralph's weapons were his jeers and threats and belittlements, not his fists.

"Well," said David. "He's welcome to try exploiting those loopholes near me, because unlike him... I *am* friends with barristers." Finally, Lennie chanced a look at him. His cheeks were flushed, his blue eyes were keen. "I say friends. They're... frankly, they're not very kind. But... they enjoy money, which is not something I lack at all."

Nowhere in David's face did Lennie see fear or revulsion after what they'd revealed, and their heart warmed as he spoke.

"Does he have any abilities himself?" Theo asked.

Lennie tore their gaze from David. "He's always kept that from me," they told Theo. "I don't think so. People who have them do look different to me. I'd guess he was raised by someone who knew about them or had them. He certainly seemed to know early that my mum could see elements of the future, and find things that were hidden. But she was transparent with him, so..." shrugging, Lennie scowled.

One did not need such powers to be an effective thief, but it helped if one could sense certain outcomes that might result from the stealing. It also helped if one had an uncanny aptitude for telling lies from truths, or noting any glittering threads that might trail between a person and their beloved heirlooms. Mum, positioned as she was as a charwoman, had been the ideal partner for a man like Ralph. He'd pressured her first into an affair, then into marriage, then into making off with valuables from her employers.

Before the marriage itself, living with a man to whom she was not married had rarely been remarked upon, likely because of her status as a poor widow with a young child. Nobody seemed to care much either way, and her employers had known her for several years and felt she was above suspicion. She moved from house to house.

No one ever connected her with the baubles, the banknotes, the small but costly things that disappeared, which was really something of a miracle. *You just had to open your mouth, didn't you?* Lennie didn't want to own to their own part in the process, and so they shoved the guilt away. They recalled the first few times they'd met Ralph and how quickly they'd disliked him. The pressure and manipulation had been subtle, then grew more overt as time passed and Mum's health waned. By the time she'd died, Ralph easily dictated her habits and had already pressed Lennie into similar circumstances.

"Lennie?" David said their name.

"Hm?"

"You know it isn't your fault."

"What's not my fault?" They fidgeted on their stool, having lost track of the conversation for a moment and wondering for a flash if David could see inside their mind, even though there was no evidence of that talent to their eye.

"That this..." a look of distaste came onto David's face and lingered. "Man. Presses you into committing petty crimes for him."

"I know," said Lennie, a little too sharply.

"Good."

Tom looked at Paul. "What do we do if he traces David here? He could." To David, he said, "Sorry. I'm sure someone has rifled through your house, old man."

To that, David just shrugged. Appearing to consider the possibilities, Paul said, "Benson has wards on the place, so if this Mr. Roylott decides to do anything untoward, he'll find it difficult."

Difficult was infused with promise. "I don't want anyone inconvenienced or endangered or..." Lennie cleared their throat. "Anyway, I don't believe he'd do much himself. He's older now, and he was rather ill the last time I saw him. If it's anyone who comes, it'll be Robbie."

It wasn't a given event, for Robbie worked doing *something*. Lennie didn't care to know how he earned his living these days, but when they were younger, he'd been a man of all work between two pubs near Elm Hill. He wouldn't be able to just tear to Cromer without losing some income, but he might try. He and his father had always possessed a troubling relationship, and Lennie suspected he often thought he could gain more of the man's affection if only he tried a little harder to be like him. It would never come to pass, for Ralph did not seem at all capable of supplying any affection, and Robbie was not so rotten.

But if he was pushed by his own flawed reasoning or his father put him up to it, Robbie might well discover where Lennie and David had gone. He could be snooping around Cromer now, for all they knew.

"This wouldn't be the first time I housed someone on the wrong side of the law," Paul said. "Or someone who needed help. It's no trouble." He was enigmatic, but he was sharp as Lennie's best knife. "Besides, if Ralph is as oily as you say, my concern is that he'll endanger you and won't be particularly interested in us. We're not wealthy."

Closing their mouth, Lennie nodded. By fleeing, they'd removed one of Ralph's resources and the person he most liked to belittle.

"He may try to do something to Mr. Mills, who *is*

wealthy," Theo said. David looked skeptical until Theo elaborated. "He's possibly already stolen from your house by now. But I also imagine he won't be pleased that you helped Lennie leave Norwich, when he figures that out."

To everyone's almost palpable surprise, David rose from his stool and came to stand near Lennie. He didn't touch their shoulder, but he stood just behind it. "Let him be displeased, then." Tom looked proud, while Theo bit back a smile. Paul, who'd never had any romantic entanglement with Mr. Mills, just had the air of a satisfied father. David continued, "What's the good in being a Cambridge toff if the law won't take my side over someone like his? He can break into my things as he likes or try to intimidate me as he wants. The police will side with me."

"This may be the first time you've said something that arrogant and I haven't wanted to hit you," said Tom. The slight drawl and the gentle joke were eloquent and affectionate. They could imagine how David might encourage one to hit him. At first glance, he seemed insistent upon all the little shows of deference to his standing.

But the more time they spent with him and watching him interact with the Apollyons, as well as Benson – all of whom should have been doffing their hats and engaging in inane social rituals that supposedly kept the world civilized – the more obvious it was that David didn't actually care.

Theo was more of a puzzle than the other men; they couldn't quite tell where in society he fell, but even that ambiguity might lead someone with David's means to treat him with condescension. David did not.

They glanced over their shoulder at him, although

they dreaded what they might see hidden in his eyes behind what he'd spoken aloud. "Thank you. I think."

There was nothing present to dread.

He just smiled, and for a second, it could have been just the two of them in the taproom.

It didn't make any difference to him, Lennie's divulgence, but he knew there were those to whom it would matter. When he was younger, he might have been among their number, not out of any malice, but because of malignant family beliefs about men and women. To David's mind, though, he should be the last person casting judgement. Beyond that, it was absurd to believe things were so very limited, that there could only be two exact ways of being.

Unfortunately, Lennie seemed cornered by someone who'd already manipulated his mother and gained access to much of his personal life, facts that he held dearly and close.

Pensively, David lingered at Lennie's side, suffused with the need to help him, but it was not motivated by pity or anything so base. Clearly, he could take care of himself. He seemed rather proud, too, but David did not wish to leave him to do so.

It was unlike what he'd felt for Tom, which had been engulfing and almost too hot to bear, or Theo, which had been less frenetic and still enticing. Yet it had never felt quite right, either. He and Theo were mismatched patterns that did not complement each other, David thought, with an internal chuckle. None-theless, it was more sustainable than the fuel-and-flame he and Tom had been.

But when he was near Lennie, things were as calm as they were galvanizing, as charged as they were grounded. It did feel correct and imperative. Yet because it was new to him, he did not know what to call it or how to proceed.

Paul beckoned him out of his thoughts, so he trailed him out of the taproom and into the shadowy corridor beyond. It was odd to see the bowels of a place he'd taken for granted all his life, and he studied the uneven floor under their shoes, then the beams above their heads. The building, though sturdy, pos-sessed a sense of arrested decay, bringing to mind a well-loved, but somewhat ragged museum.

"He can stay here," Paul said quietly. "I don't think it's wise to let either of you stay in your house alone."

David tilted his head in a question. "But he — Ralph — Lennie said he's not likely to —"

"Whenever you take someone away from an abuser, there's no telling how that person will react. I doubt he's much kinder to his son." Sighing, Paul said with a bit of a sneer, "The son might come sniffing about just to please Papa."

David fell quiet and studied what he could of Paul's face in the weak light. While the day was bright with cheerful, fat clouds, The Shuck felt prone to keeping light outside. It was rather like being on a ship, not that David had ever been in a vessel larger than a small, open boat or a punt. He disregarded that metaphor and went back to the museum comparison.

He sometimes forgot that Paul was older than he appeared and had lived a far more interesting life than he ever would. He'd always been wary of him because he had an air of knowing, of experience, that felt dangerous.

Or, mused David, it was similar to being near a particularly calm, large-clawed cat. If you kept on his good side, he wouldn't scratch, but if you crossed him, you might end the encounter bloodied.

"Have you... seen anything?" David asked. He didn't necessarily disagree with Paul's words. They made sense and he suspected Paul could be correct. But he wanted to know if he also had some kind of otherworldly foreknowledge.

"No, not how you mean. But when you first came here, I did notice he felt marked. A little like Theo did, but more familiar to me." Paul shrugged. "It's more like I imagine I feel to anybody who's adept at sensing the preternatural." He tongued the corner of his mouth and said, "You even feel different, Mr. Mills."

About to tell him about what had happened to Robbie, David halted, finding the prospect of owning that moment entirely daunting. He supposed Tom might have already told his uncle, or perhaps Benson made a quip about it to Paul before he'd left for Norwich. "Do I?"

"Indeed. I thought, at first, it was just Benson. But the sense was radiating from you. It's distinctive from how you felt last winter."

"You really don't see anything at all?"

He shook his head, dark hair unruly as he moved. "I see someone who needs help and found the right people. I see someone else who has become less of a starchy..." Paul smirked, evidently trying to decide how coarse his language should be in present company. "Cambridge toff."

Less than a year ago, David would have taken umbrage, but now, he snorted. "I suppose I was quite...

starchy." He could surmise what was meant by it, though he'd never thought about a person being starchy like a collar or lace.

"I didn't know you well when you were seeing Tom. To be frank, I was busy avoiding him. But..." offered Paul, "you appear to me much more like you were, and I think that is a good thing. You seem less encumbered."

Like he was before university, before being found out by Father, before trying to force himself to be what he was not. While most of his little retorts still came to mind whenever he was engaged in conversation — how could they not, when they were born of his need to defend himself and had carried through into his adult life — he found the thought of saying them was a little repulsive.

As though he confessed his sins to a priest, he said, "I don't know what I'm doing."

He didn't even know what anyone might be finding at his office. It might have been left open by nefarious burglars, or it might remain locked, but empty. He supposed someone would probably alert various authorities or the landlord, and some effort would be made to contact him. This was the first day in a long while that David had not dedicated himself to either work or some kind of productive endeavor, and so it would be marked and odd if he did not show up to his office. He found he didn't particularly care.

Most of his worry and all of his attention was directed at Lennie with his teasing, inviting eyes. The rest of his worry was for Musgrave, and Ellie, and Mrs. Greaves. He did wonder if they were well, or if they'd alerted someone on his account. It would be incredibly unusual for him to disappear from his home, for he was not one to take impromptu journeys.

"Do any of us?"

"I suspect you do. Even that old man — Benson. Even he seems to know better than me."

"Well, in our respective cases, we're older," said Paul, with traces of jovial banter in his voice. "And he's older than me, and has even fewer cares for what people think of him."

"That he certainly does." David pictured his bizarre attire, the way he was dressed like an ambulatory pile of rags. No one who presented themselves that way would care for another's opinion.

"I am not in the habit of giving advice, but would you like some?"

David shifted his gaze from a trapdoor set into the floor. Something about it seemed to be glowing just slightly, and when he glanced at Paul, Paul himself refracted the same hazy, gentle glow. "Hm? I... yes. Actually."

"You *have* changed." Paul actually smiled at him and it melted years from his face.

The Apollyons are *dangerous,* thought David unprompted.

Not for the reasons his father proclaimed, though it was true they were not demonstrably religious people. The danger they presented was more subtle: when they looked happy, one might become beguiled enough to keep ensuring that happiness. He could see why the same man remained with Paul for years if he kept receiving that kind of smile.

"Theo said I had to let my father die," said David, shrugging, heedless of how macabre it might sound. "Perhaps I am different having decided to do so."

But Paul didn't seem to find it macabre at all, and he nodded once. "Yes."

"What's your advice?"

"Don't expect things to make sense."

He felt the scowl cross his face. "That isn't advice."

"And yet, it's the best I can give. Don't keep trying to make things make sense, at least not in the way you've been taught. Chase feeling good." Amused, Paul eyed him. "Follow what feels right."

His scowl became more of a pout. "That doesn't make sense." However, he said it because what felt right was Lennie, and that revelation was new and untested. Lennie felt right to him, but it wasn't guaranteed that he felt right to Lennie.

Paul chuckled. "What did I just say? Look, Mr. Mills. David. I'm not a very intelligent man." David snorted; he doubted that entirely. "But I know what I value. I'm good at reading people. I value love, and I can read you and Mr. Campling like a novel. I think he crashed into your life the same way the last lover I ever had crashed into mine."

David debated telling him exactly how correct he was. "You have little idea."

"Tom can't have told you how we met; I haven't even told him. But..." With the smallest laugh, Paul said, "One afternoon, Alastair ran in here asking if he could hide in my cellar. I'd just inherited this place, and I was alone... and instantly transfixed. So... I did what anyone with no sense would do. I said yes, and down he went through that trapdoor back there."

Listening, choosing not to assert that it was glowing softly, as was Paul, David had to smile. Then he smiled a little less when he thought about one of the two dreams he recalled. He had the sense something a bit strange, one in a small parade of other strange occurrences, might be transpiring. If so, he couldn't say what it might be, and he'd rather listen to a love story than speculate.

"Why did he need to hide?"

"That's a whole separate matter, but it was also about love." Paul shrugged. "Love brought us together, and it isn't always biddable or sensible. In fact, I'd say it almost never is. Which is unfortunate for someone of your temperament, isn't it?"

"Absolutely, yes. I would love for something to be a little more within my control." Sighing, David reached for his wallet and took out enough to furnish Paul with payment for two rooms. He knew it was too much because he and Lennie had just one, but he just felt so bewildered at all of the help, and at not being abandoned, that he wanted to do something to feel less like a burden. Besides, he had been toying with the idea of asking for his own accommodation if it was insisted upon that he remain here.

He hadn't fancied staying in his house alone, anyway, even if he wasn't convinced Ralph, Robbie, or anyone to do with them would come calling to threaten him. Their type of criminality seemed sneaky and evasive, not combative.

Now he didn't want to be his new self in old confines, rooms where he'd conformed and kept silent. The thought grated in his mind.

"No," said Paul, albeit pleasantly.

David brandished the money a little.

"No." Still pleasant, Paul waved a hand in a negative gesture.

"How do you remain in business?"

"In spite of your misguided bewitchment, I somehow do."

Unamused, David said, "Yes, well..."

"Ask your selkie," said Paul, "he's keeping the books now. And when I kept them, I never had any trouble, either."

"He is not my selkie." Apart from needing to assert that, David also wondered what Paul did with his time if he was not keeping the accounts or books.

"True."

Defeated for now, David stopped trying to pay him and put away his money. "Thank you. For... putting us up. I don't know why I ran here." If he pressed himself, he did. But it was true that he couldn't articulate the reasoning with words meant for another person to hear. It didn't feel possible to explain that The Shuck had immediately felt like a safe place to run in a manner that wouldn't sound self-serving.

After all, he had been the one to break Tom's heart and to betray Theo's trust. They had reason to turn their backs on him, and although they hadn't, he still couldn't quite tell why not.

"It's probably one of those things you ought not to question, or perhaps you already know the answer." Paul moved to pass him in the corridor when the bell at the desk in the foyer tinkled gently, and David stepped aside. "If you want to eat tonight, I strongly suggest coming down to the taproom. Mrs. Lloyd would only ever bring Tom or me a tray. I think she made an exception this morning because she felt sorry for you." Paul's steps paused. "And she's a relentless gossip."

———

Lennie went back upstairs quite soon after they'd eaten and David sat with a half-gone pint before Tom said to him from across the bar, "Why are you still here?" The night was young and the room was full of what he presumed were largely regular patrons, as Tom addressed most of them by name.

"Well, your uncle won't let me leave." That wasn't the pure truth, but it sounded better than any garbled explanations involving his fear of being alone in his own house, or his dislike of the mere thought of being out of Lennie's general vicinity.

"Since when do you care about what my uncle says?" Tom reached for David's abandoned pint and drank the rest of it without asking. David raised an eyebrow in reply and received a cheeky grin. "I don't recall you were particularly enamored of him."

"Things have changed, though, haven't they?" David said absently.

"Yes. Do you want some advice?"

"Today seems to be my day for your family to give me advice."

"How do you mean?" Wordlessly, Tom met the eyes of someone behind David and moved to pour a dram, then handed it off to the person.

Impressed despite himself by the movements' fluidity, David said, "Nothing. Paul asked me the same thing earlier."

"Oh, when he pulled you aside? I was glad he did. He said something to you about wanting to keep Lennie here, didn't he?"

Tom's intuition seemed impeccable, these days, and David wondered how much of it was just self-acceptance. The rest might be his comparative lack of constant inebriation. His head had probably cleared entirely for the first time in well over a decade. Once again, David silently marveled at the strength of will Tom exhibited, because the types of changes he had enacted were not generally easy.

"Yes, he did, and then he asked me if he could give me advice."

"I'll give you more, and of a more specific and immediately applicable nature, I'd bet."

"Fine."

Before he replied, Tom poured another dram. Watching, David assumed it was for another patron who'd communicated without any words, but Tom pushed it gently to him.

"I don't like whisky."

"I think even you'd like that one. It's sweet."

Dubious, David gave it a cautious sniff. Realizing it didn't smell nearly as intense as what Theo called an Islay, he took a cautious sip. "It's... gentler than I thought it would be."

"Once you've finished, go upstairs to that room."

It wasn't what David expected him to say, so he spluttered with a bit of the whisky still on his tongue. "I'm sorry?"

"David, he's nervous... and I'm sure he's a little scared of his stepfather, no matter what he says... but it's so plain he wants you."

Clearing his throat, trying to rid it of the burn, David said, "It's not plain to me."

"Yes, because you have the romantic aptitude of a starfish," said Tom. Patiently, he added, "Which is far better than I'd expect of a man with your cold father. You're just not the best judge of others' regard for you."

Wanting to take offense yet knowing Tom was mostly correct, David met his eyes. "All right." He sighed and stood, careful of those around him.

"Finish the whisky."

"Should figure out how to curse *you*," said David, but his heart was not in it at all, and he did as he was told. Proud he did not wince as he drank, he slipped Tom an abashed smile before he turned and made his way for the stairs.

15

I t was quiet and calm up here, secluded enough from the ground floor to feel very private; Lennie relished it. This had probably been more talking than they'd done in weeks, for they were actually a solitary person and it didn't bother them much to keep to themself. Some might wonder if it were due to their ability to sense others, but it really wasn't enough to merit isolation. They were just content to keep their own company.

But this evening, their mind kept straying to David and the idea that they might have inherited acquaintances, perhaps even friends. Nobody seemed inclined to judge them or toss them back to Ralph, and they sometimes knew how David felt possibly better than David himself knew.

"Lennie?" David knocked on the door gently and since they didn't expect anyone but him, they didn't startle. Anyone more nefarious wouldn't bother knocking, anyway.

"Yes?" They didn't bother rising from their chair. Although it wasn't cold, they'd lit a small fire for the comfort and had finally relaxed enough to enjoy it.

There was a pause before David asked, "May I come in?"

Whatever was going to happen here, or rather, down in the taproom, hadn't occurred yet. That would have to unfold in its own time, and it could be the most mundane of things once it finally did transpire. They had no way of forcing the knowledge to become known to them. But it was easy for them to glean what David was experiencing and sorting through, and thankfully he had not been drunk or ill again.

It was invasive to feel too much of it, so they gently kept erecting barricades within their mind to stand between his and theirs. Mr. David Mills was an intense sort of man. He just didn't exhibit much of the intensity.

"Yes."

At their word, he entered. An aura of tentative, inquisitive arousal preceded him. "You know, I could get another room."

"No, it's all right." Lennie wanted to say they'd prefer it if David stayed, but the words couldn't find their way out. Despite understanding David felt something for them, it seemed too vulnerable to actually speak about their own feelings. They watched as David came closer, the firelight burnishing his face and the fine clothing that he'd been wearing for longer than he probably normally wore it.

There was so much about him that signified a different world, including the clothes and undoubtedly the education. Lennie knew they were clever, but they weren't in possession of a university degree. Mum had been insistent upon schooling and reading often, but after Ralph entered both their lives, it was expected Lennie would earn their keep, so schooling stopped.

"You're certain?"

"Yes," said Lennie.

"It wouldn't do for you to be uncomfortable."

"I'm not."

Charmingly flustered, his hands restless at his hips, David said, "Tom sent me up." He sat on the edge of the small, well-hewn table beneath the window, close enough for Lennie to reach over and touch him. The top of his thigh, or the dip of his waist. They didn't, but a smile crept onto their mouth. Maybe the soft-spoken innkeeper was trying to help them. "What?" asked David after a blink.

Their smile grew. "Nothing. Did he send you to bed because he was cutting you off? You don't smell like ale. I mean, you do smell like a pub, but not as though you've been drinking much." Experimentally, they rested the flat of their palm on the table just near David's leg. He glanced at it, then their face. "I'm sure I smell the same, though." Lennie hadn't bathed since before arriving here, nor had they changed their clothes. Overall, hygiene felt the least pressing compared to breathing and sleeping and eating.

They wondered if the lack of primping and washing bothered David; it seemed as though it could. But perhaps he was made of sterner, more pragmatic stuff.

"He sent me up because I have the... what did he say... romantic aptitude of a sea star? A starfish."

"Never seen a starfish in the flesh, as it were. Only drawings."

"Well, they're apparently not ideal Romeos," David said. "Or I was just being teased. Likely that."

"I wouldn't want a Romeo, anyway... that play is awful." They'd seen it performed once, back when the idea of someone dying for them had been a romantic one. Now, they'd much prefer someone lived for them.

And they were quite happy being romantically unentangled. Or they thought they would be until they'd stolen from this man.

Snorting, David shifted on the table, resettling mostly where he'd already sat. "Never heard Shakespeare called 'awful,' but I'd tend to agree in this case. What the hell is romantic about both of them dying?"

"David?"

The impact of his name seemed to still his restless fidgeting, as it often appeared to, and he looked at them. "Yes?"

"Will you kiss me, or should we keep shitting on Shakespeare?" Once the question was out, it couldn't be taken back, so Lennie merely kept themselves still and tried not to look *too* eager. They didn't care that certain things hadn't been discussed, or that David knew little about them other than they were a pickpocket with a stepfather who capitalized on their rather strange aptitudes while essentially blackmailing them into compliance.

Then, they had their answer. In an abrupt movement, in David coming forward from the table to meet their lips as they sat in their chair. In the room itself feeling smaller, warmer, and all the more bearable.

—

Somewhere in the ether, all of his witch-hunting relatives were plotting their direct revenge against his temerity.

David didn't care.

Any wraith could appear in this room and he'd merely put his hand, his fingers, to them as he had with Robbie, and he was sure that unlike a flesh-and-blood man, they'd dissipate rather than become unconscious. Perhaps it was because he knew everything was out of balance anyway now that he'd missed an entire day of normalcy or the hours drifting by in the office on Upper St. Giles, but when his lips met Lennie's, he knew he wanted more than a kiss.

Any other carnal or romantic experiences that had led up to this exact second were inconsequential, yet they had prepared him for what he presently experienced. Bliss of a sort he'd never encountered, though he might've come close. Still, there was a madness and urgency to it that he was certain could have killed him if he wasn't properly prepared by other circumstances.

Then the table creaked and he halted, mumbling, "I'd have thought the chair would've given out before this table."

"Kiss me like that and you can break whatever you want." Lennie got up himself, eyes smoldering, and before David could protest at all, had clambered into his lap. Without thinking, David put his hands on his waist, but could only look up at him with some bewilderment.

"You wanted me to kiss you."

Scoffing, Lennie said, his eyes bright and his face mirthful, "No."

So engulfed by the feeling of having Lennie on top of him, it took a moment for him to realize he was being teased. This seemed to be a common thing amongst those who liked him. He allowed a second for it to settle, then said, "Are you... do you... is there anything you want to discuss?" But he hastened to add, because he did not want Lennie to think any of the answers would disgust him, "I don't *care* what your stepfather thinks or believes. I only care about what *you* tell me."

A bit breathless, Lennie said, "I dress like a man, whatever that means. And sometimes..." he smiled. "No, oftentimes... most of the time. I feel like one." He chuckled. "Whatever *that* means." His eyes were guileless. "I know for certain I'm not a woman. Not at all."

With alacrity, David nodded, fingertips on Lennie's hips. "No." Then he thought, *He isn't. They aren't?* That much was clear.

Exhibiting no small measure of relief, Lennie sighed and studied him. "Really?"

"Yes, really. How... should I talk about you? Or to you?"

Lennie thought about it. "I'm much closer to a man, but I'm... also somewhere in between. So... if it's just us, I'd like to be reminded of that." Hearing this, David inferred neutrality was best and endeavored to embrace it. "Anyone else, though? Those who don't know me well? They should address me as a man."

Feeling slightly as though he'd been blessed with these insights, David nodded. "All right."

"If I start to feel less... between, I'll tell you."

"Good."

"Robbie, believe it or not, never butchers it," Lennie said, clearly musing a little on the subject. "He's never said 'she,' not after I told him the truth."

To that, David only grunted. He knew nothing about this or how it felt, but it seemed the least Lennie's sibling could do.

Maybe mistaking the grunt for a different kind of annoyance on David's part, Lennie said, "I know it's different. Me, I mean. But you don't just see me as some... oddity? For you to..."

David's answer to *that* was another kiss, then reassuring words. He could see this was an area of vulnerability. Given the nature of what Lennie discussed and how they had been treated, he couldn't blame them. "I was intrigued immediately when you bumped into me outside of my office. And I *don't* think you're an oddity."

Lennie's tongue flashed along his, almost as a reward for what he'd said. Or perhaps words were too difficult. David groaned quietly.

"Come to bed?" they asked. "And don't go to your fancy house, tonight."

He nodded.

—

This morning, compared with the one when they'd woken up sick with too much drink on David's behalf, was idyllic. It was also almost perfect, although they felt the bed was a little small to share with someone who stretched out as much as David. Lennie hadn't realized until being in such small quarters with him, but he was quite tall and long limbed. They were on an upper corner of the bed and facing the wall, but they were so warm and content that they would've taken being much more cramped than this.

They imagined that asking for any bathwater *now* would be met with knowing looks, but even that didn't matter in the face of how sated they felt. Eying David in the warming, rising sunlight that shone through the window, they admired his back and smiled at his musculature, which was surprisingly defined for someone who generally kept books or conversed with shopkeepers all the day round.

"You're awake, aren't you?" David mumbled.

"No, not at all."

"Liar," he breathed fondly. "How do you feel?"

"Sublime," said Lennie, after contemplating it for the barest moment.

"Good," said David, and he flung an arm over their chest. He was on his stomach; they were on their back and the limb's weight was most welcome. It felt like something that could keep them safe from interference. Lennie gazed at the chaotic heap of clothing on the rug between bed and hearth. "I hope you don't plan on moving."

"No," Lennie said. It was almost wistful, filled with all the desire they had to remain in bed until every problem they possessed was solved, preferably by someone else, but they knew such leisure wasn't possible.

"Stop worrying so much," said David, the sleep heavy in his smooth voice. Lennie didn't know if he could sense their feelings, or if he just had a precise understanding of their body language. What they felt coming from David was much mellower, and it seemed as though this could be the result of consummation — he might be less strained and peevish overall. But, they'd also taken pains to be less attuned to him, so it was hard to say.

"Fine. But I would like some tea, and... well, not to put too fine a point on it, I need to piss," they said. "But neither of those needs are imperative right this moment." They hugged his arm, peering at his closed-eyed face. It seemed David was hard to rouse after he'd slept the night with someone.

"I won't stop you."

"What the hell do we do all day while we're just... waiting? I keep wondering. I know I said I needed to get away to think, but now I'm away... I can't even think." Much of that did have to do with the lovely man next to them.

"Hm," mumbled David. "I can think of a few things, though I doubt they're of any use." He sighed and rose up a little to look at Lennie. "I know I should speak with Paul today. But it's nothing to do with your stepfather. The only reason The Shuck was so fresh in my mind when we needed somewhere to go was…"

Lennie traced his jaw with their fingertip. "What?"

"I've bewitched the place, supposedly. And while we're here, why not try to fix it."

"You're a witch. Makes sense."

"I don't… I didn't… do it on purpose. I think I know *when* I did." David went almost cross-eyed watching their fingertip on his own flesh. "Benson seems to think…"

"Thinking isn't very much use with things like this. Or maybe you're already fixing it by thinking about it. Who knows."

Falling quiet, David took a few breaths. Then he asked, "How did you come to know about what you could do… what your mother did?"

"She just told me about it, the same way you'd learn about colors or speech. Is Tom?"

"A witch? No… he's closer to you or Paul. Well, maybe. Yes. I suppose."

"Many would lump us all together, even if that Benson doesn't." Lennie smirked. "And what's Theo? He's something."

At that, David chuckled and grasped their wrist gently. "I think you're much more equipped to hear it than I was." He kissed their earlobe and they shivered. "He's a fucking seal. A selkie. You… know what they are, correct?"

"Yes."

Another kiss to their earlobe, paired with a little nip to the same flesh, dissolved their resolution to explore how David had come across the knowledge.

16

Two more days passed without any alarming incidents. No one had broken into The Shuck, and neither had anyone been caught skulking near it. A back window was found mysteriously ajar, but there was no sign of forced entry, so Paul rationalized it as a trick of the breeze or perhaps the building settling.

There was no sense in saying David had found a routine. He hadn't been here long enough for anything about it to feel normal. The constants were the small, shared space, passing Theo in corridors as he went about his work in Paul's study, and trying to get Paul to spend more than five minutes alone with him in a room. He dearly wished to talk a little about his thoughts on his own abilities, but it seemed Paul was unwilling to have a private conversation.

It did, however, feel like David had never been without Lennie. Waking next to them was now the way he wished to start all of his days. As with most of what he thought when it pertained to softer feelings, he had not said so.

Earlier this morning, the closest he got to mentioning it was bringing up clothes.

"I wonder," said David as he was buttoning his shirt, "if we might be all right to go back to Norwich, or if at the very least, it might be all right for me to go to my house here and find some clothes." There had to be some secreted somewhere, even if they were out of fashion or old.

"Is it bad of me to say I don't particularly want to go anywhere?" Lennie replied, resplendently naked and making something of a show of gathering their clothes from the back of a chair. David enjoyed it, but he also knew their bravado was itself a show.

Ralph still disturbed Lennie enough to put off a return journey, even though they acknowledged they'd have to go back soon. They didn't want to distress their landlady, whom they seemed fond of, and while they were visibly unnerved by their stepfather, they admitted it would be best to make this final payment to him. Sever the ties, as imaginary and disingenuous as they were.

From David's perspective, Lennie was under no obligation to Ralph at all, particularly because there was no family money, no business to inherit – and most importantly, Ralph had been nothing but a menace to Lennie throughout their life. However, David doubted many people knew better than he did the lure of a venomous father, so he also empathized with Lennie's quandary. And when one's self was leveraged, it was painful.

For David, this had been by omission and ice, and for Lennie, it was by belittlement and thorns. But he still understood the pain itself, and wished to spare Lennie the experience.

He appreciatively gazed at the elegant lines of Lennie's back. "I know I haven't said so, yet, but I'll go with you when you meet with him. Call on him.

Whatever he chooses it call it." He was sure the man called it something genteel or cozy, rather than what it was: intimidation. Lennie sighed and seemed as though they might protest, so David pressed on. "I know... you haven't known me long, and I have no reason to do it. But you can trust me."

"I do."

Blinking, purely because it wasn't what he expected Lennie to say, David said, "You do? Good. You should."

They turned back to face him and he struggled between wanting to caress them and wanting to listen. "I need to tell you something."

"Naked?" It emerged on a croak.

"I can put clothes on, if you'd rather, but it won't take me long to say it if you keep your hands to yourself."

"I don't know if I can promise that."

Lennie took a few steps closer to him, and he was acutely aware of how sensual it was to have them completely naked just before him while he was almost entirely clothed. "I've seen you in my dreams," they said.

"That may not be the best way of starting this revelation, if you want to finish it," said David. "Depending on what sort of dreams." He was, of course, thinking about lewd ones.

They chuckled and stroked the side of his wrist. "It's true. I dreamt about you before I met you outside your office."

"Before you robbed me."

"I gave it back."

David dipped down and kissed them softly. "And what else?" He didn't refer to the attempted pickpocketing. Lennie smiled against his mouth.

"We're here. Always here. Talking to Paul downstairs, who... I recognize now. Whatever that conversation is, it hasn't happened yet. I never remember exactly what we say, but I know it's... not now. It's... later." They kissed him with a gentle touch. "That's why I followed you into the Sir Garnet. I didn't want to put you off, you see, if we were supposed to meet."

"All right." David held them at the small of their back. He found he felt nothing less than serenity. "Of course, we could have met anyway... but... I am glad you met me then."

"Truly?"

"Oh, yes. You've rewritten my whole story, I think."

"Haven't even known me that long," grumbled Lennie.

"Then come stay with me, and we can take our time."

—

Because he had almost said what he wanted to say to Lennie, he was emboldened enough to ask Paul if he thought it might be all right to go to his house and procure some of his own clothing. Most of it was still in Norwich, but he thought to go to the house in Cromer. So he lingered in the ground floor common area after taking only tea at breakfast, knowing he hovered, but feeling it would be more intrusive to wait outside Paul's flat.

Around eleven in the morning, Paul finally appeared, just as David was thinking of going back upstairs.

"Good morning," he said, blinking as he registered David sat in the tufted chair.

"You're not my jailer, I know, but do you think I could step out and get some clothes from —"

"Must you?" Paul had a large book under his left arm, which he placed carefully on the mantelpiece, seemingly just so he could scowl unencumbered at David. Yet again, David wanted to ask what his experience was with crime or the criminal element.

He could guess there might be some Apollyon family ties to free trading, perhaps, for a lot of it did take place on the coasts. There was less now than there had been a generation ago, thanks to stricter laws.

Father, of course, had seethed about the matter. But from what David had heard, most of the local operations hadn't been massive or violent undertakings. It was expected that he take a hard stance against it, too, but the older he grew — and especially the more he rubbed shoulders with Tom — he was less convinced it was as odious as his father's ilk said it was. After all, it wasn't all infamous pirates and dastardly highwaymen.

Like many opinions he held contrary to those who'd raised him, he'd kept it to himself. It was only the David of right now who could openly declare what he truly thought about something, although it still made him nervous to do so. He hoped that, over time, he might get better at such expressions.

"Yes," he said truculently. "I know you might not care, but I care very much what I'm wearing. And I think I've had rather enough of my life upended... it's a small thing to want a change of clothes. I'd like *some* sense of regularity."

"Restoring that sense by going to your own house might well lead someone back here," said Paul.

"We've no proof of that."

"Isn't it better not to take the chance?"

Exasperated, David leaned forward and spoke emphatically. "You won't even talk to me about what I can supposedly do, so the least you can allow is for me to go on a little walk to get a new shirt."

Little had been said about witchcraft. Initially he'd attributed this to the larger question of housing a stranger and himself when he hadn't been much of a friend to the Apollyons. But the few times he'd tried to raise the topic with Paul, the man deftly avoided it, shifted discussion to something else. David knew he was working, of course, but it was a slightly unexpected reaction.

There wasn't much Lennie could say about charms or bewitchment, other than explaining those who could do it studied quite abundantly to practice with precision.

Since it wasn't what they could do, there wasn't much they could illuminate.

It was possible that Paul was in a similar predicament, and anyway, he had been spending the bulk of his leisure time alone. Tom remarked that it wasn't unusual. It did mean, though, that combined with his apparent reticence, David's opportunities for cornering him were limited.

Rubbing at his stubble with slender fingertips, Paul sighed. "Benson will be back today. He's your man. I promise you, I'm only steeped in folklore and philosophy. I can't teach a fledgling witch anything useful, and I won't have you destroying our livelihoods."

"What?" About to say something else, David's voice rose slightly. "Destroy? You think I could *destroy* all this?"

Apologetically, or the closest David had ever seen him be, Paul said, "Just in case. I don't know what you're capable of and I wouldn't know what to do to instruct you. It could be as benign as you singeing off your own eyebrows, or you could bring down the whole building."

David wanted to say it was absolute fantasy, all pure shit. As with other things of late, he knew that it was not. "Well, what are fledgling witches usually capable of?"

"There's no 'usually' in these matters, is there? Take Benson. He's good at seeing what others can't. He can sniff out the unseen... bewitchments... or ghosts, for example. Though spirits and seances aren't his bread and butter. I think he's a little frightened of them, actually, though he'll never admit to it. Just after Alastair died, I often considered asking if he might try to find him."

"Ghosts?" David hadn't considered ghosts being directly part of witches' lore, but he supposed it made sense.

"Yes."

"You'd have wanted the man you loved with you, even like that?" Irresistibly, David thought of Lennie.

However, Paul obviously wished to change the subject. "He's adept at protection, too."

"Perhaps, then, he's attuned to... people? Life? Spirits?" David hardly knew what he said. Philosophy was one of his favorite subjects of study, but it presented too many unanswered questions. Or too many answered ones that were not decided to his satisfaction.

"It's possible. Why not?" Paul leaned against the wall, gazing at David with speculation. "I've met witches attuned to water, or fire..." he shrugged. "I can't just *tell* you what you have a knack for. Anyway, I don't think it works like that. Trying to say what someone is, only off their look... it would be asinine."

David tried to think about all of this with a level

head. "I see." He moistened his lips slightly, for his mouth and tongue had gone dry, and said, "You might've explained that to me at the outset. I thought you were just withholding for the sake of it, maybe to punish me a bit. I know I haven't always been friendly."

"No," Paul said. David didn't want to know if it was directed at the thought that he hadn't been particularly kind, although he did not think so. Paul did not suffer fools or mistreatment, that he knew. But neither did he seem to hold grudges. That felt apparent, or he wouldn't be here still.

"Are you afraid of me?" he had to ask.

"I am not," said Paul with a smirk. "Not at all, if you want the truth. Doesn't mean you can't accidentally set something aflame or create some other nonsense."

A little peeved at what he perceived as dismissiveness but could have been mild bantering, David said, "I did bewitch your pub."

"Mostly, you broke my nephew's heart. But you didn't entirely damage my business, you just made it a bit... drab and dismal. What you *did* was give it a preternatural head cold. Most of us can still get on with things when we have colds."

He smiled reluctantly at that, finding he liked the metaphor. Thinking about broken hearts, he leaned back in his chair. "Theo mentioned that you were thinking of going to visit Alastair's grave. He said he had more notes for you about Edinburgh. I'd just caught him on his way out, so he asked me where you were... and I asked him what he had." Paul exhibited the smallest of winces, but no more distress than that. "I'm sorry. About everything."

And he was. He had just the faintest recollections

of Alastair, having been far more interested in Tom than his uncle or anyone else who worked at The Shuck. He could only sneak there sporadically, so he wanted to make the most of his time when he did. The man had also left, well, died, when he and Tom were sixteen, and they'd only been flirting around then. Mostly just flirting.

He couldn't imagine what Paul experienced. Which was saying something indeed, because he was acquainted with numerous petty and rather cruel men who might have done the same as Alastair's son had done to him.

"Thank you."

Unbidden, Lennie's image came to his mind, the way they'd looked spent and stretched out on the bed. He blushed, hoping that his high color wasn't too obvious. What he felt for Lennie was distinct from lust, though there was a vast amount of it warming his blood. He knew, as silly as it might sound to others when they'd only been acquainted for so short a time, that if someone were to keep him from Lennie the same way Paul had been kept from Alastair, he'd be no less broken by it.

This was a less daunting prospect than he'd expected it to be. It was far more comforting.

"Will you go?"

"I haven't decided. I keep waiting for him to come to me, in a dream, maybe. I've never been the sort who can see specters."

Rather startled by the intimacy of the assertion, David had the sense it was easier for Paul to talk to someone who was not a total stranger, but who didn't know him very well. Perhaps Theo had heard more of this, too, than Tom ever would.

"You want him to tell you what to do?"

"Well, he'd know better than to try that," said Paul, with the barest smile. "I suppose I want to know if he misses me, the same as I do him. I want to know if it would make him happy to see me, the way I'd be happy to see him."

In an instant, David understood how charlatans could entice crowds to attend seances. Or how, if one truly could communicate with the dead, they might command deep loyalty from those who wanted their services. There was such raw need in Paul's gentle voice that it moved him. Beyond that, though, the rawness roused something outside both Paul and David. Noting it as it shifted in the dark, David said, as though some spirit commanded him to, "He does."

It wasn't a lie or trite words. He knew it; he couldn't explain how he knew it, but something woke around them, like a bygone scent that released from old wood paneling under the right conditions.

Covertly, David watched Paul for any sign of acknowledgement. Then, finding none, he simply waited for Paul to speak.

"I wager you don't even recall him much," said Paul, but he tempered it with a smile and ducked his head a little, almost like a timid boy. "But... it's a lovely sentiment. You're less aloof than you want people to think."

"I always was," said David wistfully. He kept a smile of his own at bay, reflecting upon how Paul had, only moments before, enumerated some of the things witches might do. Yet he also seemed unable to judge that the atmosphere in his own public house had shifted. Or accept that David might actually *know* Alastair missed him.

"If you wish to determine what it is you're talented at doing, preternaturally speaking," said Paul, after a moment of silence between them, "You could think back to childhood."

"I hated my childhood."

Giving a dry chortle, Paul stood straight, easing away from the wall. "Perhaps that's a clue in itself. But, I'm serious. Think about coincidences. Maybe there are patterns that can help you realize?"

This seemed like a much more empowering option than simply waiting for an old mystic who smelled of gin to walk in and start dictating to him what he was. Besides, he had already mused on such things, or started to, after Lennie made a similar comment while stroking his back as they lounged in bed late last night.

"You probably know more than you think," they'd said, which just added to what Theo had told him as he'd been hungover in a comfortable bed that wasn't his own. "I'm sure you've been doing eerie things your whole life and just never realized. Even something strange can be normal if you do it all the time, right?"

Releasing a breath, David nodded, taking into account what his three friends had said. Then he said to Paul, sincerely, "Thank you. Again. For... housing me and feeding me and talking to me about patently mad things. Even if you question my wanting another shirt."

He didn't add, *And for housing and feeding Lennie and talking to them about patently mad things.* But it was implied.

Paul's words were just as earnest, though as ever, they were shaded with his usual dryness. "Couldn't live with myself if I'd turned you out. I seem to be something of a beacon for lads in need, and even though I've seen neither hide nor hair of him for years... if he can see me wherever he is, I want to keep him proud."

He didn't have to replace *he* with *Alastair* for the meaning to be present. Then he smirked and glanced at the ceiling as though speaking to the air, murmuring, "I *am* sorry I never got a cat to replace Sally."

David chuckled, gathering that Sally had been a beloved creature, and he followed Paul as he went through to the taproom with his book once more under his arm.

He was about to volunteer the mouser at his own house as a pet for the pub, as he wondered how Mary was getting on with just a caretaker anyway. She'd always seemed rather sociable when he and Theo were both in residence there. But the same hazy glow he'd noticed the last time he'd spoken to Paul in the corridor had reappeared, emanating from the end of it where the trapdoor was located in the floor.

Rather than ask Paul if he wanted a cat, he started to ask about the light, then halted himself when he noticed a tall man standing directly atop the trapdoor, face tilted downward and obscured by a wide-brimmed hat.

17

"I s there... was there someone waiting to be served?" David spoke to Paul's turned back.

"How do you mean?"

David stared at the man in the corridor, who neither moved nor spoke to acknowledge them. It would've been strange, not to mention rude, to just linger there and David was struggling to see how someone could have been present the entire time. Everything about it felt askew. He said, one foot on either side of the threshold, "There's someone in the corridor."

"If there is, there shouldn't be. There's naught for customers back there." Humoring him, Paul doubled back and poked his head through the doorway they'd just passed through. Quiet, David tried to ground himself in the mundane sounds just outside the windows. Someone shouting amicably as they matched pace with a friend, the calls of gulls, clattering wheels on stone.

"Nobody," said Paul.

Disbelieving his certainty, David looked again. Indeed, nobody was present even to his eye, but the semidarkness seemed charged and he didn't trust it.

"Trick of the light, perhaps." With a frown, he said, "I shall go for a walk after all, and if I *happen* to come back with a few clean things to wear, then..."

"Fine, but it's on your own head."

The tick of the clock on the wall punctuated his words, and David couldn't tell if he was in earnest. "Were you always so dramatic?"

"I prefer thinking of it as pragmatic. Go if you have to, but don't linger. I wouldn't tempt fate, and remember... Benson will be here soon. I'm certain we'll all be able to move forward better with him." Surrounded by a place he'd run most of his life, and one where he'd lived all of it, Paul spoke with the reassuring authority of a calm father.

One, thought David, who was remarkably better at voicing dissent and displeasure than his own father. He was aware Tom and Paul hadn't been close until recently, and it was possible to present various facets of oneself to different people. But the more David spoke to Paul, the more he liked his company, even if Paul was so direct. He found it easy to speak to him and he liked his perspective.

Nodding, he turned to leave. "I'll certainly try to... oh, fuck." Benson was just outside the window and swanning toward the pub, so David halted. There was no mistaking his profile or the voluminous silhouette of his clothes, and the glass was neither dirty nor warped enough to obscure identities. "Of course."

"Oh, take heart," said Paul, smiling when he realized the reason for David's dour words and tone.

"Why?"

"You need to listen to someone who knows what he's on about, *and* he should have news about your staff."

That was something. In retrospect, he was grateful

Benson had been commandeered into the effort. He did wish to know what had transpired with Mrs. Greaves and Ellie in particular, having concluded with reasonable certainty Musgrave must have known what was good for him and stolen away from the to-do Robbie had caused. Robbie had been breathing and physically unscathed when they'd left him in that doorway. But faced with Musgrave's quick and unpredictable responses, he might not have remained so lucky. The unbalanced, kind veteran must've just left.

"I hope so."

"He's rather useless at daily matters." Paul set his book safely aside on the bar. "But his brother isn't, and I'm sure he helped Benson ask the right sort of questions."

"Subtle ones, I should think," said David. He appreciated that Lennie didn't think Ralph was pervasive in his influence, but subtlety couldn't hurt.

Resigned, he sat at one of the empty tables. Presumably by way of consolation, Paul brought him a pint. At least it would give him something to hold, because he didn't really want a drink. The air still felt weighted like the breeze before a storm, and the sense that he and Paul had unearthed something while talking about Alastair lingered.

When Benson entered, he didn't glance in David's direction; he just declared cheerfully as he set his filthy bag on the bar, "Your Mrs. Greaves lives on Magdalen Street very near my brother."

David blinked; Norwich wasn't nearly as parochial as some could make it sound, yet it wasn't so hard to believe that his cook would live close to Benson's relative. "Does she?"

To Paul, who was shelving some bottles, Benson said, "Gin, please."

"Lovely to know she's still with us," mumbled David. He hadn't thought Robbie would have brutalized her, necessarily, but he was in a frame of mind that might lead him to assume the worst within an instant.

"Oh, yes, though she's not happy with the way your door was ruined, I can tell you."

"That was Lennie. And anyway, they said they'd pay for it."

"Well." Benson drank half of the gin he'd been supplied, then spoke up. "Even so, she wanted to tell you she went back the next day and didn't notice anything being burgled, but that might've been because she alerted the constabulary after she heard an intruder enter the house. Snuck out the garden, she said." He drank the other half and Paul tutted. "The police have put a guard on the place."

"And Ellie?"

"Right, the maid. She snuck out the garden, too. Didn't come back with your cook to inspect the premises, but I'm assured she's well."

That left Musgrave, who was much more akin in his habits and disposition to Benson himself. "There's a man called Musgrave, and..." Well, Benson was possibly less mentally adroit in some ways.

"You care a lot about those who're under you," said Benson. He toyed with his beard, which had no seed pearls or wee charms at all, and hadn't since the night David had gotten absolutely pissed. David decided they'd never been of the world itself.

"A habit my family never understood, I promise. Don't worry, most of us are all the same," replied David with a slight sneer.

Easing back from his observation, Benson said, "They took him well in hand, Ellie and Mrs. Greaves."

"What does that mean?"

"Got him to go out of your house, too."

Sighing with relief, David permitted himself a drink of ale. "That was wise of them. He's not entirely well in his mind. I expect if he had noted an intruder, someone would've been shot. Him, perhaps."

At length, as though he had momentarily forgotten but knew he needed to remember, Benson said, "Timmy, that's my brother, he thought to tell the police you were well and unharmed."

"That was well done of him."

David was plotting how best to open the topic of witchcraft when Benson said, apropos of nothing anyone had mentioned, as was seemingly his custom, "Feels different in here."

"Does it?"

Twisting around to sit on his stool while gazing at David, Benson nodded. "Like a thunderstorm." He grinned, displaying only a few teeth. "*You're* the lone tree in a field, lad. I'd best watch myself, if I were you. Ready to talk, then?"

Letting go of any illusions of what was expected, or what he expected, David took a deep, desperate sip. "I am."

"Good. Thought you'd bolt like a hare when I entered a room."

Struggling not to be insulted, David said, "I'm not bolting, now." He wanted to know what could possibly be so complex that Paul wouldn't speak of it with him without Benson present, he wanted to know why he was able to send a spark through a man's chest, and he wanted to know why he suddenly saw a man who apparently wasn't there at all. "Tell me what you know."

"It'll take you a lifetime to know, to understand,

and even then, you'll die at the end of it all. Best not take it too seriously, you know?"

About now, David was poised to fling himself across the room and pummel Benson into the bar. "I don't."

Thankfully, Benson ended his pronouncements more constructively than they had started. "I can start to teach you how to keep yourself in check. I can, perhaps, show you where you're best aligned. It'll take time, though."

"Aligned? You can... tell me what I can... do?" There were moments when all of this still felt so utterly farfetched that he could hardly track what he said.

"Maybe, maybe not." Taking a pipe from a hidden pocket, or an unseen aspect of the world that neither Paul nor David had any access to, Benson lit it, dropping the still-smoking match to the bar.

"I was hoping he wasn't... one of those fire or... water people," said Paul, carefully flicking the match into the nearby hearth from where he stood. "Just to be safe, I waited for you. You've charms to protect against everything, haven't you?"

"He's no water witch. It's too bad he's no makings of a fire one, either... could've become a blacksmith." The man was mad; blacksmiths were becoming more obsolete by the year as technological advancements edged them out of their trade. David reached for his ale.

"I'm sorry, Mr. Mills," said Benson. "You're more my kind of character." With a pipe leaking obnoxious smoke, he eyed David as seriously as a judge delivering a sentence. "Called you a witch when I spooked you, but I think you could be more of a witch-hunter after all."

At that, David stood, still holding his pint. *Witch-hunter* was too close to what Father took pride in. "I won't hurt people. Won't hunt them." Even as he said it, however, he knew he could be induced to hurt Ralph or Robbie. As hypocritical as it might be, he couldn't rouse the same sense of justice when it came to them.

Since he'd been given to believe witch-hunters were ruthless, the antidote to witches, he wanted no part of them. All he'd read convinced him that his perceptions were correct, for they seemed like terrible men insistent upon violence or fraud. Though witchcraft and the preternatural were real, David knew that not every supposed witch who'd been tortured or executed could be, which almost made the idea of a witch-hunter even more repugnant.

It would help if Benson might explain his own ideas on the matter, for clearly he did have some. And David would call him many things, but ruthless or violent – or fraudulent, for that matter – were not terms that came to mind when he thought of Benson.

A little of him was begging to have his biases dispelled. He wanted the initial belief he'd had in witches and witch-hunters being quite similar to be reaffirmed.

"Sit down, lad."

"No."

Paul frowned and looked, for an instant, like he wanted to interject. He seemed to think, then he said, "We know you won't."

"What?" David glowered at him.

"Well, look what you've already done. You're protecting Lennie. Took him here."

"You can choose to be different. I do." Unbothered,

Benson inhaled from his pipe, then exhaled with his chin tilted up at David. "I don't hunt or hurt anybody."

"Then what do you do? Besides sit around and deliver odd proclamations."

"A lot," replied Benson. He was still calm, but David thought he sensed a bit of annoyance in Benson's speech. "I see enchantments, and spells, and curses, and ghosts. I can talk to what others don't hear, though I'm not as blessed in that respect and I don't like the dark, so ghosts aren't my favorite of beings."

"What else?" He felt there had to be more, but even if there was not, he wanted confirmation.

"I can cast them... enchantments, spells, curses. It's not the shit out of fairy stories. It's a subtler art than that, always."

"That all sounds like what witches could do," said David, and he shook his head. "How are you any different from them?"

With a smirk, Benson said, "Point of view. My relations were all told they were witch-hunters, and so that's what they called themselves. I won't claim every witch-hunter in history has possessed a knack for witchery, but some have. Like can find like, and if it's hunt or be hunted, things can become twisted. Compassion might be forgotten."

It was a surprise how helpful this was to hear. "But you've never..."

"You have my word. I've never harmed, or hunted."

Quietly, Paul said, "Things aren't always what they seem. Nobody's calling you a monster."

Deliberating, but only because it was Paul who spoke to him this way, David let his mind fall on the suggestion that Benson saw things others missed, that he was capable of protecting things rather than destroying them. After a few seconds ticked by on the clock, he sat down again. Took a drink.

Benson mumbled, "Now, can *you* tell me about this shadow man lurking in the corridor, Mr. Hand of Glory?"

"How the *hell* could you know about that?" David protested. He couldn't even take issue with the nickname.

"He's poking his head round the doorway," said Benson, as though it was a fully normal thing to discuss.

David, who'd been instinctively avoiding the merest glance in that direction, resisted the urge to look. "I don't know what there is to tell." He felt helpless, for when he'd finally had the mettle to sit near Benson and discuss the preternatural, it seemed nothing would be direct. "He was over by that trapdoor. Couldn't really make out a face because his hat hid it." Benson must have seen the man a little differently than he did.

Paul had stopped moving completely, standing with his forearms on the bar, his face frozen in a dimly terrified expression reminiscent of a child's trying to work out a puzzling equation. Benson was looking at Paul with compassion, which unsettled David. He knew they were friends, but he hadn't really seen Benson exhibit such a soft emotion toward anyone.

Bemused, David demanded of Benson, "What's that to do with me, though? I didn't *cause it*, surely."

"Dunno if you caused it, exactly. I think... in a sense, sort of, you did." Benson's eyes narrowed in thought, then he dared to smile. "You've lifted your own bewitchment. That's why it feels so different."

"Christ, I created a ghost where there'd been a... curse?"

David still wouldn't look at the doorway and just hoped someone of flesh and blood would come through it. Preferably Lennie, who was presumably still upstairs reading, or even Mrs. Lloyd, who was working somewhere in the building. Theo was in Paul's private study; David had seen him before he'd gone up to the flat.

Hell, he'd even welcome the sight of Tom's scowl, though his scowling was admittedly much less present than it had been.

"It was never quite a curse," said Benson.

"Pardon me for not knowing the difference between a curse and a bewitchment."

"And you didn't *create* a ghost. You've just let it come through after keeping it from doing so. You're not dead, are you, and you haven't murdered anyone."

"I may be tempted to, if you keep speaking." The only person he'd thought about killing had been Father, back when he was quite young, but there hadn't been any teeth in the feeling. Lennie's stepfather roused more of a true drive toward violence than his own father ever had.

Benson just shook his head and fell quiet, closing his eyes. Even Paul, who was quite used to his idiosyncrasies, seemed rather perplexed by this behavior.

With a long sigh and after a full span of several minutes, during which David wondered what to do or say, Benson returned his attention to Paul.

It seemed he'd been silently testing the air for currents only he could know, or listening to someone only he could hear, but he did not seem distressed. Only full of gentle regret. That concerned David more than any of his customary blithe levity.

"Well, Mr. Apollyon... I think you might've gotten your wish at long last."

18

Lennie had never been more bored and more invigorated in their life.

Bored because they weren't given to idleness, which was what sitting around reading for a good part of the day felt like, yet invigorated by the presence of so many new beginnings. The start of friendships, and whatever might grow between them and David, neither of which they'd sought. Really, these potentials were what had kept them here longer than the day or two they'd originally envisioned staying. It had not been terribly longer than that, but to someone who rarely had leisure time and made their living by their wits, it felt like half a century.

They went down the old stairs and followed the voices below, hearing what they thought were David's studied, polished tones in conversation with others. It was still early in the afternoon, and though The Shuck seemed to have a few boarders and did brisk trade in the evenings, the afternoons had been fairly quiet.

When they walked into the taproom, they might've cut the tension like the strawberry jam topped cake they'd been brought on their first night. Paul was, as he always seemed to be, behind the bar, staring at

Benson. David, meanwhile, was sitting at one of the several tables, a mostly empty pint near his left hand.

Lennie decided immediately that they could do with one of Paul's ales, which they'd found to be stronger than many other landlords' and preferable to most others they'd had. Whatever was going on, it couldn't be good. Heedless of the tautness between the three men, or at least disregarding it in the hopes of defusing things, they went to Paul. "Pint, please? The same I had last night."

They did not present any money, which still felt very strange; he hadn't and seemingly wouldn't take it for food or anything else. Whenever this was all resolved, they were going to leave the Apollyons at least twice of what they were owed.

Paul looked abstracted, but he did focus on Lennie. Without a syllable of acknowledgement, he pulled the pint and gave it to them.

"Thank you," they said.

"Paul," said Benson, "I think it's him."

Lennie slipped next to David and took a seat. It was the gentlest, most tentative way they'd heard Benson speak, though they hadn't heard him speak overmuch. "Who?" they asked David quietly.

He glanced at them and grasped for their free hand, about to reply.

But Paul spoke with rancor first. "Rubbish."

David gave Lennie's hand a little squeeze. They sipped their pint to give themself something to do, unsettled by the bitterness in Paul's voice.

"It's not," Benson said.

"You're quite correct. It's not rubbish; it's shit," said Paul. "You've been back less than an hour, and you come in with your cryptic little phrases and glib humor... how the fuck do you know?" His arms were crossed over his trim chest and he was breathing deeply. Lennie did not know him well, but they knew enough to understand he was a mild-mannered person who was not prone to charged displays like this one.

"Who else would it be, and now?"

"Why him, and why now?" Paul countered.

Utterly perplexed, Lennie looked to David for some clue and he shook his head minutely, as though helpless. "I... we... we'll... we should leave you to it," he said, his eyes on the two men.

Neither Benson nor Paul looked at him, each seeming intent upon willing the other to understand something that was not actually being said aloud. David stood carefully. Rather than relinquish his hand, Lennie rose too, but took several gulps of their pint before setting it upon the table. They eyed it wistfully and wished Paul might consider taking a rather old apprentice, or at least tell them how he did it.

"Well, there's been a disruption." Benson jerked his head in Lennie and David's general direction. "It's them who brought it. Maybe Mr. Mills' bewitchment had him all repressed and whatnot. It's only been starting to lift within these last few months, and now he's here." Benson gave a little shrug. "Maybe them coming here was meant to happen."

At that, Paul did look at David.

Lennie felt compelled to step between them due to the severity of the expression. So they did, a little, edging just in front of David's taller form. "Who's *him*?"

Instead of answering the question, Paul said to Benson with his burning gaze still on David, "Alastair's not here."

Benson countered, "He could be." Lennie read

nothing but sympathy in Benson's rheumy eyes. "It looks a bit like — definitely feels like — him, to me. I can't hear him, yet, but give me a little time. It's been a while since I've done this, and I don't particularly like it."

Meanwhile, Paul's voice was desperate. "That's all very well for you, but I can't feel a damn thing. Can't see a damn thing. Can't hear a damn thing." He inhaled sharply, looked like he was going to say something more, then shook his head with marked vehemence and quit the room in a silent rush of dark clothes.

Lennie still could not tell what was transpiring, but they didn't move away from David, taking comfort in his ambient presence just behind them. Benson murmured, as though sharing a grave confidence with both of them, "I am glad you came here. Both of you, but you, Mr. Mills, in particular."

"Why?"

Sharing the confusion, Lennie agreed with the one-worded question. It felt as though they and David had actually created more of a problem for Paul, if he'd been induced to flee like he just had.

As he seemed to gather his thoughts, Benson spoke slowly. "Since January, I've been experimenting with how to lift what you put on The Shuck. It wasn't horrendous, as you know, but when you made it, you were angry and frightened and heartbroken." Benson's thick, gray eyebrows rose. "And young. Nobody wanted you to suffer while I was lifting it, so I worked as gently and carefully as I could."

"How would I suffer?"

"If someone like you or me sends something back to whoever made it, it can create recoil. Think of firing a rifle."

Lennie, although the words were not directed at them, nodded. Mum had explained something of the kind. Magic generated its own energies, but it took from a person. "If you had just done away with it yourself, David would have known it... even if he didn't know why. He'd have felt ill, or tripped over his own feet and hurt himself, or... something like that." Benson inclined his head in an affirmative. They thought that if David had not intended to do anything to The Shuck, which he hadn't, the tax on his body wouldn't be so very high. But it would still be noticeable.

David frowned and Lennie wanted to kiss the disgruntlement from his face. They did not. He said, "How does that follow?"

With a patience Lennie would not have expected from Benson, he said, "It's yours. You were supplying it. You've been continuing to do so until, well... not precisely this moment, but... very recently. Between what I was doing to understand the bewitchment, and whatever you've been doing to feel more..." Benson's eyes swept David. "Yourself, I think you've finally recanted it."

Lennie was only sorry they could not feel a shift in energies to verify what Benson explained. They did believe him, for nothing he said was outlandish after growing up with their mother.

Continuing, Benson said, "When Alastair first died – I never told Paul this, because I didn't wish to add to his heartbreak – I did sense him here. For a bit. After that presence dissipated, I assumed it was only the natural order of things. Ghosts are common after a death, whether they're echoes or sentient. But..." he gave David a shrewd glance. "Perhaps you, in laying your unintentional little not-curse, drove him out."

"If he's back. Why can't Paul see him?" David asked. "Or feel him, like you can?" He added, and Lennie was proud he included himself, "Like... I can."

"I'm no great thinker, lad, so I can't say. But I'd guess it's hell on them both."

"You knew him better than I did, of course," said David, and he took a seat again, brushing his palm against Lennie's hip as he did so. Lennie sat, too, and rather than interrupt, they took another drink. "I was only ever here for Tom, and frankly... even though I'm sure I'm not picturing his face properly, Alastair scared me a bit."

"To the likes of you, he'd be terrifying." David narrowed his eyes, yet didn't speak up for the honor of toffs everywhere as he appeared ready to do. "But he was a kind man. Bit troubled, though, and tighter than wax about why." Looking to the doorway as though he'd sighted someone, Benson said, "He's not distinct to my eye, yet, but I could make out the outline of his hat and hair. Kept it long, you see, and the hat was old but he loved it."

Appearing lost in his own thoughts, David nodded.

Running his fingers along his dry lips, Benson sighed, thoughtful rather than truly distressed. "More than that, though... doesn't matter what I see. I expect to turn around and see him. Seems like he's entered the room."

"Theo told me what happened."

"Oh, yes. Awful." Gruff, Benson relit a pipe that had rested before him on the bar. If Lennie didn't know better, they'd say Benson seemed nervous.

"What happened?" Lennie said. "Who's Alastair?"

"Paul's lover, who happens to be dead," said Benson. "He's often said he wouldn't mind being haunted."

"We were talking before you returned, Benson, and he did..." David paused. "He mentioned it. But then he said he wanted to know if Alastair missed him, the same as he missed Alastair, and... I told him he did."

Lennie was still contemplating the thought of someone's dead lover coming back to haunt their public house, but as David spoke, they were pulled back into the present moment. "Why?" they asked. David's tone seemed to be implying this went beyond the benign well-wishes you might give to a bereaved person.

The idea of specters didn't bother them much, if there was one hovering about. They'd always been more occupied with the ills the living could create. Then again, though, the tales Mum had told usually involved the ghost telling living people something urgent.

Rather at a loss, David said, "I knew it. I didn't hear anyone say it, but it felt like someone... nodded their assent as soon as Paul had spoken. Told me to say it. Then, not long after that, I saw a man standing over that trapdoor, the one that leads to the cellar."

Avid as a bird of prey, Benson said, "You really are more like me than you'd like to be. When he's calmed down, have Paul tell you how he met Alastair."

"He already has. What has that to do with anything?"

"Well, it involves Paul hiding him away down there, doesn't it? Makes some sense you'd see him nearby."

"Do you think it's a bad sign if Alastair is around, again?" Lennie asked. They couldn't help but feel it did have something to do with them and the factors they brought into Paul's life.

Benson breathed out smoke through his nostrils and waggled his head.

Impatiently, Lennie pressed, "Do you?"

"Could be an ill omen," said Benson. While he didn't seem especially concerned, Lennie felt mounting nervousness. They tried to concentrate on the lifted not-curse being the cause of Alastair's presence, and found it was not enough to placate them. "Probably isn't. I think he's back because the bewitchment is gone. But I won't know for certain until I talk to Alastair."

Even David seemed somewhat swayed by Lennie's question. "It might be too much to be coincidence. In fact, I've rather given up believing in chance. Someone's going to have to convince me it exists, actually."

Fighting a lurking sense of betrayal, for they'd wanted to count on David's sense of pragmatism, Lennie said, "I can leave. I meant to leave, anyway. If I go, then Ralph or Robbie or whoever else won't come sniffing around Mr. Apollyon. That's one risk we can eliminate."

"That's not necessary, surely." David was adamant. Anyone could read it in his voice or his words, but Lennie also felt his utter resolve in their chest, their bones. Really, it was gratifying that he didn't want to be parted from them.

Still, they were adamant, too. "It's one thing I feel like I can control. And in most of the ghost stories I've heard, the ghost usually wants to avert disaster."

———

They were making the bed when soft footfalls came and stood in the doorway to the room. It wasn't David. His were heavier and louder. It could be the ghost of a dead lover; if it was, Lennie would explain they were going and Paul Apollyon would be safer once they were on a train back to Norwich. They'd also explain how Ralph wasn't likely to retaliate once they'd just abandoned their own pride and paid him.

It felt like capitulation, but it was better than letting someone who seemed inordinately kind potentially fall afoul of a petty man with a collection of pistols and terrible opinions. They couldn't let Paul suffer for their own weakness. They weren't a child whose existence depended upon a stepfather; they could put their foot down and have nothing more to do with Ralph. Perhaps they'd been wrong to assume ignoring him, avoiding him, would yield the same results as confronting him.

And even if he wanted to report them to someone, who would it be, and who would care? If he set foot in any learned man's office, a doctor of the body or mind's, it was obvious that he couldn't pay for any services. He certainly couldn't pay for any kind of incarceration or continued care.

They shuddered at the thought. There was no money to be had from Ralph, and they suspected that lack would go a long way in protecting them.

If only taking that risk felt less frightening.

They tried to view it logically and succeeded only minimally in calming their nerves. *Even if he tries to tell everyone he knows about you, failing having you locked up or worse... who does he actually know?*

It wasn't as though they had any place in society, either, or any family or friends to speak of. No one would turn their backs on them; no business matters would be compromised. There was Robbie, they guessed, but he already knew all about them. They plumped a pillow with a rather enthusiastic punch,

musing on Alastair and what David had said on the
train about him, the renaming of the Apollyons'
public house.

He came here, so why couldn't they just go where
he'd come from? Luckily, their skills were tremen-
dously portable.

"What're you doing?"

It wasn't a specter. Lennie finished smoothing the
linens and turned to face Paul, whose cheeks were
pale and nose was red. "You move like a cat."

"So my housekeeper tells me all the time."

"I should thank you for your hospitality."

Inexpressive but for the preoccupied look in his
eyes, Paul asked, "Did Benson spook you?"

"No. It would take someone far worse than him
and his odd ways to scare me."

"Then... if you're going... why have you decided to
leave, now?"

Warily, Lennie said, not wishing to seem as though
they were drowning in self-pity, "If David... Mr. Mills...
hadn't brought me here, everything would be simpler.
Less... fraught."

"Would it?"

No. Even if they hadn't come here with David, they
would have to confront their stepfather or wait for
him to die. But they'd tried ignoring him and received
nothing good from it. "Probably not. But it would just
be me caught up in it."

Running his hand along the doorframe, Paul murmured, "You don't have to be alone, you know, for
everything to turn out well."

They swallowed, their throat suddenly a little dry
with looming dread, and disregarded his words. "I
don't believe you're in any more danger than you were,
because as you've told me... this place is protected."

To that, Paul blinked, then nodded to the chair within the room. "Might I?" Lennie was surprised he asked permission in his own establishment, but they nodded and he crossed the threshold to sit in the chair near the fireplace. "Is that what Benson thinks? That the ghost of my dead beloved is some kind of omen?"

Hesitant, finding it next to impossible to explain that it was their own fear, as irrational as it might be, Lennie said, "No." Then, they sighed. Mussing their hair idly, they added, "I'm as blind to spirits as you. Nothing feels different to me. I'm not like Mr. Mills or Benson."

"You can call him David."

"Of everything I've just said, you're addressing that?"

"It's the one thing I can address with certainty. I don't see ghosts. Never have, probably won't. But for years, I wanted so badly to summon him. Until this year, I kept my flat all the same as it was when he was alive." Paul's face tightened for a second, then relaxed out of a wince. "It didn't bring him back. But I succeeded in driving my nephew away when I could've helped him." He smiled briefly at Lennie. "Promised myself I'd stop pushing away people who needed me."

Implicit in Paul's kind addition and his smile, Lennie thought, was how he believed they needed him. *Maybe I do.* But what did it matter, if all they did was run away and pretend their problems weren't there to be contended with? They could hardly expect Paul to employ them, for example, when he was already employing several people including his nephew and Theo.

"I need to settle things with my stepfather," they said. "I'm to blame for how he treats me, anyway." They pressed their lips together. It was too much to say and they hoped Paul would just be genteel and ignore it.

Naturally, he didn't. "Can't imagine how anyone would be liable for another's ignorance... or any of its pernicious impacts."

"No, not... he *is* enormously horrible." They threw their arms out a bit in emphasis. "But *I* was the one who suggested my mother could steal from her employer because she had the sight. She could see things and find things."

That night by the meager fire was rich in Lennie's memory. In a fit of pique, they'd made the suggestion in front of both Ralph and Mum, and if it had been just Mum, all would have been well. They were young and rebellious, and hadn't liked their mother's new husband almost from the outset. He was too supercilious, too eager to let Mum work while he did very little, the minimum amount he could for whatever job he'd undertaken that week or month.

Ralph was not as dull as he purported himself to be, or perhaps Lennie had misread him. He was certainly more manipulative than he first appeared, or he became emboldened by the security granted by his recent marriage. It had started as a tryst, and Ralph hadn't said a cruel word or raised his hand to her, so it ended in a proposal.

Because Mum had already trusted him and nattered to him about her ways, he knew Lennie was not being fanciful or silly when they demanded, one momentous night, "Why can't you just *take* Mrs. Thorpe's pearls and her baubles even if they *are* hidden? Perhaps we'd be less hungry if you stole and sold them off somewhere. She'd never blame *you*, Mum."

Paul took a breath and it interrupted their pensiveness.

He said, "We're all reckless when we're young. Hell, David — *Mr. Mills* — managed to bewitch a whole public house. Even if you did give Ralph the idea to take advantage of your mother... or you... you're not to blame for anything he does to you. Says to you."

"Or makes me do?" Their smile was shaky, and they could see that the implications of what they said caused Paul some distress.

"What does he make you do?" The question was asked as though it might end in Ralph's murder, and Lennie was very grateful for the protectiveness.

"Oh, no, not like that. Thank fuck. My mother made no secret of her abilities or mine, and unfortunately, he knew I could do similar things." Lennie chuckled darkly. "She can't have stolen from *all* of her employers or she would have been ruined, impossible to hire." Paul nodded a little. "He had me start to follow wealthy folk years ago, observe them and pick-pocket them. He wanted the income from Mum *and* from me."

Frowning in thought, still seated, Paul stretched out his legs before him. "Can he see anything himself?"

"No. He's mostly just a bully with a handful of pistols, and a son from his first marriage. At least Robbie never insults me the way his father does, though." Ruefully, Lennie thought, not for the first time, that had Ralph been less pernicious overall, they might have had a chance of being allies with Robbie.

They'd found their own place to live with great relief, but residual guilt did linger. It wasn't in their nature to believe others didn't deserve help just because they hadn't received any.

"Don't leave."

"You've only just met me. I'd *make* me leave if I brought me all this tumult."

"Then... it's fortunate I'm not you." Running a hand through his hair, Paul smiled a little. "In truth, I would be vexed if you left on my account. *If* there's a ghost, and *if* it's Alastair, and *if* it's some kind of harbinger, I won't hold you responsible for anything that happens to me."

Premonitions aside, witches aside, specters aside, Paul was truly one of those men with integrity. Lennie sat on the bed they'd just made. "I've seen The Shuck before. I've seen you before."

"In dreams, I wager?" He chuckled. "Or do they sometimes come out of nowhere and incapacitate you for a moment?"

"Dreams, mostly, but I can kind of... only sometimes... I can experience things others feel or do." Lennie huffed. "I don't know if that's foresight, though."

Lifting a shoulder in an eloquent shrug, Paul said, "The way I see it, it's probably from the same source, not that I have any idea what the source itself is. Why else would there be overlap between witches and seers and whoever else? Regardless." His mouth lifted into a gentle smile. "You have seen me."

"Yes, downstairs. But whatever that is, whenever that is, it hasn't happened yet and," they added hurriedly, "it's not bad. It's just... we're just talking." Though they'd explained it to David in brief already, it felt no less confusing that what they remembered was only the setting itself and the barest idea of a discussion. They usually recalled their dreams.

Still, even if they did not remember the exact words or even the general topic itself, they knew through instinct that it was yet to occur. While they had immediately recognized The Shuck as soon as they'd set foot inside, then knew Paul as the man they'd seen, they hadn't had any sense of events repeating.

But would they really be repeating? This was something they often pondered, because contemplating the logistics of their abilities was appealing. Did things happen for the first time when they dreamt them, or did they only happen for the first time when they were awake? Smothering a chuckle, they already suspected that such talk would confound David.

"Then that must mean I survive any danger headed my way, if it hasn't happened and the discussion doesn't seem bad." Paul's smile grew. "This is all much too interesting for me to demand you go, you know. Even if I was the sort of man who could turn his back on you, I don't think I would prefer you left."

Appreciating his matter-of-factness even if they were mystified by it, they nodded, ducking their head a little out of slight embarrassment. For so long – most of their life, not that they were even so old – they'd assumed it would be wisest to count only on themself. It would be wrong to say they were bitter, for they weren't, not by most measures. Lonely, perhaps, but not given to resentment.

For this almost stranger to be offering calm strength and camaraderie without any suggestion of manipulation was almost too much to bear. "All right." They endeavored not to let him regret his generosity of spirit.

19

Some hours after they'd gone to bed, Lennie was roused by some phantom sounds that compelled them to creep downstairs. Mostly to satisfy their curiosity, and partially because until they'd done so, they knew they wouldn't be able to sleep again regardless of how thoroughly David had exhausted them.

Drawing from years of practice at stealth, they made it without any creaks or clicks of their own. "You heard it, too." Paul's voice came from the dark common area nearest the stairs, and they jumped very slightly.

When Lennie looked at the closest chair, they could make out his form and the glint of his eyes. They took the final step down and crept to his side. "I don't always sleep very well," they murmured. "Ironically. Or perhaps I do and I'm just easy to wake." They'd slept better these last several nights alongside David than they had in years, but nearly a lifetime of being easy to rouse couldn't be shaken. In addition, they did feel nervous the longer they stayed at The Shuck, yet could not bring themselves to leave. Some of that agitation likely leaked through into their sleeping brain.

"I guess this means David is a heavy sleeper when he's satisfied?"

To that, they raised an eyebrow, although he was correct and wasn't being crude. "It's probably not gentlemanly for me to say."

Paul grinned. "No, but I'm no gentleman, even if you are." Then he said with more seriousness, "If there's anyone here who shouldn't be, Benson is useless this late. Old age and alcohol. I've another two men who live here all the time, but one of them is off with his mother in Great Yarmouth and the other sleeps like the dead. The other two guests have gone, so those rooms are empty."

"What did I hear? I was half-convinced I was hearing things." They didn't entirely trust their sense of what Cromer should sound like; they'd never visited previously, and their present visit was not normal enough to give them a decent sense of the place. "What did *you* hear?" He must have a deep sense of what sounds were right for the place down to the hour of the day or night.

There probably couldn't have been an intruder inside the pub, or he would not be so calm. Then again, thought Lennie, as their eyes adjusted in the dark, his calmness could've been due to the pistol in his lap. Immediately, they regretted not taking the pistol David had brought with him.

"Hard to say for sure. Do you know, I've never had a robbery here? I'm sure there has been one, but it would've been before my time. Before my parents' time... perhaps in my grandparents' time."

"Is that because of the sigils and charms?"

Paul was going to reply until they both listened to

a creak that radiated from the direction of the kitchen. He cocked the pistol and held it steady; Lennie was poised to jump at an intruder. How they were going to avoid being shot did not occur to them until several seconds after they'd heard Paul's gun click. But it was only Mrs. Lloyd, whose room was nearest to the kitchen and back door.

That creak was the most noise she made while walking, for she approached without any other sounds and said to Paul when she was quite close, "I heard someone sneeze."

With a small frown, Paul answered Lennie before he answered her. "Could be. No magic in the world can promise safety, but it can discourage would-be thieves."

"Perhaps my mum's employers should've considered hiring a witch of their own."

"Whoever it is," said Mrs. Lloyd, "if it is indeed someone... I thought I heard them turn for the back stairs."

While Lennie couldn't be utterly sure if Paul was musing on the possibility that his Alastair was haunting The Shuck, they felt the longing was expressed on his face. They had observed that he was really the only person who used the rear stairs, for the stairs led from outside directly to his flat. He and Alastair both must have used them when the latter was living here. It seemed the building, perhaps because it was old, had undergone different renovations and additions in its lifetime. Though charming, it had a logic all its own, such as Mrs. Lloyd's room being a former cupboard, and one of the landings containing a small door that opened to reveal only a wall rather than storage space.

Lennie gazed at Paul with compassion.

Setting his jaw, Paul nodded and stood up. "Shall we go take a look, then? If we take these stairs..."

"I shall go to the base of the others and wait," said Mrs. Lloyd. Lennie hadn't seen her makeshift weapon until just then. It was a very sensible brass candlestick. It might've been pewter, or silver, but regardless of what it was, the metal gleamed slightly. Her delicate hand tightened around it as she spoke.

"Very good." Paul seemed satisfied enough with her ability to hold her own. In a fight, Lennie would have backed Mrs. Lloyd, too.

Lennie followed Paul up the stairs, past the floor where their and David's room was located, and stood outside the door to Paul's flat for the first time. Though David did not seem to know much about it, he'd told Lennie the flat had supposedly been untouched since Alastair's death, something even Tom hadn't known for certain until several months ago. It had been a sort of local legend, the tale of the eccentric proprietor whose rumored lover left him and never returned, rendering him not quite right in the mind.

Then Paul himself had told Lennie he didn't touch anything, hoping it might help Alastair make his way back.

Lennie nervously chewed their lower lip as Paul listened for a moment, lingering near his own closed door. His hand was on the doorknob; he tested it gently and grunted when he ascertained it was still locked. Gingerly, pistol still in his other hand, he positioned the key and unlocked it.

"I shall go first," he breathed. Lennie didn't like the idea. If anyone should go first, they thought, it should be them. They had a funny, ill feeling about this entire affair.

Nonetheless, they nodded once, their eyes on the old wood before them, and murmured, "All right."

The door came open and Paul barely nudged it with the back of his knuckles.

Lennie waited for a gesture, any small movement to indicate it was fine to proceed.

But a muscular, sleeved arm snaked out from just beyond Paul's left side. As soon as he was just inside the room, it pulled him close to an unseen body. About to cry out for someone, anyone, or charge forward to protect Paul themself, a familiar voice stopped Lennie cold. "Make a noise, Lennie, and I'll slit his throat," Robbie said quietly.

Quickly, they came inside the flat and didn't bother to take in their surroundings more than the brief amount it took to make sure they wouldn't trip.

"Shut the door."

Lennie obeyed Robbie, thinking as adroitly as they could. He held Paul fast against himself, a wicked knife at his neck. Not for the first time, Lennie cursed Robbie's size. It did leave them at a considerable disadvantage. And Paul was not a substantial man. He was admirably serene, though, seeming quite aware that he could neither overpower this stranger, nor shoot him anywhere without being killed as he did. Lennie's eyes were on the blade itself. They had no doubt it was kept sharp.

"Now," Robbie said, his lips just next to Paul's ear, "If you'll be so kind and put the pistol down on that little table, just there." He meant a delicate, round table of the kind kept in a lady's parlor. Paul, barely moving more than the hand holding the pistol, complied and set it down carefully.

Metal clattered on varnished wood, and all Lennie could hear after that was Paul's deep breathing, almost like it was their own. They resented that Robbie would use their scruples against them. He would know they wouldn't want someone hurt on their account, and whatever he wanted, he would try to get by leveraging that threat. Though they weren't sure if he'd come under duress or his own volition, he was here.

Deciding now wasn't the right time to ask, Lennie waited for him to speak again.

"Thank you," said Robbie. "I've no quarrel with you, you see." His eyes met Lennie's. "I don't even have one with you, really. I just want you to come home."

Lennie found their voice and said carefully, "It's not home to me."

"No, well, I can't blame you for thinking it isn't. He's not a kind man and he was never kind to you at all. You know, I don't think you're strange. Live and let live, eh?"

As children, Robbie and Lennie never scrapped beyond some normal spats between siblings. As they grew older, Ralph had stepped in and made his prefer-ence for Robbie clear, but that had quickly shifted to make way for his avarice toward Lennie's particular skillset.

While Robbie had been jealous at first of what he saw as his father colluding with his sibling, as time passed, he realized they were not particularly close to each other. He'd witnessed how poorly Ralph spoke to Lennie, something that only continued as they chose not to conform to what was expected of them.

He just didn't know how to stand up to Ralph, even if the cruelty seemed to disturb him. Lennie couldn't blame him, but they had wished he'd try until finally, the hope just died. They ventured a cautious guess at something that might compromise Paul's safety if the answer made Robbie angry enough.

"Is he not being kind to you, now?"

His answering laugh was brittle. "He doesn't always know what's really going on. I've kept him even more unaware of your little adventure. He just thinks you've been taking more time to rob your toff blind. Thinks there'll be lots of money after this one is done. He's *proud* of you."

"You've been covering for me?" Incredulous, Lennie wanted to keep Robbie talking.

"Of course. What did you think was going on? He'd have my hide if I told him you'd left the city." Robbie scoffed. "I woke up after that toff did something to my heart. I assume you two dragged me off to that doorway?"

Mutely, Lennie nodded.

"I knew if I went and told Father the truth, he'd be livid. His golden goose escaping? He can't have that."

Paul's throat must have been dry, or more constricted than Lennie could see, because he gave a little cough. "I didn't know he still cared that much about what I brought him," they said. "Thought he was just doing it to be cruel, because he can, because I'm..."

Petulantly, Robbie shook his head. "He's fucking lazy, and you know it. That man will never do things for himself; he'll just keep dragging us into his affairs until he dies. And he's not well, so it's only going to get worse even if it's not forever. I need help."

Willing themself to stay still, though they wanted to try to rush at Robbie and grapple with him until Paul was able to get free, Lennie asked, "What do you want from me, then?"

"Take whatever you want from Mr. Mills, all he's got. We can take anything valuable from this flat, too. And come back with me."

"Why?"

"I told you. Father would be... upset. If he lost you."

Surely it didn't matter so much. Those days felt finished, and Lennie had believed they were done when they'd started to rent their own rooms and live more autonomously from so-called family. Then, it came to them. "He's made you *responsible* for me." The small play of vulnerability on Robbie's carved features, only there if one knew how to see it, said they were correct. "You're going to be punished if he can't find me whenever he wants to."

At that, Robbie did nod, and he appeared more like the little boy they'd met before Ralph and Mum were married. Lennie wanted to harden their heart against him, and they were vigilant and furious, but it was impossible to fully hate him.

"He's old. He'll be gone soon. Then you'll never have to see me again." Whether out of subconscious emotion or calculated malice, Robbie pressed the blade more pointedly into Paul's neck. "Come along, Lennie. I can tell you don't want me to hurt him. Don't know who he is to you, but if you didn't care, you wouldn't still be talking. You'd just run, like you ran away from us, and like you ran here."

Us seemed more like *me*. Lennie winced when a thin, dark line started to seep from broken skin under the knife's point. It wasn't so difficult to see up here in the flat, for Paul had left the curtains open. The moon, though it was not full, created just enough ambient light. They tried one more verbal defense, or perhaps it was an offense. "You're not a killer."

It was a gamble, for certain, because in the last two years they had been out of the house, they didn't actually know what Ralph expected of Robbie. Initially, it had just been pickpocketing and thievery, none of which involved murder even if it had involved making threats.

"No, but my father could be. His brain's gone funny of late. He's more aggressive."

"Look, I'll go back with you. I'll tell him whatever you want. I'll take all of David's money, anything he has on him that's worth something. But you have to let Mr. Apollyon go."

Paul started at Lennie, and once again they admired his coolness. If they were in his position, they likely would have been stabbed by now while trying to get free. Better stabbed than pinned, from their perspective.

Their sincerity seemed to be softening Robbie a little.

He stopped pressing the knife's tip into Paul's flesh. "You're not lying."

"Swear on my mother's grave."

Robbie knew they wouldn't, unless they were serious. "All right." But he didn't lower his arm or stop restraining Paul. "We'll have to come up with a story on the way back, something believable. You're unpredictable, though, so I think he'll believe you just took off for a bit of time alone."

"Of course," said Lennie impatiently. "Let Paul go. You have my word and you don't need to hurt him to make your point."

They breathed a sigh of relief when, at last, Robbie relaxed his hold and Paul gasped.

What they didn't quite expect was for the slight innkeeper to position himself adeptly enough to deliver a quick hit to the chin that spoke of much practice. Who he'd practiced with was a mystery, but it did seem whoever taught him made sure he knew how to compensate for his comparatively smaller stature.

Inarticulate at the sight, they gawked as Robbie crumpled, the wall behind him taking his weight as he slid into a lifeless heap.

Once the heap came to a stop, Lennie remarked, "Well... that's... efficient."

"He shouldn't have held a knife to my throat," said Paul hoarsely. "I may feel sorry for him, but there's just no need for that."

20

U nder the false assumption that a bit more light would make everything feel more manageable, Lennie found a candle and some matches. Striking one, they lit the candle and held it out toward Paul, who was quietly righting himself as he gazed down at Robbie. "Who taught you to hit someone that way?"

He licked his lips slightly before he glanced up at Lennie and replied, "Well, if your husband had been a, um, free trader before he ended up keeping a pub with you, you'd probably learn to fight, too." There was a wickedly amused look in his eyes. "He always said I should learn on account of being a runt. I take his point, now."

Lennie tried not to laugh and didn't succeed. It was the combination of the shock of seeing Robbie, Robbie holding a knife to Paul's throat, and all the guilt they felt that it was happening in the first place. They chuckled, then devolved into giggling. "I'm sorry."

Tolerantly, Paul smiled. "He's your stepbrother, I take it?" It was more of a rhetorical question, one being used to expel some of the tension and nerves he must have felt.

Taking a breath, Lennie said, "Yes. He's younger, though he may not look it. I was the runt, too."

Paul said, after a pause, "I don't envy his life."

Surreptitiously, Lennie stepped closer to him and used the candlelight to inspect his neck without touching him. The wound wasn't awful, but it had broken the skin and caused a moderate amount of bleeding that was already clotting. Most of the surrounding redness was from the pressure and friction of metal on skin. "I don't, either."

"Still, it's quite rude to break into someone's home and threaten him with a weapon."

"David has his gun, so I suppose the knife was just what he had at hand." Lennie realized they were shaking slightly and set the candlestick down next to the pistol. Their thoughts strayed along four or five different paths, so the only thing they could think to ask was, "Are you going to involve the police?"

In profile when he spoke, Paul's words were fairly neutral. "It might make him a jailbird for life if I did."

If Lennie understood correctly, he voiced a subtle question in the observation. They knew that if they wished for Paul to do so, the police would be summoned, but they also surmised he was giving them that choice.

"He... doesn't deserve that," Lennie said, at length. "Even if he's been busy finding me and watching me and..." They scowled and nudged one of Robbie's legs with the toe of their scuffed shoe. "I don't know what his plan was. Break down every door in here until he found me? Then what?"

"Knock you out?" Paul said blandly. "Carry you

off? I don't think planning seems like his strongest quality, even if he did have to track you down. I imagine he was able to get something out of David's house that helped him. David *has* sent a few letters here, recently, and it's possible he'd left some out somewhere. Brute force, though..." Carefully, as though not to startle them, Paul tapped Lennie's upper arm. "Take the knife. I'll find something to bind his hands. We can try to reason with him when he wakes."

"You think he'll want to?"

"I think he's as keen on getting away from his father as you are, so..." he was opening a bureau opposite the door and rifling through the contents of one of its drawers. Even with the minimal light provided by one candlestick several feet away, he seemed comfortable enough looking for what he wanted to find. "Yes. Call it an instinct."

Spurred into moving, Lennie knelt and safely relieved Robbie of his knife, holding it rather limply in their free hand. He didn't seem likely to wake quickly. Maybe Paul was correct and he would be desperate enough to talk things through, rather than bludgeon his way to what he thought he wanted.

"Sometimes..." said Lennie. "I don't know why I have premonitions if I can't see shit like this." They hadn't seen Mum die, they hadn't seen Ralph demeaning them for the first time.

"I wondered about that at least once a day after Alastair was gone," said Paul, as he returned with a quantity of thin, hardy rope. "All I could conclude was, maybe some people who do what we do are never surprised." He knelt and shifted Robbie's arms so his wrists and forearms were parallel, resting in his own broad lap. "Maybe some *do* see everything. But I wouldn't want to live that way; I think it would drive me mad."

Too expertly, Paul then bound Robbie's wrists.

"Is that something else your dastardly husband taught you?" Lennie approved of Paul calling Alastair his husband, even if the church would not recognize such a union.

"Yes, but we practiced knots under much more, well, carnal circumstances than these." Paul smirked and stepped back from his finished work, leaving Lennie voiceless in an impressed manner. Knots were knots, they felt, and Robbie was effectively restrained.

"Mr. Apollyon, what on *earth* happened?" The door opened to admit Mrs. Lloyd and David, the latter of whom was slightly bleary-eyed but did bear Robbie's pistol. Lennie couldn't recall being happier to see someone.

"Mrs. Lloyd, how many times will I have to tell you that I don't need the formality?"

"When we were only friends rather than employer and employee," she said primly, her eyes on Robbie and full of questions, "it was quite all right. Now I don't think it would be the done thing."

"*Clemence,*" said Paul, and Lennie gathered that was Mrs. Lloyd's given name, "I thought you were going to wait at the bottom of the back stairs."

"When no one came down that way, including you two, I feared the worst. I didn't hear much, but that doesn't always mean anything good, so I went and fetched Mr. Mills. Benson wouldn't be useful in an altercation, would he? And what good are his charms if they didn't stop that... miscreant down there on the floor." Then Mrs. Lloyd *did* know about the preternatural goings-on here, Lennie realized.

David was growing more alert, it seemed, as he

stepped past her and went directly to Lennie. "Are you all right?" But he didn't bother to wait for an answer. Instead, he looked toward the floor to see Robbie and his face darkened with wrath. Then he kissed Lennie full on the lips. In truth, there wasn't anything else they'd rather he did, for the kiss communicated more adroitly than David's words were generally capable of doing.

"Yes. But even better now," said Lennie, speaking just against his mouth.

"What the hell did he want?"

They shrugged. "For me to come back with him, to talk to his father... he's been lying for me these past several days, probably making it seem that I'm shadowing you and taking you for all you're worth."

"You are, but not in the way he'd like," mumbled David. Lennie brought a palm to his cheek. "How the fuck did he find you?"

It seemed easy enough to Lennie, but they forgot David wasn't as well-versed in the demimonde, and besides that, he was only half-awake. All Robbie would really need to do was break back into David's house or ask a few questions of locals, and he could easily trace Mr. David Mills to Cromer. While there were an assortment of hotels and public houses to choose from once there, it likewise was not difficult to determine where one might have ties. It might even be as Paul had mentioned, and maybe David had left some unsent letters out in preparation for the post.

Rather than point all of this out and frighten David any further, Lennie said simply, "A bit of sleuthing paired with a bit of luck."

They imagined he'd likely been lurking about for a day, maybe two. Likewise, this was not something they wished to bring to David's attention. If they knew how to observe people without being observed, Robbie certainly knew, too. Lennie thought of one of the back windows that had been found a little ajar, and suspected their stepbrother might have had something to do with it.

"Shall I send someone for the police? Or I can go myself."

"No," Lennie said.

"What?"

Sighing, Lennie said, stroking his cheekbone as though gentling a startled animal, then taking their hand back, "The way he was talking, I think Ralph may be taking advantage of him. Mistreating him."

"That isn't your affair!"

As though she was trying to be discreet about it, Mrs. Lloyd cleared her throat and said, "Mr. Apollyon, would you like some tea?"

"I'd like something much stronger." Paul made as though to go downstairs. Both of them clearly wished to give David and Lennie a semblance of privacy, which Lennie appreciated. But it felt strange that Paul would be obliged to leave his own flat.

"We can talk somewhere else," Lennie said.

"It's no bother for you to stay here. Just keep an eye on him. I'd be surprised if he woke soon, but he could. Move him to the sofa under the window if you're feeling charitable, or just leave him. I'll be back upstairs soon enough."

With that, Paul and Mrs. Lloyd left them, and Lennie kissed the side of David's mouth, which was pulled into a frown. "I feel like I need to help him."

"Why? When has he ever helped you? He *broke into* my house! He did the same thing here, looking for you, which means he somehow put together where we'd gone... and he was probably watching The

Shuck." David was more furious than Lennie had ever known him to be, but they couldn't divine why his usual wariness, so thorough that it was nearly trepidation, had transfigured into fury. Perhaps he was just overly startled, but it seemed uncharacteristically emotional.

"Well," Lennie breathed, "when we were children, he never liked how his father treated me."

"That's not the same as stopping it from happening. It's not the same as standing up to him."

"And you'd expect a child... a poor child, mind you, because we weren't wealthy... to do that? When his father could harm him?" Lennie wanted David to understand. They didn't wish to hurt him, but they were starting to grow rather agitated. "Throw him out with nothing?"

"Yes!"

"This isn't about Robbie, is it?"

"And it's not about me, although I'm sure that's what you assume," retorted David. "Of course I wish I'd done things differently with my own father."

Lennie wanted to believe him, but they were skeptical. Softly, they said, "Then what's the problem? I'll go back to Norwich, I'll talk to Ralph and make sure Robbie's not murdered for his trouble, and..." They grew quiet. None of this appealed at all, and it still made them want to vomit when they thought about it.

"I love you." David's words launched forth like a bullet. "I think."

Stopped mid-thought, Lennie stared at him. "Oh."

He looked more awake now in the lone candle's light; his eyes were earnest. "I know it's not been long." Scoffing, perhaps more at himself than anything else, he added, "At all. You don't have to say it back. You don't even have to feel it in kind. I just don't want *you* to be murdered because you're trying to help someone who, frankly, I don't even like."

"I don't think I'll be," said Lennie faintly, marveling at how elated they felt at the prospect of David loving them. But if Robbie were to be believed, his father's behavior had grown worse of late. They cast aside that consideration and resolved not to worry David with it. "Murdered, I mean. But I should see Ralph. At the very least, I have to do it to remove myself from him entirely."

They could tell David was disgruntled, beyond disgruntled, but he didn't fight them. He kissed them with more force than was necessary, which they enjoyed. As they were both relaxing into the feeling, he nodded and said, "I think I almost understand, even if I hate it."

"Let's go back," said Lennie, "and I'll stay with you, if I can be so bold." David smoothed some hair from their forehead. They murmured, conspiratorially, "I want you to ride me in your bed." His fingers paused and trembled a bit. They smiled. "I know it won't solve everything, especially not all of this, but it'll feel *good*, won't it?"

"Yes," David murmured.

"Just think of me sinking onto your prick, and that should make up for any of the shit we have to confront."

David's response was yet another kiss, this time one that was delicate and thorough. Their Mr. Mills was more adept at the art of kissing than speaking.

———

It had been David's idea to put Robbie in the cellar before he woke — so that when he woke he would be terrified. But what David didn't explain to Paul, Lennie, or Mrs. Lloyd was that the ghost was there too, and his presence had emboldened him. It stayed largely out of sight, but David had caught a glimpse of a tanned man with long, dark hair gone mostly to gray before switching his attention to the living man at his feet.

Robbie stayed unconscious longer than David would've thought. He'd known boxing blues at university, so he had some idea of how long a man might stay under when he'd been rendered unconscious.

Granted, his sense of time was skewed down here, but he felt more had passed than not. "Hello," he said, once Robbie had started to stir. A handful of moments went by before Robbie, who was on the floor near the base of some kegs, blinked his eyes open and even acknowledged him. When he did, it was nonverbal and scared, an expression of fear, which was exactly the reaction David wanted.

He took a few steps and looked down at Robbie as he seemed to become aware that his hands were tied together and he was on a cold floor somewhere dark. A window that was half-level with the road let forth a little light, and they could both hear ambient noises from the taproom above. But David suspected it would be petrifying to be in this situation no matter what little bits of the outside world floated through.

He wanted Robbie to know that terror because he wanted to make himself clear and terror would emphasize his point. What was more, the ghost wanted it, too. Alastair, he supposed. He could call it such. Benson seemed to think so, anyway, and even if he couldn't trust his own instincts just yet, everyone looked to Benson as a preternatural authority.

It felt correct to intimidate Robbie this way. The sentiment emanated from the space, permeating what David could corroborate by sight and smell and sound. Everything was heightened, sharper, and it all felt a little timeless or out of time.

"Fucking toff," hissed Robbie, which showed admirable pluck, considering he had woken both bound and in the relative dark only to see a man who'd caused him to lose consciousness with a shove. He did not know that David couldn't manage it at will, like a child still learning to speak and expanding their vocabulary.

"Yes, well," said David. "We can't help what we are, can we? Are you listening?"

"Don't have much of a choice, do I?"

"None, in fact. How'd you find us here?"

"Please. It's not hard to follow the likes of you, David Mills."

"That isn't an answer."

With the air of one who was being inconvenienced, Robbie said, "When I came to, there wasn't a watch on your house yet. I got back in through a window and found letters addressed to men at this place. You hadn't sent them, obviously, but I figured it was a place to start looking."

With a blink, David briefly wondered if it was worth it to lock up all of his correspondence in the future. He would definitely consider new windows, ones that were much harder to wedge open. Unless Robbie had just broken a window, although it didn't seem like he had. "I see." It was almost insultingly simple.

"Where's Lennie?"

David couldn't even be pleased that Robbie, unlike his father, he imagined, used Lennie's name. It mattered, but it was the smallest gesture of politeness and it wasn't enough for him to look favorably upon Robbie. "They're upstairs. They want to go to see your father with you, you know. So, listen carefully to me."

Apparently somewhat placated by this, Robbie rolled over and looked up at him from his back. He seemed to understand he wouldn't get very far if he struggled or got to his feet to initiate violence. Or perhaps he felt unwell. David didn't care if he wasn't feeling quite the thing, but he definitely liked that Robbie was so prone. Maybe he was actively remembering how David had felled him with a spark. That would be fine, too.

"I'm listening."

"Good lad." David crouched next to him and spoke quietly. "If you do *anything* to endanger them, you'll have me to answer to." He glanced upwards, toward the darkest corner behind Robbie. The tall form of a man lingered there, all the lines of his body vigilant and interested despite being draped in shadows. Rather than being frightened of it, though at this moment he could not entirely make it out, David took strength in its appearance. "Understand?"

He wondered if Alastair watched because he could do nothing, or if he watched because he was about to do something. There was a sense that the prior was true, and if any of the seeping rage David felt from that corner was anything to go by, Alastair did not enjoy being so weak.

He and Alastair had that in common, although David felt he'd been ineffectual almost his whole life and had only just shed the trait. He didn't imagine Alastair possessed the same problem until after death.

Mulishly, Robbie said, "I think I do."

David teased a finger near his sternum. "You know I can hurt you." Robbie flinched. Just a little, but enough to make David feel satisfied he was being taken seriously. He wasn't used to intimidating anyone in this manner, but he could see why one might enjoy doing it habitually.

"I don't want anything bad to happen to him. Them. I just want to be rid of my father."

Smiling, a little sharpish, he imagined, David nodded. "*That* I can understand. Or even help with."

"Help? How can you help us be rid of him?"

An idea had coalesced as he watched Lennie sip their tea in the dawn light of this morning. Though he'd surprised himself with his vehemence, it was a conclusion of years of repression, instances of emotion or fury he'd shoved down to fester with his sense of belief. Like faith or whimsy, anger was not something he'd allowed himself to cultivate. While he could not go back and protect or avenge himself, he could do so for Lennie now. The knowledge was galvanizing.

"It doesn't involve paying him off."

"Someone like you could keep him in comfort for years, not that he has many of those left, I'd wager."

David was rather tired of hearing what someone like him could do. He'd had enough assumptions leveled at him for a lifetime. "Oh, that I could. But I won't. I mean to say, I'll give you two enough money to appease him for a bit... we both know that it won't be enough. He's greedy, isn't he?"

Robbie peered at David, then he sighed. "Greedy, and ever since Lennie started to..." He didn't have to finish the sentence. David understood that Robbie meant something along the lines of, ever since Lennie became more comfortable and open. "It's not so much that Father *really* cares who they are, see, and it's not that he's religious or... or scientific. Neither of those." Patiently, David gazed at him, hooking his left thumb in his own front pocket as he still crouched. Robbie said, "He's just a bastard. He knows that he can scare Lennie if he makes like he'll have them committed or examined..."

"He'd never." The thought of Lennie in a cold, callous place where they were not free to live as they should cemented the choice he was about to disclose to Robbie.

Who must have been terrorized by the look on David's face, because he hurriedly added, "Even though he could never come up with the means to do it! He keeps scaring Lennie because he knows, one way or the other, Lennie will bring him money. It's one of the few things he can keep straight in his mind, now."

Quietly, David said, "And you let him do it. Repeatedly."

"How do I stop him?" The question seemed genuine and under other circumstances David would be more sympathetic. But right now, it roused disgust. Even if nothing came of his and Lennie's acquaintance, he would still believe it was better for someone like their stepfather to be dead.

"You're not a child." Robbie was, in all honesty, probably only a handful of years younger than him. "At the least, even if you can't stop him, you could walk away from him. You could tell Lennie that he's full of shit." David knew that if he allowed himself to be distracted by the revulsion he felt, this discussion would never end. Robbie had been conditioned throughout his life just as Lennie had. "Regardless... it will stop with me."

"You just said you weren't going to keep paying him."

"No." David released a breath, then said the most audacious thing he'd ever said. He wasn't sure if it was more for Lennie or for himself, but he could interrogate his reasoning later. "I'm not going to pay him. I'm going to kill him."

Robbie made no reply. But his eyes were round. Growing more confident, David said, "And you're going to help me."

After he seemed to adjust to the thought, Robbie nodded once. "Fine."

As though the word was magic itself, David unbound his hands.

21

While they both could have stayed indefinitely at The Shuck, Lennie decided that the best course of action would be to go back to Norwich that same morning. Although David had seemingly relaxed around the thought of his business calendar being disrupted, he still looked relived when Lennie told him they were ready to depart.

After everything in Paul's flat, Robbie had been put in the cellar for reasons only David knew, for even Paul seemed surprised by the flinty tone in his voice when he said he wanted Robbie to wake frightened and cramped. Lennie, still shocked that their sibling had even come here, decamped to their room and dozed off with their cheek on David's coat simply because it smelled of him.

It was impossible to say how much later, but it couldn't have been too long because the light had only started to change, David woke them with a careful hand on their shoulder and they sleepily said it would be nice to let Mrs. Peters know they were all right.

"Who?"

"My landlady."

"Ah," David had said with a smile. "Then..."

"I'm ready to go home, I think." Even though it was unnerving.

Voice suffused with relief, David said, "Yes."

Then again, perhaps that relief wasn't because he wanted so badly to return to his usual life.

Lennie yawned, believing there wasn't any going back to that, for anyone present in the taproom at this moment. They hoped, quite secretly but also quite ardently, that David wanted time alone with them and that was why he'd exhibited relief upstairs, before they each made their way down for warm drinks and toast.

Robbie had been hauled up from the cellar after a surprisingly short discussion with David and he was visibly subdued, but also strangely peaceful. As Lennie eyed him, they had so many thoughts on the matter of why Robbie had come that it was hard to settle on just one of them. Four days had passed since they demanded David stop drinking and it felt like forty years.

They might've felt more awkward watching their sibling look so tense if it weren't so gratifying. Presently, David was granting him the privilege of eating breakfast under supervision. Lennie still had his knife; David still had his pistol.

Benson, who was at Lennie's side like a talkative cat and had been apprised of the situation while he ate some toast and marmalade with his gin, said, "Mr. Mills may kill him before you all reach the station." He chortled at the unlikely scene across the taproom.

"It would simplify some things," said Lennie. "But then I'd feel terrible. Robbie wasn't treated much better than me. He's responsible for himself, but..." they fell quiet, reflecting on how sickening Ralph actually was overall. They tried to come up with something to redeem him, and the best they could say was he wasn't as bad as others.

That meant very little. Nothing at all, in context. Ralph had never physically hurt them, but the amount of disquiet, terror, and self-doubt he'd generated was immense and it had impacted their life to a degree that they'd never allowed another person to match. David might come close, but that would be for far better, purer reasons, and it would be consensual.

"Says only good things about you, then," said Benson. "I don't have foresight, but I think you're doing the right thing not giving him over to the police. *If* such a thing as the right one exists."

Smirking, Lennie said, "Well, I have it, and I can't tell what I'm supposed to be doing. This just feels like the right one." They took a drink of tea as something else occurred to them. "Has David's bewitchment *really* dissipated?"

"Oh, yes," said Benson. "He's done it, your lad. I might've started the process, but he's finished it. I say it's funny how the untrained can manage things."

Perplexed, Lennie said, "How? How did he manage, I mean?" They did not object to David being termed theirs. They also knew that if they pressed Benson, he would definitely not detail anything at all. *I wonder if he'll tell David more about it.*

"Sounds trite, but he's acted in accordance with himself. He's doing right by him, by you, by Tom, by Paul. I think... in the end, that's what needed to happen, because he caused it in the first place by being hurt and spiteful. I don't know how else to describe what I know, but it..." Benson drank again, then said, "If I were to have removed the thing myself, it's... amputation. Abrupt, shocking. If he does it, it's... healing.

Takes time, can be slow. Doesn't always look the way we might picture. Magic never does."

Lennie thought they understood. "Wait," they said, as another question came to them. "Your charms. They didn't really protect The Shuck, did they?"

"Didn't they?"

"No." Peering at him, Lennie didn't think they needed to elaborate. If the charms were effective, there wouldn't have been a break-in, for one thing.

"I'd say you two were protection."

Aghast, Lennie was about to protest more, but found they needed to stop speaking or they'd start seeing Benson's logic, and they were not certain they wished to yet. It was too convoluted and there was too much room for argument, but in the end, Benson was not entirely wrong. *I still feel I caused the trouble in the first place, but I guess I can say I protected Paul from Robbie.*

And who knew what David had done in that cellar. Something about what he'd seen in the flat, Lennie standing above Robbie's unconscious form and Paul with the livid red line on his neck, had tempered him into a stronger substance. The moment itself felt alchemical, for he was different in the second after than he'd been in the second before. Was his love for Lennie the origin of that shift, or was the cause something that had been growing for far longer?

Lennie knew David felt deeply and he felt much, and they also knew tamping down on such intensity could be harmful. They'd just witnessed such a thing in Robbie, who had felt so trapped he'd resorted to brutal measures.

It hadn't been one thing, one instance of abuse that led to him taking those measures; it had been years of abuses and slights exacting their toll from him. Lennie couldn't ignore a nagging sense that David was standing near a similar precipice, but had to trust he was flanked by more love than rage. Robbie, though, had had nobody but Lennie. His father had probably alienated anyone else who tried to befriend him.

They shook their head and went to David where he stood. Wordlessly, he slipped an arm around their waist. Paul brought him some coffee, which they didn't prefer and hadn't even been sure The Shuck offered.

But it seemed it was available the morning after a jarring night. If that was the price of coffee, they'd never like it.

—

"I realized something while a man had a knife pressed to my throat," said Paul, and if it had been anyone else, David might have inferred immense ill-feeling behind the calm words. There wasn't any present at all; it was just his droll way. "And I think I shall go to Scotland."

It made sense to David. He had not been in the flat while Robbie threatened Paul, but Paul had been cornered in the one place that must have seemed a sanctum until that exact point. He'd lived there with his beloved, the person who'd changed his habits and his life. To be threatened with death there would have been sobering, and either transformative or crushing.

"To visit your husband's grave." Lennie smiled at Paul without any reservation, and David found himself lost in their expression even though it was not directed at him. "The one who taught you to fight. And... who tied you up."

"Quite," said Paul. "I should."

Surprised, David gazed at Lennie but he didn't question the term. Or the assertions. He found himself wanting to ask what kind of fighting, and what kind of being tied up, but he also thought he already knew the answer to both: Robbie had been out cold when he'd come upstairs, and the knots on his wrists looked uncannily more like those used in a bedroom rather than on a ship.

So, he asked a different question entirely. "Will Tom run The Shuck while you're away?" he asked. This was the strangest conversation he'd ever had before departing to catch a train. He let his eyes rove over Robbie, who was now sullenly drinking a pint at the end of the bar under Benson's deceptively watchful eye.

He wanted to share Lennie's belief that the lad was redeemable, but he was more cautious about the matter.

In an endeavor to trust the person he loved, he was truly attempting to see the best in him. The trouble was, he wasn't very used to seeing the best in anyone to begin with, and when a man readily agreed to patricide, that man probably wasn't very kind.

"Oh," Paul said, "I think he's more than ready."

Neither Tom or Theo had been in since yesterday evening. Hours before Robbie executed his plan. Both were in for a shock, David believed. No one had been harmed and even Paul's neck looked less angry than it had an hour ago. But David felt that Tom in particular wouldn't take any of these events in his stride. Theo would be much better at integrating all the new developments.

Knowing Tom, he'd probably also wonder at the efficacy of Benson's supposed protective charms and slip in a few rude comments about them.

But the fact of the matter was, David wished to get

home and to his own bed in far less time than it would take to ask for, or supply, explanations.

Besides, he'd been told several times lately, more or less, to stop trying to make things follow common logic. It had been hard enough for him to shed his father's dictates and he felt like he finally had. He knew there was so much left to discover, to learn, but the prospect did not frighten him any longer.

"I agree," murmured David, earning a look of respect from the elder Apollyon. "Well... shall we?" He lifted an eyebrow at Lennie, who blushed slightly.

"I suppose. The journey won't become any less awkward if we delay it."

"Come back when you feel rested," said Paul to both of them. Then he cocked an eyebrow at Lennie. "And after you've dealt with your fucking stepfather. I don't think all of this is over, just yet."

With more than a little disquiet in his heart, David agreed. "It isn't." They'd come back, indeed, after Lennie's fucking stepfather had been dealt with permanently.

—

Dusk had never looked so beautiful in his bedroom. It was made all the more beautiful by the knowledge that there wouldn't be any trespassers, and some semblance of his normal days would be restored shortly.

Dusk was rendered *supremely* beautiful, however, not by the absence of the threat of interlopers, but by how well Lennie bloomed from his attentions. They were, for now, alone with each other.

He'd sent word to Mrs. Greaves, with further instructions to inform Ellie and Musgrave that they could return to service the next day. According to Robbie, who'd been a great, if reluctant, source of knowledge on the train home, Ralph himself never had known where David lived. He hadn't known a thing about Lennie's interest or ties to him, and he hadn't known Lennie had come crashing inside his house.

Evidently, Robbie had made good on his word of covering for his sibling and would continue to do so. David had to be satisfied with his word, since his commitment to David's rather chilling words in the cellar seemed sincere. Looking back, he felt they should have dragged Robbie off somewhere very far away, not left him so local that he could then make a point of tracking Lennie, even if it was for his own purposes.

Lennie, however, had mused that perhaps things were unfurling as they should, which sounded too close to Paul or Benson's ambiguous musings for David's tastes.

He was indulging in his tastes at the moment, and couldn't have been more content. He met Lennie's eyes as they still trembled from an intense orgasm. It had felt intense to him, at least, and although he was shaking a little from the effort to be self-disciplined, he was happy not to have reached completion himself just yet.

He grinned and rubbed his hands up Lennie's back, encouraging them to lay back down on top of him. "I think, all things considered, I like you on top."

Chest heaving as they caught their breath, Lennie chuckled slightly. "I like all of it."

He laughed a bit. "Fair. That's fair."

Then they slowly relaxed enough to drape along his body and he kissed their neck as they settled. "You make my cunt feel so good," they said, pensively.

He understood voicing the word was a mark of trust and endeavored not to take it lightly. "Well, I always want to, so..." he smiled, not making fun so much as giving a calm, intimate dictate. "Tell me if I don't, and we'll figure out how to remedy it."

"You know I'm not shy. I'll tell you if I'm not satisfied."

He brought a hand just under their chin, tilting it gently forward, and kissed them softly. "Yes, and I love it."

As he had and would continue to do, he pushed away his own insecurities. That, he was still practicing. His unanswered questions were still numerous, but they always had been. They'd just taken a different shape now. He still had no plausible explanation for how he'd knocked out Robbie, who was still terrified by the very idea. And ever since Alastair's presence had ebbed into The Shuck, David was still waiting a little fretfully for the shadows in his own home to transmute into his father, even though this was not his father's house.

Pausing for a bit of breath, he asked, "When are we seeing your beastly stepfather?" He knew a thing about beastly fathers and figured a beastly stepfather wasn't so different. They definitely weren't recognized any differently under the law.

"We aren't. I am. Well, Robbie and I am. He thought this Friday."

They had only been back in Norwich briefly, but within that time David managed to almost straighten out his scheduled appointments and send a message to the surprisingly accommodating Mr. Davies, who'd replied almost immediately that afternoon and seemed to understand the sudden nature of *family problems.* In the end, that was what they were; David's just looked different from the usual examples.

"Don't be so tense." Lennie peered down at him, and he knew he couldn't hide exactly how overwrought the subject made him. Probably no matter what the context, but definitely not when they were both joined like this. "He just wants money. That's really why he's so adamant I see him. It's why I took your wallet in the first place, isn't it? I thought for certain you'd have what I was after."

"I did."

"Well, not just materially," Lennie said with a smile. "Most of them who look like you... they have more money on them. Arrogant bastards, aren't they..."

"I'm *glad* you chose me. Well, I am now. I sort of was at the time, too. But you have to admit, you can't be *too* pleased if your wallet's gone missing. Even if the person who has stolen it is achingly gorgeous."

They stayed for some time in silence, and David basked in the sensation of being so ensconced.

Lennie said, and he felt their speech against his chest, "Have you ever thought of living in Cromer? I... liked it."

Carefully, David said, because he didn't want to make Lennie think he wanted a time that no longer existed for him, "Yes. Before my father caught me with Tom, I had thought of it. All the business is here, but that doesn't necessarily mean I need to be here." He understood that, finally. "If I thought of a different way to run things, I'm sure I could go. To Cromer. Everyone goes to London or Cambridge, don't they? But I like Cromer very much."

David liked London, though he'd probably never choose to live in it. Too many people, ones he didn't want to see, rubbed shoulders there. He'd take his leisure days at the British Museum without having a home in Mayfair or Bloomsbury.

"I'm sorry he caught you," said Lennie, kissing the

center of his sternum. "That's no way to be seen by anybody, much less a mother or father."

"Thank you. It... he... I suppose some fathers would be... better than he was about it."

"Not mine, and the only one I had was Ralph. He's the only one I recall, anyway."

"He sort of excommunicated me from the house in Cromer. That was my favorite place to be, Tom Apollyon aside. And he knew it. I wasn't welcome there again. But... when he started to lose his faculties and I needed to begin caring for him..." Lennie kissed his sternum again and he trailed off, blissfully distracted. "And especially when I became responsible for all of his legal decisions... I could come back to it."

"That's not the same as coming there to just enjoy it. Not that I'd know anything about having a second house."

David smiled and glanced down at the top of Lennie's head. "No. I mean, no, it wasn't the same."

"He didn't die there, did he?"

"No. He held on to the family home here for as long as he could, and he died there not long after he spent his last winter in Cromer. I don't know why, but it was a Mills thing to winter there... sort of the inverse of what all the other odious wealthy people with second homes do."

"So this is... yours. This house."

"Yes. I wasn't upset to sell where I grew up. Would have been much worse to lose the one in Cromer." Satisfied, astonished at the sheer pleasure of having a mundane, familiar conversation like this while he was embracing someone, while he was inside them, even, he fell a little quiet again.

"David?"

"Yes?"

"Could we live there, do you think?"

It might be a welcome change, thought David, to reside there happily. If Lennie were there with him, he would be less nervous to be himself within it. "I suppose so, yes." Then, he chuckled. "You said 'we.'"

"Don't let it go to your head. What do we do next?"

He trailed his hand against the base of Lennie's spine. "More of this."

"I meant more in general."

"Truly... more of this." He smiled, but then thought of the best way to answer their question. The truth was, he couldn't promise exactly what they would do, apart from the most obvious responses. "Then we can talk of moving house."

They would do more of *this* so long as they both wanted to, but they hadn't yet discussed much more than David's displeasure at the thought of Lennie being in the same room as Ralph. That did seem to be the closest and most pertinent issue: something about it felt off to David, though he did not want to say so.

He couldn't very well say he planned on removing Ralph as a factor just yet, and it also seemed there was no way around letting Lennie go to him. David had his suspicions that they would take issue with his solution to their problems, which was fair. Objections to murder were likely the most humane response. But that didn't make it any easier to come out with his intentions, despite knowing it would be the right thing to do, to own the truth. At least Robbie was too wary of him to tell Lennie unprompted.

The fact was, David could not countenance allowing Ralph to continue his abuses and killing him did seem to be the most expedient way of ensuring he couldn't hurt anybody. *It isn't as though you make a habit of considering it an option.*

Part of him knew that was a very flimsy consolation; he shouldn't be considering it at all.

But when he thought of Lennie left to the whims of such a loathsome person, it compromised his reasoning. And he felt that if Ralph's own son hadn't put up much of a resistance to the idea, Ralph couldn't be salvageable.

"Are you really all right with me staying with you?" Lennie's pensive question brought him back to the present moment.

"Yes. Only if you want to."

"I do," said Lennie. They shifted against him very slightly and David held his breath. While a great many things could be solved with the activity that was bound to follow, he understood this was an important thing to discuss. So, he wanted to try. He winced with delight and listened as Lennie said, "But I don't belong here, do I? I don't dress right, for one thing... my coat is so old that... and my hat..."

When Lennie was distressed, it seemed they fidgeted. He grumbled. When they also clenched a little around his prick as they fidgeted, it had an inordinately effective impact. He held them still at the waist and they blinked, meeting his eyes.

"I'll take you to the best tailor and it won't matter how old anything you own is," said David. "I promise. He'll make you look better than anyone you pass on any street." Beaming, then, feeling proud he could make light of himself, he added, "You have to trust me. I'm vain, you see." He did have in mind the perfect tailor, one he'd used for years.

"I don't know about vain, but you *are* interested in your clothes, for certain."

The first thing he'd done upon arriving home was bathe, then change and douse himself in cologne.

Even witches, or witch-hunters, had to be well-heeled. He nodded, saying, "That all right?" Then, on a breath, he added, "Please stop fidgeting."

Puzzled, Lennie asked, "Why?" Almost as quickly as they'd asked, they said, their voice lowering with pleasure when they realized David was still hard, "Oh. But is that actually a problem?"

With the most mischievous of gleams in their eyes, heated as bronze in the sun, they moved off him. David sighed, feeling a bit bereft, but silently admitting it was for the best. Until he found his mouth falling open slightly as Lennie trailed down his body on the bed, pushing aside the covers and coming to rest in a crouch between his thighs.

"There are probably a lot of things we *should* discuss, but," they said, kissing the very edge of his left hipbone, "Can they wait until later?"

He nodded, endeavoring not to think too far ahead. He knew he wouldn't be alone in whatever did come next, and he was jubilant to be able to navigate his own mind. That knowledge was more valuable than anything else could be, for it would only help him do right by both himself and Lennie.

—

In a fit of foolishness or brilliance, Lennie strode confidently to knock on Ralph's scuffed door, caring very little that it was late and not the hour for social calls. Their people had never been the sort for propriety, and Lennie didn't see the point in starting now. The street was generally rowdy, so any altercation wouldn't rouse much interest. If anything, somebody might shout insults and additions of their own, but Lennie doubted anyone would take issue.

Lennie wanted this finished. They didn't want to

be caught in this purgatory any longer, not when life was ushering in so many good things.

Perversely, they also wanted to see how Robbie reacted to the unannounced visit. Part of the desire was driven by lingering resentment over what he'd done to Paul, but mostly, Lennie wanted to make sure Robbie was more on their side than his father's. A slim chance existed that he could have been lying about Ralph's state to garner sympathy. Although they didn't think so, they wanted to be certain.

"What?" Robbie opened the door and his scowl slipped into a look of shock.

"Happened to be nearby," said Lennie. They hadn't; they'd only decided to do this five minutes after David's snoring was consistent enough to attest to how dead asleep he was. Since the sleep was postcoital, he wouldn't wake if someone practiced their piccolo right next to his head, leaving Lennie the possibility of sneaking out of the house.

"I thought we were doing this on Friday."

"What, I can't be friendly?"

Lennie shouldered past Robbie into the small room. The house itself had once been one home, then was split into two residences at some point, likely when its surroundings became more of a slum. Quarters were cramped, always had been. Seeing it now, Lennie couldn't help but question how four people had fit into a tiny kitchen, this room, and the adjoining one, even when two of them had been children. There was no gas laid in the house, certainly no electricity, and the effect of the two lit candles was cheerless. Lennie would have rather sat in the dark.

Still, as similar as it was to what they remembered, the reek of urine was new and the floor was much dirtier. When they'd lived here, they'd cleaned be-

cause they'd always helped Mum do it. It was possible
that Robbie still tried, but he'd never been as attentive
to the maintenance of tidying.

When they saw their stepfather in the bed in the
corner, they saw why cleanliness wasn't a priority.
Ralph looked blatantly unwell, far more so than he
had two years ago, and though they strongly doubted
Robbie let him wallow in filth, he was still less than
presentable.

Lennie had been waiting for Ralph's customary
spleen to make its way toward them as soon as they
came past Robbie. Then they wondered if perhaps
Ralph was out, because that used to be the only
reason for his silence. But it was evident the sleeping
man in the old bed preferred resting to going outside.

The change was stupefying. Ralph had always possessed boundless vigor, not that it was benevolent or
he put it to any good use. Lennie had not seen him at
all since they'd procured their own accommodations,
having gone to great lengths to avoid anywhere he
might frequent, and they wouldn't have imagined him
in this state.

"He sleeps a lot."

Lennie didn't realize they were mute and staring
until Robbie broke the silence. They looked at him
with no sense of what their own expression resem-
bled. It wasn't that they pitied Ralph. But he was almost unrecognizable. Perhaps better light could make
him look more as he had, yet Lennie didn't really
think so.

They eyed their stepbrother. Ralph and Robbie
had always been somewhat similar in build, but Ralph
had lost weight. Likewise, his hair had once been
black tinged with blue. Now, it was the hue of tar-
nished silver.

"Does he?" Lennie was still reconciling with the lack of verbal derision, the sheer absence of echoing, nasty words inside the house. They had to take several steadying breaths through their mouth. "I thought you said he'd gotten worse. Um, aggressive. That he was more aggressive."

"When he's awake, yes. He shouts and spits and tries to fight me, oftentimes. And he doesn't look it, but he's still strong." Diffidently, Robbie put his fingertips on Lennie's arm, resting them on their coat. "Come on. Let's go outside. I can't stand the smell. I try to clean him up when he... well..." He sighed. "But the smell lingers."

They nodded and preceded him out the door. After Robbie closed it behind him and stood closer, Lennie said, "Well, I have money... you can take it and give it to him." This was not how they'd expected the encounter to go by any means, and it seemed their body didn't know what to do without the energy of a fight. Listlessly, they adjusted their hat.

"Why'd you even come?" said Robbie.

"Thought I could just... pay him and have done with it. Get it over with."

"Does your toff know you're out?"

"No. He doesn't want me to see Ralph at all."

Robbie worried his lower lip with the edges of his teeth. "We still doing Friday?"

Lennie sighed and handed him the banknotes surreptitiously. With the ease of experience, he took them and they vanished. There was no telling who might be eavesdropping or watching from the shadows. "I... I don't know." Robbie's exhaustion and the deadened look in his eyes had convinced them of how desperate he was, how trapped he felt.

Rapidly, they wondered how bad it would be to

convince Robbie simply to leave Ralph alone until he expired, presumably in his own piss if the stench was any indication. Robbie could find a new place to live.

Then they studied their sibling and knew, despite the fatigue and the misery, he was not ready to leave his father. Mum would have been ashamed if Lennie condoned such an action, no matter how justified, but that was far less of an element in their decision not to push the option. Robbie just couldn't have handled it.

"Yes," Lennie said. "Friday. When is he awake and less aggressive?"

"Mornings. He seems better in the morning."

"Better? He's never been 'better' to me."

"Well," said Robbie. "Remember what I said. He's proud of you for stealing from a toff."

Discarding their urge to sneer, Lennie shrugged and acquiesced. "All right. Friday morning. I'll be here."

A long pause reigned, then Robbie whispered, "Thank you."

Lennie nodded, having little more to say while they digested the circumstances. As they walked away, heading home, they didn't think the impending encounter would be for them, but more for Robbie.

They cautiously hoped that illness had defanged one of the most insidious monsters under their bed.

Once they slipped in through the front door – using a key and the lock like a respectable person, even locking up behind them – David's house was still and soundless. Instead of unnerving Lennie like the lack of Ralph's customary insults had, this silence calmed them. They went upstairs, returning to David's bedroom, and proceeded to undress carefully, forgoing a nightshirt.

David's quiet snoring continued until they slid

under the bedclothes next to him. Roused by the movement, he snuffled and squirmed closer to them, and they savored the contact.

"You can't possibly want to go again, can you?" he asked.

They had not replied before David said, "Well, we could, just give me a moment..." and fell back asleep within the next two breaths.

Lennie grinned and smothered a chuckle in their pillow. So much was left to be said and decided. But for the moment, they would enjoy their toff, and revel in the warmness of his eyes when he woke in the morning and realized they didn't wear a shred of clothing.

It might have been folly to think so, but here in the dark with David's breathing to anchor them, it didn't feel wrong to believe Ralph's schemes and cruelties were of the past.

EPILOGUE

"I felt in me five manner of workings, which be these: enjoying, mourning, desire, dread, and sure hope."
—Mother Julian of Norwich

The strangest thing about being both dead *and* aware was the lack of interaction he had with anything physical. It rankled, not being able to do anything at all. And perhaps worse, nobody – or almost nobody – could even hear or see him. Worst of all, this was the second time he'd found himself in this exact situation.

He reached out and idly tried to touch a half-full glass on the bar. Though he saw his fingertips resting on the smooth surface and he remembered what glass should feel like, he felt nothing. For someone who had been an epicure in life, it was almost infuriating: he wanted to smell the ales, put his hand on the banister as he walked up the stairs. Run his fingers through Paul's hair, which was much grayer and a little wilder now.

Hell, he didn't even *walk*, really. Walking would imply that his feet connected with the floor, and although they did not go through it, he had little sensation of being grounded on anything solid.

Even in death, Alastair Gow realized he was not quite ordinary in his thoughts or approach to anything. He imagined most people, if they were somehow summoned from a void back to where they had once been happiest, would be terrified by the change. While it had been quite jarring to find himself in The Shuck again, he found it more curious than troubling.

Whatever it had been that brought him forth, here he was. Something about Mr. Mills must have proved crucial to his being here, for he was the only thing that had changed. Even Benson hadn't been able to bring him out of the dark, which was unexpected. Then again, he mused, Benson had spoken about ghosts before, but he never seemed particularly keen on making a living as their interlocutor.

The fact of the matter was, Alastair did not remember where he'd been before. He hoped, because he had not been a man of faith when he died, it was not somewhere bad. Although if he could not recall, perhaps it did not matter if it was heaven or hell.

He did remember dying, for there had been a second when he was out of his own body, hovering above it, looking down at himself and Paul next to him in the bed they'd shared for years. He was torn that it had happened while they were both asleep; it meant nobody had to see him expire and he felt no pain at all, but he also did not get to say goodbye properly. Not that everyone got to say their goodbyes, or that there would have been an acceptable way to say goodbye to Paul. Their abrupt division still ached like a lingering bruise.

After that moment, that odd, floating purgatory, he

was still in The Shuck, confined to its walls. That hadn't lasted too long, although he would be pressed to determine how long, exactly. He did know it felt terrible to watch Paul shatter. He wished for nothing more than to piece Paul back together as James, his grown son by marriage, arrived and took custody of his body, denying Paul any knowledge of where he was to be laid to rest.

He'd tried to box James' ears, that was for certain, but like anything else, there was no contact. James didn't so much as blink.

It was the same when he tried to kiss Paul on the cheek or embrace him about the waist. Nothing at all. Alastair hated interacting with his old life that way. He felt like the lingering scent of food that had been brought through a kitchen to a dining room. The smell was there, but it was ineffectual and not at all satisfying.

He *had* gotten to understand Paul's nephew much better than he ever had while alive. He watched the lad experience his first deep heartbreak as his uncle went through one that would last the rest of his life. That knowledge, at least, was something, and knowing more about the family helped Alastair feel even closer to the man he loved.

Then, after who really knew how long, his mind went blank. He saw nothing, knew nothing. It was rather like a deep sleep and more like being knocked unconscious.

So this return to The Shuck was about as inexplicable and abrupt as the first. But if he'd learned anything in his too-brief life with Paul, it was that both the best and worst things could be inexplicable and abrupt.

It did feel different, being back this time. Things

seemed rather brighter, and while he hadn't eaves-
dropped too much on Benson and Lennie, or Benson,
David, and Lennie because he was too preoccupied
with shadowing Paul, he gathered some kind of bewitchment had been resolved.

Frowning at the thought, he went to a table in the
corner, the one nobody seemed to take because it always caught a draft when the door opened or closed.
No one seemed to notice him as he walked, took a seat
on the chair whose hard surface he remembered and
did not quite feel, and stretched.

It pained him to think of leaving Paul alone and
his calm, careful seer had turned his grief inward for
too long. He'd glimpsed a calendar and knew the year,
although time felt as vaporous as it had right after
he'd passed. He cared to mark it by Paul's wrinkles
and the state of his hair, not bits of inked paper.

Over his week or so of wakefulness, his solace and
burden was being able to watch Paul. All he could do
was watch or wander the building, and he'd indeed
watched as Paul knocked that odious, strapping
Robbie fellow out cold.

Lennie, who Alastair greatly liked after witnessing
all of it, had done an admirable job keeping Robbie
talking and deescalating the tension. *That* had been
infuriating, being unable to do anything but stare as
somebody held a knife to his beloved's throat. Had he
been capable of it, Robbie would have been dead then,
never mind Paul's laudable talk of reasoning with him
when he woke.

Mr. Mills, David, had the correct idea, in his opinion. Alastair had *still* been unable to do a damn thing
down there in the cellar when David had spoken to
Robbie. He'd tried to be a proper howling ghost, and
he'd tried rattling the ladder and the trapdoor. None

of it had worked, so he gathered he also couldn't try his favorite option: going directly for Robbie's throat and constricting him until he no longer gasped for air.

Paul entered the room, probably coming from the kitchen, for he dusted his hands off on his trousers, shedding what looked to be flour. Alastair sat straighter. He thought his heart might burst as Paul served a young man who hardly looked capable of drinking a pint. *You don't have a heart.* But merely being near Paul again made it feel like it still existed and hadn't rotted away with the rest of him.

Confronted with the suggestion that Alastair was present, Paul had said with such despondency, "I can't feel a damn thing."

But Alastair could.

"Can't see a damn thing."

Yet Alastair could.

He saw too much, really. Saw a man who was as steadfast as he ever had been but was irrefutably crushed, even if he had offered safe harbor to two people who'd needed it. No, Paul had not changed. All he wished to do was embrace him, kiss him, spend one night with him and halt his tears, all shed in private. But he knew through a relentless, internal itch that he was present to do more than pine for what he could not have.

He supposed he should be trying to find someone who could see him, could communicate somehow. He had a bevy of questions. Thus far, that had been David, whose abilities weren't honed but were keen enough that he was aware of a presence and could sometimes see him, or Benson.

As David had left The Shuck and was apparently intent upon committing murder, and Alastair could not blame him for it – he would have volunteered to help had he been corporeal – Benson was presently the viable candidate.

The trouble was, both of them had only seen him sporadically. Benson mentioned a shadow man, while David seemed innately capable of seeing Alastair more as he was. He glanced at his hands. David could pick up on his feelings, of that he was positive. After all, as he'd lingered in the cellar when David insisted upon talking to Robbie alone, David had glanced in the corner where he lurked as though seeking reassurance. There'd been no fear, no nerves, in his eyes.

Still, all he'd been to either David or Benson was something resembling a man, so he was impatient to discover what might let him become intelligible.

When Benson came in with his usual flask, Alastair did not expect much. The taproom was not dark, but it was perfectly capable of being a bit shadowy in its corners in the evening, and Benson's eyesight could not have been excellent at his age. There was nothing to suggest a specter was loitering and trying to assuage his desires using proximity.

The old loon came directly to the table. Alastair thought nothing about that was abnormal, for it was an empty one. Or it was to most gazes.

Then Benson looked him squarely in the eyes; Alastair froze.

Only after a long drink from the flask and settling in the chair across from his, Benson said, "Mr. Gow, isn't it wonderful of you to join us? Glad you've taken a table. Got so much to catch you up on."

"Fuck's sake," Alastair said with relief. If he'd thought it through, he might not have wanted the first thing he'd uttered in years – that someone else could hear – to start with *fuck*. "You can see me."

Perhaps Benson couldn't hear him.

"Yes. Tattoos look good for a dead man's. Your hair is admirable, too. *And* I can fucking hear you."

That cleared it up. He already knew it wouldn't bother Benson to be seen talking to thin air. They knew each other too well for Alastair to be under any impression that he wished to appear sane. "What the hell is happening?"

"As to that," said Benson. "Just a question for you, first."

So pleased to be conversing, Alastair glanced at Paul, hoping with everything he could summon that Benson was not the only person who could hold a conversation. But he knew better than anyone what Paul was capable of, and talking to the dead had never been one of his talents. "Fine."

"He can't," Benson said, following Alastair's line of sight. A remarkable amount of compassion flowed from the two words. "It's absolutely killing him. No offense meant given your present status. He might rather be dead with you."

"No, he's too sensible for that," said Alastair.

"Too stubborn, more like."

"What's your question?" Reluctantly, Alastair looked at Benson instead of Paul.

"You were here before. After you expired, I mean." It wasn't asked like a question, but Alastair knew Benson wanted confirmation.

"Yes. Only for a while. Then I was... not."

Sipping whatever infernal juice was in his flask, Benson gave a nod. "I did think so, but I couldn't bear adding to Paul's... well. I didn't know if it would actually *help* him to know you were around." Off what must have been the scowl on Alastair's face, he added, "I don't know if that was the correct choice. But what's done is done, and you're here now."

Releasing a breath that was nothing but the memory of air, Alastair said, "Why?"

"I know the 'how' – Mr. Mills bewitched this place by accident some years ago. I believe that's what took you away. He's just very recently gone and lifted it. And I reckon that's how you're back."

For Alastair, none of this was bizarre. He'd experienced too much in life and death to belittle anything preternatural. He accepted it without hesitation.

He did wonder a little at the person in question being David Mills, who seemed better suited to keeping ledgers than drawing sigils. He'd also wondered at David's apparent ability to sense specters, too, but beggars shouldn't be choosers. Distantly, he remembered being told about a certain type of witch whom spirits sought out, often to the witch's detriment, so the idea wasn't foreign. Only the person exhibiting the aptitude was odd.

"That... all right." He'd heard about some of it, anyway. "But if that's *how*, what about... why? Why am I here?"

"I don't think it's only the dead who ask that question," Benson said cheerfully. "But let's start with what might bring you closure, hm?"

Gazing once more at Paul, who was now accepting an elderly woman's payment in exchange for her glass, Alastair preferred this sweet and sustained torment to closure.

Almost.

ALSO BY CAMILLE DUPLESSIS

Threads of the Wyrd

Kraken and Canary

Like Silk Breathing

The Only Story

Unfair Winds

ABOUT THE AUTHOR

Camille is a thalassophile who sadly spent too long residing in Chicago, where there's just a very large lake and no sea. An enquiring and possibly over-educated mind, she's been described as "the politest contrarian." Though everyone believes she's tall, she's not. Likewise, she doesn't dress in all-black.